PENGUIN CLASSICS

THE SONG OF THE CID

BURTON RAFFEL is Distinguished Professor of Arts and Humanities Emeritus and Professor of English Emeritus at the University of Louisiana at Lafayette. His many translations include Cervantes's *Don Quijote*, Rabelais's *Gargantua and Pantagruel* (winner of the 1991 French-American Foundation Translation Prize), Chrétien de Troyes's *Arthurian Romances*, Balzac's *Père Goriot*, and Chaucer's *Canterbury Tales*. His translation of *Beowulf* has sold more than a million copies.

MARÍA ROSA MENOCAL is Sterling Professor of the Humanities and Director of the Whitney Humanities Center at Yale. Her books include *The Ornament of the World: How Muslims, Jews, and Christians Created a Culture of Tolerance in Medieval Spain* and, as coauthor, *The Arts of Intimacy: Christians, Jews, and Muslims in the Making of Castilian Culture.*

T0200888

The Song of the Cid

A DUAL-LANGUAGE EDITION
WITH PARALLEL TEXT

Translated by
BURTON RAFFEL

Introduction and Notes by
MARÍA ROSA MENOCAL

PENGUIN BOOKS

PENGUIN BOOKS

Published by the Penguin Group

Penguin Group (USA) Inc., 375 Hudson Street,
New York, New York 10014, U.S.A.
Penguin Group (Canada), 90 Eglinton Avenue East, Suite 700,
Toronto, Ontario, Canada M4P 2Y3 (a division of Pearson Penguin Canada Inc.)
Penguin Books Ltd, 80 Strand, London WC2R 0RL, England
Penguin Ireland, 25 St Stephen's Green, Dublin 2,
Ireland (a division of Penguin Books Ltd)
Penguin Group (Australia), 250 Camberwell Road,
Camberwell, Victoria 3124, Australia (a division of Pearson Australia Group Pty Ltd)
Penguin Books India Pvt Ltd, 11 Community Centre,
Panchsheel Park, New Delhi – 110 017, India
Penguin Books (NZ), 67 Apollo Drive, Rosedale, North Shore 0632,
New Zealand (a division of Pearson New Zealand Ltd)
Penguin Books (South Africa) (Pty) Ltd, 24 Sturdee Avenue,
Rosebank, Johannesburg 2196, South Africa

Penguin Books Ltd, Registered Offices: 80 Strand, London WC2R 0RL, England

This translation first published in Penguin Books 2009

Translation copyright © Burton Raffel, 2009
Introduction copyright © María Rosa Menocal, 2009
All rights reserved

ISBN 978-0-14-310565-7
CIP data available

Printed in the United States of America
Set in Sabon
Maps by Virginia Norey

for Elizabeth—
splendid critic,
passionate reader

Contents

THE SONG OF THE CID

Introduction

It begins with weeping, the open sorrow of a man riding into exile. Soon we hear its distinct echo: the weeping of those who remain behind, and who line the streets to see our hero and his band of loyal followers, all men forced to abandon their homes, and their homeland. There is more weeping: the good citizens along the route openly lament the injustice of it all, and they decry the irascibility of their king, who, they say, has not only banished from the kingdom a better man than himself, but also threatened to rip their eyes out from their heads should they open their doors to these fugitives, this company of sixty men who ride out with their proud banners, following the man they call Cid.

But the king cannot prevent the men and women from opening their hearts to the Cid. Just what has so angered the king, just what the Cid has done to earn himself this calamitous sentence, is never mentioned, and will never be explained, but from this dramatic and poignant beginning forward there is never any question of where our sympathies lie. For the length of three cantos, out of the old Castilian capital of Burgos and into the proverbial deserts of exile—which here means all that lies beyond the Castilian frontier—we follow Rodrigo Díaz, our hero. We are often reminded that he is from Vivar, a small town some five miles to the north of Burgos. This is very much the heart of Old Castile, the Christian kingdom that ultimately conquers the lands of the peninsula that had long been Islamic territories. But Rodrigo Díaz is known mostly by his unambiguously Arabic name: Cid is a direct rendering into Castilian of *sayyid*—Lord, or Commander. Sometimes he is also called by his strongest epithet, *Cid Campeador*—the Champion, or the Warrior. By any and all of his names, from

the start there is no doubt he is our hero, as we listeners, or read-
ers, are easily welcomed into his first little troop of lucky few, who
so possessively, and with such palpable endearment, often call
him *mio Cid*—my Cid.

The *Cantar* or *Poema de Mio Cid* has survived some eight hun-
dred years as a written poem, and perhaps decades longer than
that as part of an oral poetic tradition. Long regarded as Spain's
national epic, it recounts the clearly fictionalized life and deeds of
a charismatic historical figure who played a role in some of the
dramatic episodes of the tumultuous eleventh century. *The Cid*
has particularly strong kinship with other national epics (includ-
ing the American Western) that recount mythologized historical
events believed to be vital to the formation of a people or a na-
tion. Central to many of these is an acting-out of the passage from
the almost wild universe of unruly frontiers and their attendant
injustices to the new world—the new community, the new nation—
where a newly crystallized society is instead governed by laws, and
where justice reigns.

The Cid's roughly 3,700 lines are divided into 152 stanzas
(called *tiradas* in Spanish, and *laisses* in French, and sometimes in
English) of irregular length. These are in turn part of three major
subdivisions called *cantares*, powerfully suggesting the work's in-
extricability from the tradition of singing (*cantar*); in English, *can-
tares* is easily translated as "canto." Much else about the poem's
form—its single lines broken into half lines, its oft-repeated for-
mulas, its irregular meter, its use of assonance—also suggests
that the poem that comes down to us was composed and per-
formed orally, and transmitted orally for some time, before being
committed to writing. But the poem's occasional learned and
ecclesiastical expressions, and its detailed understanding of im-
portant legal traditions, suggest instead that there were written
sources of various sorts at play in the creation of the poem, and
perhaps even that the version we read today is a text originally
composed as a written poem.

In either event, one of the poem's most distinctive features is its
relative proximity to the historical events narrated. The roughly

contemporary *Song of Roland* recounts the overtly mythologized story of Charlemagne and his troops crossing the Pyrenees in 778, returning to France from Spain after the siege of Saragossa—events removed from the mid-twelfth-century audience's lifetime by some four hundred years. Regardless of whether the *Cid* poet was a wandering and illiterate blind bard, whose masterpiece was most canonically performed in the last decade of the twelfth century before being recorded by a scribe, or instead a cultured lawyer, who had studied in France and even read some of the French epics, such as *The Song of Roland*, and who finished writing his text in 1207, he was evoking a past that was not far beyond living memory, and that was still well enough known that any number of its salient historical milestones did not need to be retold in the poem in order to be understood.

The historical Cid died in 1099. He had lived out his life of military prowess and fame during a particularly momentous period of Spain's history: The last quarter of the eleventh century was pivotal in the Iberian peninsula, much of which had been an Islamic polity for nearly four hundred years. After several centuries of grandeur and cultural achievement, the Caliphate of Cordoba collapsed at the beginning of the eleventh century, torn apart by civil wars provoked by crises of succession, as well as a series of ideological rifts—contemporaries poignantly called this era the *fitna*, or times of troubles. What remained after the demise of the once powerful central state of Cordoba were dozens of often warring city-states, called the Taifas, from the Arabic *muluk at-tawaif*, meaning the kingdoms of divided parties, or factions. Although they continued and even expanded many of the great cultural traditions of the past, especially poetry, these fractured kingdoms became increasingly vulnerable to the military incursions and ambitions of the various relatively small Christian kingdoms of the north.

These now-expanding Christian polities—Asturias, Galicia, León, Navarre, Aragon, Barcelona, and, of course, Castile were the major ones—often regarded one another as rivals, and most of them had long had all manner of contacts with the Islamic world that lay just over porous and ever-shifting borders. There were military confrontations, perhaps most famous among them the incendiary attack on the pilgrimage city of Santiago de Compostela in 997 by the infamous usurper al-Mansur, a pivotal figure in the downfall of the caliphate. But the complex relations between Islamic and Christian states also included much that was not hostile, including alliances of one Christian kingdom with the Islamic state against their Christian rivals, as well as intermarriages of royal and other important families across the Muslim-Christian divide. And beginning in the Taifa period of the eleventh century, when the events of *The Song of the Cid* take place, weakened Taifa cities began paying *parias*, or tribute money, to Christian kingdoms, in return for protection against all enemies, Christian or Muslim.

At his death in 1065, Ferdinand I of Castile and León—father of Alfonso VI, the king who exiles the Cid, in both history and our poem—was receiving occasional tribute money from the large and important Taifas of Seville and Valencia, and quite regular *parias* from others: Saragossa, Badajoz, and Toledo. The abundant tribute, paid in both coin and goods, as our poem insistently details for us (the Cid collecting such tribute at every turn, as kings did), made some of the Christian kings and kingdoms ever wealthier, and increasingly powerful. And none more so than the Castilians.

Here was a land poised for far-reaching changes, with dramatic shifts of power around almost every corner. Despite the fact that Ferdinand had spent his life and kingship struggling to unite various rival Christian kingdoms, he ultimately chose to leave the land as a divided inheritance to his three sons: the youngest, García, inherited the least central and least desirable kingdom, Galicia; Alfonso, the middle son, received León, considered the richest prize; and Castile went to the eldest brother, Sancho, whose entourage, the historical record reveals, included a rising star, the prominent warrior and courtier Rodrigo Díaz. Not surprisingly, the brothers were not content to share what they had already seen could be a formidable unified kingdom, and they spent most of the decade after their father's death in a series of few-holds-barred struggles against one another. When the dust settled it was not

Rodrigo Díaz's sovereign, Sancho, but rather the middle brother, Alfonso, who emerged as the victor, and who was able once again to create a single united Christian kingdom. But this was achieved only at the expense of his brothers and, in fact, not until Sancho was murdered in 1072, while putting down an insurrection in the dramatically sited city of Zamora, the inheritance and the dominion of Ferdinand's daughter, Urraca. Some believed that Alfonso—who at the time was in exile in Toledo, driven there by Sancho—was directly implicated in the regicide of his brother, perhaps even in collusion with Urraca. These melodramas go unspoken in the poem but are nevertheless understood as the causes behind the exile of the Cid, an exile that is not only the dramatic opening but also the very heart and soul of the poem itself.

Also unspoken in the poem is the cardinal political event of the Cid's lifetime: In 1085, Alfonso—for over a decade now the powerful Alfonso VI of the unified kingdoms of León and Castile—took Toledo outright, suddenly making this glorious old Taifa city no longer part of the Islamic orbit but the new center of Castilian life. Here was a city far larger and vastly more cosmopolitan than any of the older capitals to the north, a brilliant new jewel in the crown of this ambitious and increasingly powerful king. But it was not just Toledo's prosperity that made it of incomparable value, and its conquest a palpable turning point. This was no less a place of profound historical and symbolic importance: Toledo had once been the ancient capital of the Visigoths, the Christian rulers overrun by invading Muslim armies centuries before, and the capital of the church in Spain.

Very little of this escaped the Taifa kings. Although for several generations they had bitter relations among themselves, and many had been militarily dependent on Christians, paying them *parias*, the various Muslim monarchs of the peninsula grasped that the outright loss of Toledo was a defeat of a different order. In a rare moment of something resembling unity among themselves, the Taifa kings, led by their most prominent, al-Mutamid of Seville—who may well be the historical figure loosely summoned up in the poem's "lord of Seville" in the second canto—decided to ask for military assistance against Alfonso, who, emboldened by the ease with which he had taken Toledo, clearly had further expansion in mind. For this they turned, with considerable trepidation, to the Islamic state in power just across the Strait of Gibraltar, a recently ensconced Berber regime called the Almoravids. Led by the imperious Yusuf Ibn Tashufin—the basis for the Yusuf of the poem, against whom the Cid fights the memorable battle to defend Valencia—the Almoravids crossed over to Spain in 1086, just one year after Alfonso had taken Toledo, and helped the Andalusians deal Alfonso a decisive defeat at Zallaqa, one of the most famous battles of the age. They headed back home, but before long the Almoravids were back on the Iberian peninsula, this time to wage war on their erstwhile allies, the hapless Taifa kings, whose kingdoms they now coveted, and who ended up appealing to Alfonso himself for help in what turned out to be their ultimately unsuccessful struggle against these invaders.

Heady times, these, for a warrior, and especially for one like Rodrigo Díaz, who was at odds with Alfonso after the murder of his own king, Sancho, and more often than not was very much his own man. The historical Cid was exiled not once but several times, for reasons that, on at least one occasion, clearly had to do with what Alfonso felt was egregious lack of loyalty—the virtue the poem is devoted to establishing and repeatedly praising—and for embezzling the *parias* he had gone to collect for the Castilian king from al-Mutamid of Seville. And in history, the great Castilian warrior fought at the head of virtually any army that he could muster (and frequently these were "mixed" armies, with both Christian and Muslim soldiers) or that would hire him, including that of the Muslim Taifa of Saragossa.

These details are but the tip of the iceberg of differences between what history records and what the poem narrates. The poem is a work of historical fiction, a literary masterpiece that paints its original stories on a vivid historical canvas. Some events in the poem are wholly imaginary, such as the marriages of the Cid's daughters to two fictitious noblemen and the sequence of events that follow from that dramatic plot turn, but even these are saturated with historical allusions and truths, spun out of a dense fabric of historical concerns, including those of the moment at which the poem crystallizes, a century after the events narrated. Some would say that, as with most other historical fiction, it is really the political and social dramas, the anxieties and preoccupations, of the poet's time, rather than those of the events narrated, that lie just beneath the surface.

Arguably the most notable historical concerns that have long colored readings of the poem are not from the eleventh century, or even from the twelfth or the thirteenth, but from much later centuries, when Spain no longer had Muslims living on the peninsula, and when implacable religious enmity between the two peoples was believed to have always driven encounters between them. Popular beliefs about the poem deeply affect readings of it, as well as of the history it may reflect. Because this is a text long perceived as central to understanding the national character, there are distinctive claims made as to what it is about—the Reconquest, the ideologically charged struggle of the Christians against the Moors—that are difficult to find in the poem itself, a poem, it is vital to note, that contains a single character—a Frankish churchman, to boot, rather than any Castilian—who speaks and behaves as a wild-eyed Moorslayer, as the later mythology tells us all Christians did.

Writing about *The Song of the Cid* in *El País Semanal* in 2007, the year of the poem's eight-hundredth anniversary, Javier Marías, one of Spain's most prominent contemporary writers, remarked that it is one of those books that few know but that most believe they have read. Many surprises await those who imagine, before actually reading the *Cid*, that the poem pivots on the epic struggles between Christians and Muslims in medieval Spain, much as the famous Old French *Song of Roland* pivots on its epic struggle between "Christians and Pagans." Although the Cid is indeed a warrior of epic skills, and although his exploits on the battlefields from Castile to the outskirts of Saragossa and ultimately to Valencia can be seen as the stepping-stones of the plot, the heart of *The Song of the Cid* is not at all in its warfare. And while many, perhaps most, either in Spain or abroad, are likely to say that the Cid is a hero because of his role in reclaiming Christian lands, an attentive reading of the poem reveals that this is scarcely an issue at all, and that while our hero may be a pious Christian he is not driven by anything like religious zeal in his battles and conquests. Both the Cid and his poem have other preoccupations, and other problems to resolve.

Exile, as well as the opportunities for triumph and redemption that exile provides, is the poem's principal concern, and that of its surprisingly tenderhearted warrior-hero. The Cid's first stop on his way out of Castile is the monastery of San Pedro de Cardeña, some half-dozen miles to the southeast of Burgos. His wife, Jimena, and their two small daughters, Elvira and Sol, are already there, and as Rodrigo leaves them in the care of the abbot Don Sancho—for clearly the Cid cannot take them into the rough unknown that his political banishment forces him to face—we witness scenes of unembarrassed familial passion. We also hear the Cid's profound concern not only for their immediate well-being, but just as much for what might seem, at first glance, to lie in a distant and peripheral future: his daughters' eventual marriages.

The question of what will become of Elvira and Sol will turn out to be not distant at all but indeed quite central—the Warrior's enduring concern, from this beginning until the final lines of the poem, which celebrate the extraordinary matches finally and triumphantly made. When we ride with the Cid out of Castile and down those roads he is forced to take, to build a new life for himself after he has been cast out, and his whole universe thus scattered, we grasp that the poem is preoccupied with the ways and means of re-establishing the order and justice in the universe that were lost when the Cid was exiled. Exiled unfairly, as a host of voices in the poem invariably remind us, our hero must display publicly, over and over again, his abundant good qualities in order to make things right. And while some of these good qualities are the virtues one would expect of a legendary warrior—utter fearlessness and great physical prowess—others are those that make him an appropriate hero for a society whose affairs are conducted largely off the battlefield: transparent honesty and dignity; belief that justice prevails; and exceptional generosity to all, including the king who has banished him. The Cid's unflinching loyalty to Alfonso, despite the unfair exile, and his quest for justice, to reclaim his rightful place in society, are perhaps the most vivid and omnipresent strands in the poem, and tightly interwoven.

Once out of Castile, the Cid and his men begin their quest for a new life, which means they will attack and raid one town after another. This war-making is motivated neither by politics of any sort, religious or otherwise, nor by the desire to conquer the lands attacked and make them his own, at least until Valencia is reached in the second canto, some three years after his having been forced to flee from home. It is only then, when the Cid takes one of Spain's greatest cities, *Valencia la clara,* "shining Valencia," that he feels he has found a new home for his family. Up until then, the goal was far simpler: the accumulation of ever-greater wealth. Some of the material gains come directly off the battle-fields, and we quickly learn the very great value of horses, as well as their saddles, and of tents and, of course, of the great swords of kings, two of which he will win in combat: the first, taken from the Christian Count of Barcelona, is named Colada, while Tizón is won from Búcar, the Muslim king of Morocco who first appears at the beginning of the third canto. A great deal of the gain also comes as coin, both silver and gold, the tribute that mimics the *parias* that defined relations between Christian and Muslim king-doms, here paid outright to the Cid either because he has taken a place or, once his fame begins to precede him, to prevent him from attacking.

And his fame does begin to grow immediately, from his first raid (dangerously made inside Alfonso's Castilian territories, as they are on their way out) onward, and with that renown, and with the wealth that increases with every raid and conquest, more and more men will flock to his side. Within a few years, the war-rior we first glimpsed as he was leaving Burgos, weeping, with a handful of loyalists at his side, finds himself at the head of a real army, all volunteers, all happy to join what has become a profit-able adventure. Our poem is always careful to have us understand that this juggernaut of success is rooted in the virtue of generosity, in the giving away much more than in the taking: The Cid is from the outset a veritable river to his men. Never, while he is traveling the roads that lead from the near despair of losing everything to the triumph of great wealth and possession of a major city, do we sense that our hero is craven, or bloodthirsty, or anything other than a man whose unjust exile is what has transformed him into this legendary warrior ("Castile's great exile had become a serious danger") and forced him to make such a life for himself and his men. In stanza 62, the Cid tells the vanquished Count of Barcelona that he will release him but not return any of the hoard he has taken from him "Because I need it for these men of mine, / Who have, like me, no other way to find it. / We stay alive by taking from others, as we have with you. / And this will be our life for as long as God desires, / Living as men must, when their king has thrown them into exile." And a considerable part of the fortune won this way also serves the vital purpose of re-establishing the Cid's standing with King Alfonso, to whom he begins to send always greater gifts from the bounty he takes with each battle, each victory.

The king, in turn, begins to see the worth of the warrior he has exiled, taking the measure of his utter fearlessness, which enables him to move easily from one conquest to the next, even when he and his men are seriously outnumbered. The monarch also sees the warrior's worth in terms of the considerable wealth he amasses, a substantial part of which then becomes his own. Although he cannot pardon the Cid with undue haste, Alfonso appears to understand his error from early on—an error, it would appear, rooted in poor counsel, the corrupt advice of jealous nobles close to him. The king does almost immediately pardon those close to the Cid and, each time he receives his always greater gifts, encourages others to band with him: "Rejoin my Cid and seek more treasure."

Predictably, however, our hero's ability to transform the original desolation of his exile into a triumph of might and growing wealth, of great fame and near-universal admiration, of personal dignity and worth in the face of injustice and duress, provokes even greater envy and covetousness among some of those in King Alfonso's court. And so it is that less than halfway through the poem its core dramas begin, when two young noblemen (who we can see in a minute are far from noble of character) persuade Alfonso to betroth them to the Cid's daughters. The rest of this animated, fast-moving, and often surprising narrative poem plays out the story of these obviously ill-fated marriages to the nobles of Carrión, and the trials of every sort that follow from them.

Virtually all of the events of the dramatic dénouement are starkly literary: the opening scene of the third canto, when a lion escapes while the Cid is sleeping, and in an instant lays bare the cowardice of the sons-in-law; the heartbreaking beating of the Cid's daughters, in a distant and dark woods, and the poignant sorrow of the father when he is told, revealing a warrior determined to seek social justice for the outrage, rather than the physical vengeance he could easily have had; the pageantry-filled court that Alfonso calls in Toledo, where every noble in the land is summoned to witness the charges and countercharges; and then the dramatic confrontation between the Cid and those among the nobility who have long sought to discredit and banish him, a showdown, we realize, that has been coming all along. The Cid, our Warrior, emerges the victor in all of these trials without once lifting his own sword.

The *Cantar de Mio Cid* has long enjoyed a seminal place in the Spanish consciousness of its notoriously complex medieval past and, thanks in some measure to the popular 1961 big-screen extravaganza *El Cid*—with international stars Charlton Heston and Sophia Loren in the leading roles—a certain place in the popular imagination beyond Spain, a kind of window into this unusual chapter in medieval European history. The text of the poem survives in a unique and incomplete manuscript that is a fourteenth-century copy of an earlier and lost one, probably from the early thirteenth century. Today considered one of the greatest treasures of the Biblioteca Nacional in Madrid, it was acquired only in 1960, after circulating for several hundred years among private collectors and interested scholars. Although the manuscript was discovered in 1596—in Vivar, appropriately enough, the legendary birthplace of the Cid—the existence of the work was not revealed to a broader public until the publication of a scholarly edition by Tomás Antonio Sánchez in 1779, an edition clearly a part of the universe of Romantic discovery and study of the medieval world. From that moment on, this narrative poem has remained indissolubly linked to very broad intellectual and scholarly disputes, and especially so to arguments, both direct and indirect, over the national origins and character of Spain, and about the qualities of its culture, arguments scarcely resolved to this day.

The peculiarities of the mutilated manuscript have, from the outset, seemed to invite persistent and divisive disputes: on one hand, the first folio—and with it probably some fifty verses—is missing; on the other, at the end of the nearly four thousand verses, there is explicit mention of someone called Per Abbat and the specific date—1207, once the calculation is made from the Hispanic to the Julian calendar—he tells us he recorded the poem in his manuscript: "Per Abbat le escrivió en el mes de mayo . . ." Most scholars agree that the Old Castilian *escrivir* here does not refer to authorship but rather indicates that Per Abbat copied the manuscript, and most also believe that this would be perfectly congruent with a great deal of what is known about the anonymity of many medieval texts and the vicissitudes of their translation from the universe of oral culture to that of the written word. All of this leaves wide open the question of authorship and, closely related, that of dating—problems not unique but in their general parameters shared by other famous premodern epics, not least the *Iliad* and the *Odyssey*. At the same time, the lacuna at the beginning of the poem—vital, among other reasons, because we tend to assume it would have told us more about the roots and causes of the Cid's exile—provoked a far-reaching practice of filling in the poem's story from other sources, as if the poem itself were merely a fragment of a larger story, rather than an autonomous artistic composition related to but distinguishable from the history that emerges from other sources.

Other sources do certainly abound. Long before the discovery and publication of this masterly poem, materials about the life of the Cid were plentiful, and some of these were roughly contemporary, going back to his own lifetime in the eleventh century, or the century or two immediately thereafter. These include purportedly historical as well as openly legendary and literary material, although unambiguous distinctions between the two are sometimes difficult to make, and not only when we are dealing with medieval material. Rodrigo Díaz was a charismatic and well-known figure in his lifetime, as attested to in fairly simple historical documents known as "diplomas" (or charters) that speak to his participation in events at various courts of the Castilian monarchy. Beyond these there are also two important Latin works, one a history, *Historia Roderici* (1140–47), and the other a historical poem, the *Carmen Campidoctoris* (*The Song of the Warrior*), which was long believed to be contemporary with the Cid's life but is now thought to be from as much as a century later. Material about the Cid's life proliferates in later histories composed at the court of the prolific scholar-king Alfonso X, from the mid-thirteenth century on, especially in the massive *Estoria de España* (*History of Spain*). These written histories themselves incorporate extensive popular and orally derived materials about the Cid, much of it clearly bound up with the vigorous ballad tradition, the *Romancero*, which overflowed with popular songs about the Cid, and was itself closely linked to a broader epic tradition that, with the exception of the *Cantar de Mio Cid*, has survived only in these indirect attestations. All of these often entangled sources further beg the question of history versus mythology, or literature, and of the relationship between the oral and the written at a period when the latter was beginning to supplant the former. But in all of this what remains indisputable is the great popularity of all manner of stories about this warrior, a popularity that has long transcended national preoccupations and reached as far as the theater of seventeenth-century Paris, where Corneille's innovative 1636 *Le Cid* proved an immediate success.

In very broad terms, these intertwined problems constitute the principal and still starkly contested grounds of questioning and belief about this singular text: Who, if anyone, composed this masterpiece? Should we understand it not as authored in the modern sense but as part of the oral tradition, an oral tradition that in Spain especially has long been concerned with historical events, and long been believed to carry authentic historical information? Just what is the poem's relationship to the history and historical characters it sings about, and what is the Cid's relationship to the historical figure who actually lived and fought in late eleventh-century Spain? And what does any of it matter to a reader many centuries removed, whether that reader is a Spaniard or an American, a nineteenth-century gentleman or a twenty-first-century student?

In the early twentieth century the towering Spanish scholar Ramón Menéndez Pidal published two works—his edition of the *Poema de Mio Cid*, which came out between 1908 and 1911, and, in 1929, his monumental *La España del Cid*—that powerfully staked out the ground for one set of answers to these questions, and shaped the vision of the poem and its meaning for generations, even to this day. For Menéndez Pidal the *Cantar*—for this is what he invariably calls it (despite the use of the word *poema* in his title), with its strong connotation of being sung rather than written—is unambiguously the product of the oral tradition. An anonymous composition that closely reflects the historical events and milieu of Castile during its formative years, from which the poem, which he dates to circa 1140, is scarcely far removed, Menéndez Pidal's *Cid* is a work of profound and direct historical veracity, revealing to us the Cid's authentic private and civic persona. To make this argument his book begins with a long and impassioned rebuttal of the work of one of the legendary Arabists of the time, a distinguished and prolific specialist in the Hispano-Arabic world named Reinhardt Dozy, whose writings on the Cid were based on, among other things, Arabic documents dating back to the time of the Cid.

Several historical texts do exist in Arabic: A native of Valencia named Ibn 'Alqama, who lived through the Cid's capture of his city, wrote an account long lost in its original form but largely transcribed into a later historical work; another contemporary, Ibn Bassam, profiled notable Andalusians in an important biographical dictionary discovered by Dozy. But Dozy's late-nineteenth-century debunking of the romanticized literary Cid threatened to undermine the Campeador's already well-established hagiography, which made him a paragon of medieval Christian values; indeed, Dozy's work even included the observation that the Cid had qualities far beyond his Arabic name that made him seem more Muslim than Catholic. Menéndez Pidal, however, unembarrassedly argued that our hero's virtues—his loyalty to an unworthy king, which is really to the nation; his open devotion to his family; his generosity to all—needed to be remembered as foundationally Castilian, and thus Spanish, and to be emulated in the difficult present. That present, of course, was the stage-setting for Spain's devastating civil war, and Menéndez Pidal's views not only won the day among most scholars, and among the Spanish intelligentsia, but were also eventually appropriated explicitly by the Franco regime, despite the fact that Menéndez Pidal himself did not share the regime's ideology. As the great historian of medieval Spain Peter Linehan points out, the painful questions about exile and loyalty that bitterly divided Spain's intellectual classes after the triumph of the Nationalists strongly echo the questions at the heart of the poem, and many interpretations of the Cid, and of medieval Spain in general, are indissolubly tied to the dramatic events in Spain's history in the twentieth century.

In 2007 even an innocent traveler to Spain might well have become aware that the year marked the eight hundredth anniversary of the *Cantar de Mio Cid*. The milestone was celebrated in ways both potentially meaningful—a rare public display, one evening, of the precious manuscript at the National Library—and overtly camp—a label, with charging knight and all, on bottles of the sparkling mineral water called Vichy Catalan. And when the Prado, Madrid's extraordinary art museum, opened its new wing to international acclaim, the commemorative exhibition of nineteenth-century history paintings in the new spaces revealed to visitors the once great popularity for painters of the scene of the Cid's daughters, beaten and abandoned in the imaginary Corpes woods. Most remarkable, perhaps, and certainly most unplanned, was the scandal that erupted over the sword long displayed at the Military Museum as the Cid's Tizón, which, along with his other sword, Colada, plays a prominent role in the events of the poem. The sword was sold for a considerable sum to the region of Castile-León, so that it might be displayed in the cathedral at Burgos, where the tombs of the Cid and of his wife, Jimena, are centerpieces of tourist interest. But the Ministry of Culture decided to have the authenticity of the sword scrutinized, and eventually announced that the sword could not possibly have

belonged to the Cid, having been made in the fourteenth or fif-
teenth century. The anniversary display in the cathedral went on
just the same.

Despite this kind of attention—or perhaps because of it—the
poem is indeed, as Javier Marías noted, scarcely read in our own
century, even by educated Spaniards, and almost never approached
outside of loathsome required-reading school lists, nor without a
series of largely negative preconceptions. In a post-Franco Spain,
justifiably proud of its social and economic modernization and of
its increasingly prominent role as one of the leaders of the Euro-
pean community, of an open and ethnically diverse society, it is
perhaps not surprising that there is little real interest in this so-
called national epic, assumed to be openly anti-Muslim and a glo-
rification of a bigoted Christian worldview, a work held up for
so long as emblematic of the Franco era's repressive values. But
these preconceptions are largely unjust and, at times, deeply
ironic, given the centrality of the question of Christian-Muslim
relations not just in Spain but also throughout the world in the
twenty-first century.

The poem itself reveals a far more complex world than most
imagine, a universe within which, among many other things, the
Christian hero's most trusted ally can be a Muslim, and where the
most odious villains are important members of the Castilian aris-
tocracy. As readers of Burton Raffel's vigorous new translation
will immediately discover, the reality of the poem is very different
from the mythology, and its preoccupations are enduring ones.
Although few readers of either the glorious Old Spanish or this
brisk and instantly captivating new English version will sympa-
thize with all of its values—and when is that ever the case with a
work of fiction?—most will find themselves transported to a world
sometimes unexpectedly familiar. Raffel's rendition serves to re-
mind readers of the straightaway power of oral narratives—hence
the choice of the title *The Song of the Cid*—and captures much of
the genius of the poem, especially its frontierlike directness and its
unashamed expression of the most fundamental aspects of the hu-
man condition: the seduction of wealth, the grief of exile from a
homeland, the unspeakable love of one's children, the anger pro-
voked by betrayals, the difficult contemplation of how to achieve

justice. And all of this plays out on a stage where warfare is a fact of life, and yet where there is a visible and central struggle to re-place raw violence with the rule of law as the ultimate arbiter of justice. Here we have an epic narrative that vividly conjures up a world at once removed and yet far from remote from us.

MARÍA ROSA MENOCAL

Suggestions for Further Reading

A vast library of scholarship and commentary on *The Song of the Cid* exists. Mentioned here are a very small selection of essential works in the history of the poem's interpretation as well as recommendations for further exploration by the general reader. Many of the works cited contain extensive bibliographical guidance.

The most influential early works of scholarship on the Cid are Menéndez Pidal's edition of the *Poema de Mio Cid* and his study *La España del Cid*, which exists in an English translation from 1934, *The Cid and His Spain*, by Harold Sunderland (London: J. Murray); both remain of considerable value and interest, and enduring influence. It is more than a curiosity to note that Menéndez Pidal served as an advisor to the 1961 Hollywood production of *El Cid* and that the story told in the film is based only in small part on the events of the poem itself but principally on Menéndez Pidal's version of the history, as reconstructed from other texts. A number of recent Spanish editions of the poem provide useful commentary on textual and historical problems, extended bibliographies, as well as fundamental readings of the poem that can differ dramatically from those of Menéndez Pidal. Among these see especially Eukene Lacarra Lanz, *Poema de Mio Cid* (Barcelona: Area, 2002), and Alberto Montaner and Francisco Rico, *Cantar de Mio Cid* (Barcelona: Crítica, first published in 1993 but republished in an anniversary edition in 2007). Lacarra Lanz was herself the author of a landmark study of the poem in 1980, *Poema de Mio Cid: Realidad histórica e ideología* (Madrid: Porrúa Turanzas), which argued, against Menéndez Pidal, that the poem is the written work of a learned man, deeply versed in the law, and concerned with the early-thirteenth-century struggles among the different classes of the nobility, and their relations with royalty.

The arguments in favor of a learned single author were expanded a few years later by Colin Smith in *The Making of the Poema de mio Cid* (Cambridge: Cambridge University Press, 1983). Smith breaks even more radically, and controversially, with the notion that the poem is the product of the oral tradition, suggesting that it is instead "a wholly new work of the early thirteenth century, by a single learned author who was not dependent either on an existing epic tradition in Castilian or on earlier vernacular poems about the Cid." Smith's own edition of the poem was published by Oxford University Press in 1972 and in many quarters—among both those who agree with his vision of the poem's authorship and those who do not—has since replaced that of Menéndez Pidal. The most comprehensive countervision to Smith's is thoroughly laid out by Joseph Duggan in *The Cantar de mio Cid: Poetic Creation in Its Economic and Social Contexts* (Cambridge: Cambridge University Press, 1989). This landmark study for the first time brought detailed attention to the vast gift economy of the poem, and to the ways in which the acquisition and distribution of wealth are intimately tied to other thematic concerns, especially the preoccupations with social morality and nobility. Duggan's book also provides a spirited defense of the hypothesis that the work was orally composed, arguing at the same time that the poetic achievements of anonymous works from the oral tradition are not primitive or inferior literary forms. Although completely at odds with Lacarra Lanz and Smith on the question of authorship, Duggan's book, like theirs, places considerable emphasis on the gestalt at the time of the composition of the literary work, and provides an excellent history of the late-twelfth-century political and social issues that inform the poem recorded by Per Abbat in 1207.

Although most of these editions and studies contain narratives of the history of Spain in the eleventh century, and of the Cid's life, none can match the breadth and depth of Richard Fletcher's *The Quest for El Cid* (New York: Knopf, 1990). This is today the fundamental and highly readable source for the life and times of the historical Cid, complete with extended discussions of the historical sources in all languages; invaluable as well are Fletcher's detailed observations on the differences between the presentation of the hero in the poem and what is known from other sources, and the ways that some traditions of scholarship have blurred the two. Other accessible narratives of the history of the period, in the broader context of the cultures and histories of medieval Spain, include Fletcher's *Moorish Spain* (Berkeley: University of California Press, 1992), Bernard F. Reilly, *The Medieval Spains* (Cambridge: Cambridge University Press, 1983), and María Rosa Menocal, *The Ornament of the World* (New York: Little Brown, 2002). Peter Linehan's 1996 article "The Court Historiographer of Francoism?: *La leyenda oscura* of Ramón Menéndez Pidal" appeared in the *Bulletin of Spanish Studies* (73:4, 437–450) and is essential reading for anyone interested in the intersection of contemporary and historical concerns in general, and especially in the life and works of the great Spanish intellectuals who survived the civil war and had to choose either exile or a return to Franco's Spain.

MARÍA ROSA MENOCAL

A Note on the Translation

My basic text has been *Poema de Mio Cid*, edited by Colin Smith. I have used the second edition, a Spanish-language text (1985), rather than the original English-language edition (1972), because the second edition has been corrected and enlarged. I have occasionally not followed Smith, particularly with regard to line sequence and the correct placement of the arabic numerals indicating a new section (*laisse*). Miguel de Unamuno's *Gramática y Glosario del Poema del Cid*, posthumously published in 1977, has often been helpful.

BURTON RAFFEL

The Song of the Cid

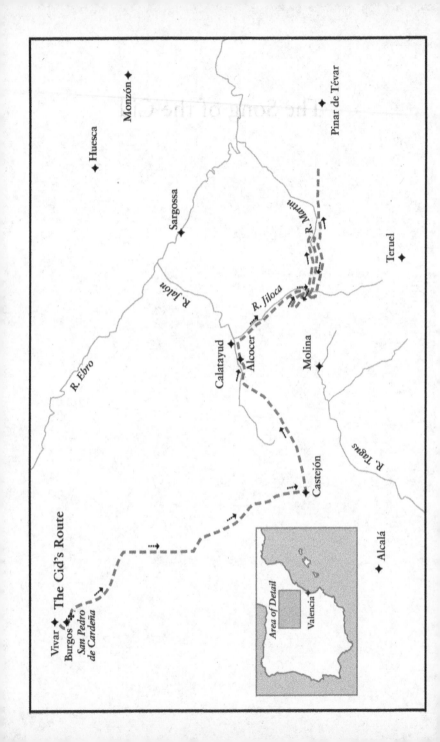

CANTO ONE

[*The beginning of the poem is lost. Historical documents show that the King of Castile had turned against the Cid and given him nine days to leave.*]

1

De los sos ojos   tan fuertemientre llorando,
tornava la cabeça   e estávalos catando;
vio puertas abiertas   e uços sin cañados,
alcándaras vazías,   sin pielles e sin mantos
e sin falcones   e sin adtores mudados.
Sospiró Mio Cid,   ca mucho avié grandes cuidados;
fabló Mio Cid   bien e tan mesurado:
"¡Grado a ti, Señor,   Padre que estás en alto!
Esto me an buelto   mios enemigos malos."

2

Allí piensan de aguijar,   allí sueltan las rriendas;
a la exida de Bivar   ovieron la corneja diestra
e entrando a Burgos   oviéronla siniestra.
Meció Mio Cid los ombros   e engrameó la tiesta:
"¡Albricia, Álbar Fáñez,   ca echados somos de tierra!"

3

Mio Cid Rruy Díaz   por Burgos entrava,
en su conpaña   *sessaenta* pendones.
Exiénlo ver   mugieres e varones,
burgeses e burgesas   por las finiestras son,

[*The beginning of the poem is lost. Historical documents show that the King of Castile had turned against the Cid and given him nine days to leave.*]

I

Tears were flowing from his eyes, then flowing faster
As he turned and looked back, just standing.
He saw the doors, swung open, padlocks gone,
Wall pegs empty, no furs, no gowns
Or cloaks, no falcons or molting hawks.
My Cid sighed, his burdens weighing him down.
My Cid spoke, in measured, well-controlled tones:
"I thank you, my Father, my Lord on high!
This is the vulture trap my evil enemies sent me."

2

They spurred the horses, let the reins hang low.
To their right, leaving Vivar, they saw a hooded crow,
But as they reached Burgos it flew to their left.
My Cid shrugged his shoulders and shook his head:
"Let it be a good sign, Alvar Fáñez, for now we're exiles!"

3

My Cid, Ruy Díaz, rode into Burgos.
His sixty men carried spears, hung with banners.
Men and women came out, when they appeared;
Merchants and their wives leaned from their windows, staring,

plorando de los ojos,   tanto avién el dolor;
de las sus bocas   todos dizían una rrazón:
"¡Dios, qué buen vassallo,   si oviesse buen señor!"

4

Conbidar le ien de grado,   mas ninguno non osava,
el rrey don Alfonso   tanto avié la grand saña;
antes de la noche   en Burgos d'él entró su carta
con grand rrecabdo   e fuertemientre sellada:
que a Mio Cid Rruy Díaz   que nadi nol' diessen posada
e aquel que ge la diesse   sopiesse vera palabra
que perderié los averes   e más los ojos de la cara
e aun demás   los cuerpos e las almas.
Grande duelo avién   las yentes cristianas,
ascóndense de Mio Cid,   ca nol' osan dezir nada.
El Campeador   adeliñó a su posada,
assí como llegó a la puerta,   fallóla bien cerrada
por miedo del rrey Alfonso,   que assí lo avién parado
que si non la quebrantás por fuerça,   que non ge la abriesse
    nadi.
Los de Mio Cid   a altas vozes llaman,
los de dentro   non les querién tornar palabra.
Aguijó Mio Cid,   a la puerta se llegava,
sacó el pie del estribera,   una ferídal' dava;
non se abre la puerta,   ca bien era cerrada.
Una niña de nuef años   a ojo se parava:
"¡Ya Campeador,   en buen ora cinxiestes espada!
El rrey lo ha vedado,   anoch d'él e[n]tró su carta
con grant rrecabdo   e fuertemientre sellada.
Non vos osariemos   abrir nin coger por nada;
si non, perderiemos   los averes e las casas
e demás - los ojos de las caras.
Cid, en el nuestro mal   vós non ganades nada,
mas el Criador vos vala   con todas sus vertudes sanctas."
Esto la niña dixo   e tornós' pora su casa.

Weeping, overcome with sorrow.
And from their lips, all of them, fell the same prayer:
"O God, what a wonderful servant, if only he had a decent
    master!"

4

They would have been glad to ask him in, but no one dared;
Don Alfonso, the king, was far too angry.
He'd sent the city a notice, received the night before,
Sealed in dramatic passion, and urgent:
My Cid, Ruy Díaz, was to be turned away,
Given nothing. Whoever dared to disobey
Would lose whatever they owned, their eyes would be torn from
    their heads,
And their bodies and souls would be lost forever.
Every Christian in Burgos was bent in fear
And sorrow, hiding from my Cid, too terrified to speak.
The Warrior rode to the Burgos house where he'd always gone;
He stood at the door, solid and bolted shut
By the people inside, for fear of King Alfonso.
Unless he broke it down, nothing would force it open.
My Cid called to them, his voice raised high,
But no one inside would reply.
My Cid rode up to the door,
Slipped his foot from the stirrup, and kicked at the place.
But no one opened what was closed tight in his face.
    Then a little girl appeared, nine years old:
"It's done, Warrior, you who have worn your sword so proudly!
The king has forbidden it, his order came last night—
Strict and fierce, harsh and sealed all over, tight.
We don't dare help you, we can't do a thing,
And if we did, we'd lose our houses and everything—
And what's still worse, the eyes in our heads!
My Cid, you'd win nothing from our misery, our death,
But may the Creator protect you with his heavenly blessing."
The little girl said this, then went back in her house.

Ya lo vee el Cid   que del rrey non avié gr[aci]a;
partiós' de la puerta,   por Burgos aguijava,
llegó a Sancta María,   luego descavalga,
fincó los inojos,   de coraçón rrogava.
La oración fecha,   luego cavalgava,
salió por la puerta   e Arlançón pa[s]sava,
cabo essa villa   en la glera posava,
fincava la tienda   e luego descavalgava.
Mio Cid Rruy Díaz,   el que en buen ora cinxo espada,
posó en la glera   quando nol' coge nadi en casa,
derredor d'él   una buena conpaña;
assí posó Mio Cid   como si fuesse en montaña.
Vedádal' an conpra   dentro en Burgos la casa
de todas cosas   quantas son de vianda;
non le osarién vender   al menos dinarada.

5

Martín Antolínez,   el burgalés conplido,
a Mio Cid e a los suyos   abástales de pan e de vino,
non lo conpra,   ca él se lo avié consigo,
de todo conducho   bien los ovo bastidos;
pagós' Mio Cid e todos los otros   que van a so cervicio.
Fabló Martín A[n]tolínez,   odredes lo que á dicho:
"¡Ya Canpeador,   en buen ora fuestes nacido!
Esta noch y[a]gamos   e vay[á]mosnos al matino,
ca acusado seré   de lo que vos he servido,
en ira del rrey Alfonso   yo seré metido.
Si convusco escapo   sano o bivo,
aún cerca o tarde   el rrey querer me ha por amigo,
si non, quanto dexo   no lo precio un figo."

My Cid knew the king was burning inside.
He turned away from the door, galloped through Burgos,
Straight to Saint Mary's cathedral, where he dropped from his
　　horse,
Fell on his knees, and prayed from his heart.
The moment his prayer was finished, he departed;
Galloping through city gates he crossed the great river, the
　　Arlanzón.
Not far from Burgos, sand all around,
He stopped, ordered tents put up, and then dismounted.
My Cid, Ruy Díaz, who had worn his sword with pride,
Was lodged, near this city now closed to him, in a barren sand
　　pile,
But with good company all around him.
My Cid, camped as if in a mountain wilderness,
Forbidden to buy food of any kind, in Burgos,
Nothing at all, and the people behind their doors
Barred from selling him half a penny's worth.

5

Martín Antolínez, that deft citizen,
Brought bread and wine for my Cid and his men—
Things he did not buy, he already had them—
So they had plenty, whatever they wanted.
Warrior Cid, mighty Conqueror, was glad,
And so were all who'd come with him.
　　Martín Antolínez spoke: listen to what he said!
"O, mighty Cid, born at a lucky hour!
Stay here tonight, and we'll leave in the morning—
Because, for sure, I'll be accused of doing what I've done,
And King Alfonso's anger will hunt me down.
If I run off with you, and stay in one piece,
Sooner or later the king will want to be friendly—
And if not, whatever I leave is dust on the ground."

6

Fabló Mio Cid,   el que en buen ora cinxo espada:
"¡Martín Antolínez,   sodes ardida lança!
Si yo bivo,   doblar vos he la soldada.
Espeso é el oro   e toda la plata,
bien lo vedes   que yo non trayo aver
e huebos me serié | pora toda mi compaña.
Fer lo he amidos,   de grado non avrié nada:
con vuestro consejo   bastir quiero dos arcas,
inchámoslas d'arena,   ca bien serán pesadas,
cubiertas de guadalmecí   e bien enclaveadas.

7

"Los guadamecís vermejos   e los clavos bien dorados.
Por Rrachel e Vidas   vayádesme privado:
quando en Burgos me vedaron conpra   e el rrey me á airado,
non puedo traer el aver,   ca mucho es pesado,
enpeñar ge lo he   por lo que fuere guisado,
de noche lo lieven   que non lo vean cristianos.
Véalo el Criador   con todos los sos sanctos,
yo más non puedo   e amidos lo fago."

8

Martín Antolínez   non lo detarda,
por Rrachel e Vidas   apriessa demandava;
passó por Burgos,   al castiello entrava,
por Rrachel e Vidas   apriessa demandava.

6

My Cid replied, he who raised his sword at a lucky hour:
"Martín Antolínez, you're a bold soldier!
If I live, I'll double your pay!
I've used up all my gold, and my silver,
You can see for yourself I've taken nothing away.
I've got to find something for these men of mine—
No one will help; I'll do what I dislike.
So lend me a hand, we'll make two storage chests.
We'll stuff them with sand, I want them good and heavy,
Covered with leather, embossed and studded just right!

7

"The leather will be crimson, the nails perfectly gilded.
Now go, as fast as you can, tell Raguel and Vidas:
Since I'm barred from Burgos, and the king is still angry,
And I can't carry what I've got—it's much too heavy—
I need to pawn it at some fair price.
Tell them to come and take it at night, so Christians can't spy.
Let God almighty see, and all his saints:
This isn't business I like; what good would it do to complain?"

8

Martín Antolínez did not sit around waiting,
But rode to Burgos, passed through its fortified gates
And quickly riding through the castle
Asked for Raguel and Vidas.

9

Rrachel e Vidas   en uno estavan amos
en cuenta de sus averes,   de los que avién ganados.
Llegó Martín Antolínez   a guisa de menbrado:
"¿Ó sodes, Rrachel e Vidas,   los mios amigos caros?
En poridad fablar   querría con amos."
Non lo detardan,   todos tres se apartaron:
"Rrachel e Vidas,   amos me dat las manos
que non me descubrades   a moros nin a cristianos;
por siempre vos faré rricos   que non seades menguados.
El Campeador   por las parias fue entrado,
grandes averes priso   e mucho sobejanos,
rretovo d'ellos   quanto que fue algo,
por én vino a aquesto   por que fue acusado.
Tiene dos arcas   llenas de oro esmerado,
ya lo vedes   que el rrey le á airado,
dexado ha heredades   e casas e palacios;
aquéllas non las puede levar,   si non, serién ventadas,
el Campeador   dexar las ha en vuestra mano
e prestalde de aver   lo que sea guisado.
Prended las arcas   e metedlas en vuestro salvo,
con grand jura   meted í las fes amos
que non las catedes   en todo aqueste año."
Rrachel e Vidas   seyénse consejando:
"Nós huebos avemos   en todo de ganar algo;
bien lo sabemos   que él algo gañó,
quando a tierra de moros entró,   que grant aver sacó;
non duerme sin sospecha   qui aver trae monedado.
Estas arcas   prendámoslas amas,
en logar las metamos   que non sean ventadas.
Mas dezidnos del Cid,   ¿de qué será pagado,
o qué ganancia nos dará   por todo aqueste año?"
Rrespuso Martín Antolínez   a guisa de menbrado:
"Mio Cid querrá   lo que sea aguisado,
pedir vos á poco   por dexar so aver en salvo.
Acógensele omnes   de todas partes me[n]guados,

9

Raguel and Vidas were together, as he knew they would,
Weighing and counting gold and silver; business was good.
Martín Antolínez knew how to greet them:
"So here you are, my dear friends? I need to speak to you, in
    private."
Without another word, the three of them stepped inside.
"Raguel and Vidas, each of you give me your hands.
Swear you won't reveal this, to either Moors or Christians:
I'm going to make you rich forever, you'll never need more.
My Cid collected King Alfonso's tribute—a fortune,
Fantastic huge amounts;
He kept most of it for himself—
Now he's been accused, and he fled.
He brought two hidden chests, heavy with finest gold.
You know he's running from the king:
He's had to leave his houses, land, and everything.
He cannot travel with those chests—everyone would know.
My Cid will leave them when he goes,
For a loan that's decent, gracious.
Come take the chests, and keep them safe—
Swear you'll leave them untouched, right here,
For one entire year."
    Raguel and Vidas whispered to each other, then stopped:
"Any business we do must earn us a profit.
My Cid went to the Moors, made himself rich;
But he who travels, burdened with gold, won't sleep at night.
Yes, we'll take those chests,
We'll keep them hidden where no one will know.
But how much does my Cid want of our gold?
And how much interest will come from this entire year?"
    Martín Antolínez knew what to answer:
"My Cid wants nothing that isn't fair,
He asks very little, putting his treasure in your hands.
People on every hand are making demands:
The sum he needs is six hundred gold marks."

á menester   seiscientos marcos."
Dixo Rrachel e Vidas: "Dar ge los [emos] de grado."
"Ya vedes que entra la noch,   el Cid es pressurado,
huebos avemos   que nos dedes los marcos."
Dixo Rrachel e Vidas: "Non se faze assí el mercado,
sinon primero prendiendo   e después dando."
Dixo Martín Antolínez: "Yo d'esso me pago;
amos tred   al Campeador contado
e nós vos ayudaremos,   que assí es aguisado,
por aduzir las arcas   e meterlas en vuestro salvo
que non lo sepan   moros nin cristianos."
Dixo Rrachel e Vidas: "Nós d'esto nos pagamos;
las arcas aduchas,   prendet seyescientos marcos."
Martín Antolínez   cavalgó privado
con Rrachel e Vidas   de volu[n]tad e de grado.
Non viene a la puent,   ca por el agua á passado,
que ge lo non ventassen   de Burgos omne nado.
Afévoslos a la tienda   del Campeador contado,
assí como entraron,   al Cid besáronle las manos.
Sonrrisós' Mio Cid,   estávalos fablando:
"¡Ya don Rrachel e Vidas,   avédesme olbidado!
Ya me exco de tierra   ca del rrey só airado.
A lo quem' semeja,   de lo mío avredes algo,
mientra que vivades   non seredes menguados."
Don Rrachel e Vidas   a Mio Cid besáronle las manos.
Martín Antolínez   el pleito á parado
que sobre aquellas arcas   dar le ien seiscientos marcos
e bien ge las guardarién   fasta cabo del año,
ca assil' dieran la fe   e ge lo avién jurado
que si antes las catassen   que fuessen perjurados,
non les diesse Mio Cid   de la ganancia un dinero malo.
Dixo Martín Antolínez: "Carguen las arcas privado,
levaldas, Rrachel e Vidas,   ponedlas en vuestro salvo;
yo iré convus[c]o   que adugamos los marcos,
ca a mover á Mio Cid   ante que cante el gallo."
Al cargar de las arcas   veriedes gozo tanto,
non las podién poner en somo,   maguer eran esforçados.

Raguel and Vidas replied: "We'll be glad to give him that much."
    "But you'll have to come tonight. My Cid needs to rush,
We need to have that money in hand."
    Raguel and Vidas replied: "We don't do business that way.
First we take, and then we pay."
    Martín Antolínez said: "That's fine with me.
Both of you come to my world-famous Warrior,
And we'll help you (as we ought to do).
Take the treasure and store it
Somewhere hidden from both Christians and Moors."
Raguel and Vidas said: "We agree.
When the chests are here, you'll have your money."
Martín Antolínez wasted no time,
Glad to gallop off with Raguel and Vidas,
Avoiding the bridge, choosing to splash through water, instead,
So no one in Burgos would see them.
They reached the famous Warrior's tent,
Kissing my Cid's hands as they entered.
He smiled and spoke to them:
"Don Raguel, Don Vidas, you surely forgot me!
The king has turned against me, he's thrown me out.
I think you've come to collect some of my treasure:
For the rest of your lives, it will give you pleasure."
Raguel and Vidas kissed his hands again.
Martín Antolínez rehearsed the bargain:
Two great chests to secure a loan of six hundred marks;
The chests would stay for a year, carefully guarded.
They swore in good faith to observe these terms,
Agreeing to waive all interest if their word was broken:
Bad faith and profit did not fit together.
    Martín Antolínez said: "Now take these chests—
Lift them up, bring them wherever
They're safe. I'll ride with you, for collection:
My Cid must leave, tomorrow, before cocks crow."
Lifting such heavy chests clearly pleased them—
Hard to lift even for two such hefty men!
Having such bountiful treasure thrilled them both:

Grádanse Rrachel e Vidas   con averes monedados,
ca mientra que visquiessen   refechos eran amos.

10

Rrachel a Mio Cid   la mánol' ba besar:
"¡Ya Canpeador,   en buen ora cinxiestes espada!
De Castiella vos ides   pora las yentes estrañas,
assí es vuestra ventura,   grandes son vuestras ganancias,
una piel vermeja,   morisca e ondrada,
Cid, beso vuestra mano   en don que la yo aya."
"Plazme," dixo el Cid,   "d'aquí sea mandada;
si vos la aduxier d'allá;   si non, contalda sobre las arcas."
En medio del palacio   tendieron un almofalla,
sobr'ella una sávana   de rrançal e muy blanca.
A tod' el primer colpe   *trezientos* marcos de plata echaron,
notólos don Martino,   sin peso los tomava;
los otros *trezientos*   en oro ge los pagavan;
cinco escuderos tiene don Martino,   a todos los cargava.
Quando esto ovo fecho,   odredes lo que fablava:
"Ya don Rrachel e Vidas,   en vuestras manos son las arcas,
yo que esto vos gané   bien merecía calças."

11

Entre Rrachel e Vidas   aparte ixieron amos:
"Démosle buen don,   ca él no' lo ha buscado.
Martín Antolínez,   un burgalés contado,
vós lo merecedes,   darvos queremos buen dado
de que fagades calças   e rrica piel e buen manto,
dámosvos en don   a vós *treínta* marcos,
merecer no' lo hedes,   ca esto es aguisado;
atorgar nos hedes esto   que avemos parado."

These were riches enough for the rest of their lives,
    they thought.

10

Raguel kissed my Cid's hand once more:
"O Warrior, knighted at a lucky hour!
You're leaving Castile, you'll be among strangers:
This is how your life goes, filled with honors and favors.
I kiss your hand, Cid, to ask you a favor—
A Moorish coat, a good one, with red fur lining."
"Surely," said my Cid. "Consider this a promise.
Either I'll send it, or you'll deduct it from those treasure chests."
    Raguel and Vidas, with Martín Antolínez,
Rode back to Burgos, doing their best
To proceed unseen. They succeeded.
    Then, in the middle of the floor, they spread a carpet,
And placed a snow-white towel on it.
First, they poured out three hundred marks, pure silver,
Which Don Martíno counted, but did not weigh.
The second three hundred marks were gold, and that was paid.
Don Martíno had five men with him, and he loaded them all.
Here's what he said, once that was done:
"All right, Raguel and Vidas! The treasure sits on your floor—
And I, who arranged this, deserve a reward."

11

Raguel and Vidas stepped aside, and whispered:
"Because you found us this treasure, we'll give you a good gift—
You, Martín Antolínez, famous son of Burgos!
We're deeply grateful, and pleased to show it
With enough to make you splendid clothes—
Thirty golden marks you've surely earned,
For your presence and words have truly served us,
And we are grateful for all your help."

Gradeciólo don Martino   e rrecibió los marcos,
gradó exir de la posada   e espidiós' de amos.
Exido es de Burgos   e Arlançón á passado,
vino pora la tienda   del que en buen ora nasco.
Rrecibiólo el Cid   abiertos amos los braços:
"¡Venides, Martín Antolínez,   el mio fiel vassallo!
¡Aún vea el día   que de mí ayades algo!"
"Vengo, Campeador,   con todo buen rrecabdo,
vós *seiscientos*   e yo *treínta* he ganados.
Mandad coger la tienda   e vayamos privado,
en San Pero de Cardeña   í nos cante el gallo,
veremos vuestra mugier,   menbrada fija d'algo.
Mesuraremos la posada   e quitaremos el rreinado,
mucho es huebos   ca cerca viene el plazo."

                                    I 2

Estas palabras dichas,   la tienda es cogida,
Mio Cid e sus conpañas   cavalgan tan aína,
la cara del cavallo   tornó a Sancta María,
alçó su mano diestra,   la cara se sanctigua:
"A ti lo gradesco, Dios,   que cielo e tierra guías,
¡válanme tus vertudes,   gloriosa Sancta María!
D'aquí quito Castiella,   pues que el rrey he en ira,
non sé si entraré í más   en todos los mios días.
¡Vuestra vertud me vala,   Gloriosa, en mi exida
e me ayude | e me acorra   de noch e de día!
Si vós assí lo fiziéredes   e la ventura me fuere conplida,
mando al vuestro altar   buenas donas e rricas,
esto é yo en debdo   que faga í cantar mill missas."

                                    I 3

Spidiós' el caboso   de cuer e de veluntad,
sueltan las rriendas   e piensan de aguijar;
dixo Martín Antolínez: . . . .

Don Martíno thanked them, taking the money,
And anxious to get away, said his goodbyes.
He galloped out of Burgos, across the Arlanzón,
And straight to the tent of the Warrior, born to good fortune.
    My Cid embraced him, hugging him hard:
"You've come, Martín Antolínez, my loyal follower!
O, I wait for the day when I can reward you!"
"Yes, I'm here, Warrior—and I've finished it all.
There's six hundred marks for you, and thirty for me.
Let's pack up the tents and leave in a hurry:
Let's be in San Pedro de Cardeña when the cock starts crowing,
And we'll see your wife, wellborn and wise.
We'll stay a little while, then leave the country.
We've got to hurry, the king gave you nine days to leave."

1 2

The tents came down as soon as he spoke these words,
My Cid and his people went galloping away;
He turned his horse's nose toward Saint Mary's church,
His right hand making a cross on his forehead:
"I thank you, God, guardian of heaven and earth!
O help me with your power, blessèd mother Mary!
I've angered the king, and I'm leaving Castile—
Perhaps forever, for the rest of my life.
O holy Mother, protect me as I leave,
Help me every day, lift me every night!
Do this, and if my fortune continues bright
Splendid gifts will come to your altar,
A thousand masses will be sung in your honor!"

1 3

The Warrior left, his heart steady;
They loosened the reins, gave the horses their head.
Then Martín Antolínez said:

"Veré a la mugier   a todo mio solaz,
castigar los he   cómo abrán a far.
Si el rrey me lo quisiere tomar,   a mí non m'incal.
Antes seré convusco   que el sol quiera rrayar."
Tornavas' Martín Antolínez a Burgos   e Mio Cid a aguijar
pora San Pero de Cardeña,   quanto pudo, a espolear.

14

Apriessa cantan los gallos   e quieren quebrar albores
quando llegó a San Pero   el buen Campeador
con estos cavalleros   quel' sirven a so sabor.
El abat don Sancho,   cristiano del Criador,
rrezava los matines   abuelta de los albores,
í estava doña Ximena   con cinco dueñas de pro,
rrogando a San Pero   e al Criador:
"¡Tú que a todos guías   vál a Mio Cid el Canpeador!"

15

Llamavan a la puerta,   í sopieron el mandado,
¡Dios, qué alegre fue   el abat don Sancho!
Con lu[n]bres e con candelas   al corral dieron salto,
con tan grant gozo rreciben   al que en buen ora nasco.
"Gradéscolo a Dios, Mio Cid,"   dixo el abat don Sancho,
"pues que aquí vos veo,   prendet de mí ospedado."
"Gracias, don abat,   e só vuestro pagado,
yo adobaré conducho   pora mí e pora mis vassallos;
mas porque me vo de tierra,   dovos *cinquaenta* marcos,
si yo algún día visquier,   ser vos han doblados.
Non quiero fazer en el monesterio   un dinero de daño,
evades aquí pora doña Ximena   dovos *ciento* marcos,
a ella e a sus dueñas   sirvádeslas est año.
Dues fijas dexo niñas   e prendetlas en los braços,
aquí vos llas acomiendo   a vós, abat don Sancho,

"I'll see my wife, my only comfort,
Advise her what to do, now that I'm gone.
Let the king take what he wants to, I don't mind.
I'll be with you, tomorrow, before the sun shines high."

14

Martín Antolínez turned back toward Burgos,
My Cid rode to San Pedro of Cardeña, as fast as possible,
Riding with his loyal men.
    Cocks had begun crowing, the sun was trying to rise again,
When the Warrior reached San Pedro.
Don Sancho, the abbot, a man of true Christian faith,
Was saying morning prayers as dawn rolled through the gray
Mists. Doña Jimena, Cid's wife, was there,
With five of her ladies, praying to Saint Peter and God:
"You who guide and rule us all, defend my Cid."

15

My Cid knocked at the door, his presence was reported.
Lord, how Don Sancho, the abbot, was rejoicing!
They brightened the courtyard with lamps and candles,
Welcoming the Warrior, born a lucky man.
"God be thanked, my Cid," said Don Sancho,
"That I see you here. Please accept my hospitality."
He who was born at the right time replied:
"Thank you, dear abbot, I appreciate your generosity.
Could you have food prepared for me and my men?
I've been exiled from this land, but let me give you fifty
Marks—and double that, if I live on.
There must be no loss to this monastery, on my account,
So I give you a hundred marks for Doña Jimena:
Let her, with her daughters and her ladies, be cared for here,
    for a year.

d'ellas e de mi mugier   fagades todo rrecabdo.
Si essa despensa vos falleciere   o vos menguare algo,
bien las abastad,   yo assí vos lo mando,
por un marco que despendades,   al monesterio daré yo
    [quatr]o."
Otorgado ge lo avié   el abat de grado.
Afevos doña Ximena   con sus fijas dó va llegando,
señas dueñas las traen   e adúzenlas adelant;
ant'el Campeador doña Ximena   fincó los inojos amos,
llorava de los ojos,   quísol' besar las manos:
"¡Merced, Canpeador,   en ora buena fuestes nado!
Por malos mestureros   de tierra sodes echado.

16

"¡Merced, ya Cid,   barba tan conplida!
Fem' ante vós,   yo e vuestras fijas,
iffantes son   e de días chicas,
con aquestas mis dueñas   de quien só yo servida.
Yo lo veo   que estades vós en ida
e nós de vós   partir nos hemos en vida.
¡Dadnos consejo,   por amor de Sancta María!"
Enclinó las manos   la barba vellida,
a las sus fijas   en braço' las prendía,
llególas al coraçón,   ca mucho las quería;
llora de los ojos,   tan fuertemientre sospira:
"Ya doña Ximena   la mi mugier tan conplida,
como a la mi alma   yo tanto vos quería.
Ya lo vedes   que partir nos emos en vida,
yo iré e vós   fincaredes rremanida.
¡Plega a Dios   e a Sancta María
que aún con mis manos   case estas mis fijas,
o que dé ventura   e algunos días vida
e vós, mugier ondrada,   de mí seades servida!"

Fold your arms around my two little girls:
I entrust them to you, Don Sancho,
I leave them all in your hands.
If more money is needed, for you or them,
Spend whatever you need to:
I promise you four for every mark you spend."
The abbot cheerfully agreed.
   Now see Doña Jimena and her daughters approaching,
Each little girl in a nurse's arms.
Doña Jimena dropped to her knees, in front of the Warrior.
Tears flowing, she kissed his hands:
"I call to your grace, O Cid, you who were born for grandeur!
You've been driven out of Castile by malicious informers.

16

   "Grant me a favor—you, who wear so flowing a beard!
Behold, in front of you, myself and your daughters,
Both still tiny, their lives an infancy,
And also my women, who go with me.
I see you have come in a hurry, and you'll go, and too soon,
We'll have to live alone.
For the love of our Mother Mary, tell me what to do!"
   He stretched out his hands, his heart as soft as his beard;
He picked up the little girls, and held them
Close to his breast, held them and loved them,
Weeping. He sighed from deep in his heart:
"O Doña Jimena, my wonderful wife,
I love you so much, and I always have.
You see I have to leave you, O soul of my life—
I go, and you must stay behind.
May it please God, and his mother Mary,
That some day these hands will give them in marriage—
And let fortune favor me, adding some days to my life,
To serve you, O you, my much-honored wife!"

17

Grand yantar le fazen   al buen Canpeador;
tañen las campanas   en San Pero a clamor.
Por Castiella   oyendo van los pregones
cómo se va de tierra   Mio Cid el Canpeador,
unos dexan casas   e otros onores.
En aqués día   a la puent de Arla[n]çón,
ciento quinze cavalleros   todos juntados son,
todos demandan   por Mio Cid el Canpeador,
Martín Antolínez   con ellos' cojó,
vanse pora San Pero   dó está el que en buen punto nació.

18

Quando lo sopo   Mio Cid el de Bivar
quel' crece conpaña   por que más valdrá,
apriessa cavalga,   rrecebirlos salié,
.... tornós a sonrrisar;
lléganle todos,   la mánol' ban besar,
fabló Mio Cid   de toda voluntad:
"Yo rruego a Dios   e al Padre spiritual
vós que por mí dexades   casas e heredades,
enantes que yo muera,   algún bien vos pueda far,
lo que perdedes   doblado vos lo cobrar."
Plogo a Mio Cid   porque creció en la yantar,
plogo a los otros omnes   todos quantos con él están.
Los *seis* días de plazo   passados los an,
tres an por trocir,   sepades que non más.
Mandó el rrey   a Mio Cid a aguardar,
que, si después del plazo   en su tiérral' pudiés tomar,
por oro nin por plata   non podrié escapar.
El día es exido,   la noch querié entrar,
a sos cavalleros   mandólos todos juntar:
"Oíd, varones,   non vos caya en pesar,
poco aver trayo,   darvos quiero vuestra part.

17

A glorious farewell feast was given the Warrior.
The bells of San Pedro clanged a great clamor,
Sending a message all over Castile, calling:
"He's leaving our land, my Cid, the Warrior, the great one.
Come join him!" Some left their houses, some left great estates.
That very day, on the Arlanzón bridge,
A hundred and fifteen knights crossed all together,
All of them looking for my Cid, the Warrior:
Martín Antolínez took charge
And brought them to San Pedro, to the man born at the right hour.

18

When my Cid heard new men were coming,
His forces suddenly growing,
He quickly mounted, rode out to greet them,
His face remembering how to smile again.
Each one of them reached for his hand, and kissed it.
    And my Cid said, speaking with passion:
"May God, our Father in heaven, ensure
That those who have left their homes and come to me
Will be rewarded at my hands, before I die,
Double whatever their loss may be!"
My Cid was happy to have more mouths to feed.
Everyone fully agreed.
    Six days of his reprieve already gone,
Three remained, and then there were none.
The king's men were there, waiting, watching:
When all nine days had passed, they could catch him,
And nothing would save him, neither silver nor gold.
That day went by, and then it was dark,
And my Cid assembled them all:
"Listen, you noble knights: there's nothing to worry about.
I have no riches with me, but I'll share what I have all around.

Sed me[n]brados   como lo devedes far:
a la mañana   quando los gallos cantarán,
non vos tardedes,   mandedes ensellar;
en San Pero a matines   tandrá el buen abat,
la missa nos dirá,   ésta será de Sancta Trinidad;
la missa dicha,   pensemos de cavalgar,
ca el plazo viene acerca,   mucho avemos de andar."
Cuemo lo mandó Mio Cid,   assí lo an todos a far.
Passando va la noch,   viniendo la man,
a los mediados gallos   piessan de *ensellar*.
Tañen a matines   a una priessa tan grand,
Mio Cid e su mugier   a la eglesia van,
echós' doña Ximena   en los grados delant'el altar,
rrogando al Criador   quanto ella mejor sabe
que a Mio Cid el Campeador   que Dios le curiás de mal:
"Ya Señor glorioso,   Padre que en cielo estás,
fezist cielo e tierra,   el tercero el mar,
fezist estrellas e luna   e el sol pora escalentar;
prisist encarnación   en Sancta María madre,
en Beleem aparecist   como fue tu voluntad,
pastores te glorificaron,   oviéronte a laudare,
tres rreyes de Arabia   te vinieron adorar,
Melchior   e Gaspar e Baltasar
oro e tus e mirra | te ofrecieron,   como fue tu veluntad;
[salveste] | a Jonás   quando cayó en la mar,
salvest a Daniel con los leones   en la mala cárcel,
salvest dentro en Rroma   al señor San Sabastián,
salvest a Sancta Susanna   del falso criminal;
por tierra andidiste   *treinta e dos* años, Señor spiritual,
mostrando los miráculos   por én avemos qué fablar:
del agua fezist vino   e de la piedra pan,
rresucitest a Lázaro   ca fue tu voluntad;
a los judíos te dexeste prender;   dó dizen Monte Calvarie
pusiéronte en cruz   por nombre en Golgotá,
dos ladrones contigo,   éstos de señas partes,
el uno es en paraíso,   ca el otro non entró allá;
estando en la cruz   vertud fezist muy grant:
Longinos era ciego   que nu[n]quas vio alguandre,

Be wise, and do what must be done:
In the morning, when crowing cocks have begun,
Quickly saddle up your horses.
Don Sancho will ring the bells for morning prayers
And sing us the mass of the Holy Trinity.
And when that mass has been sung
We'll leave, with a long ride still to come."
So it was settled; when morning came, it was done:
As the cocks crowed their second call
They were saddled and ready, one and all.
   At that moment, the matin bells resounded;
My Cid and his wife entered the church.
Doña Jimena knelt at the steps in front of the altar,
Praying every bit as hard
As she could for God to keep my Cid from harm:
"O glorious Father, high in heaven,
Who raised the sky and made the world, and the next day the sea,
Who made the stars and the moon, and the sun to warm us,
You who were incarnated in our Mother, Saint Mary,
Who, as you chose to, appeared in Bethlehem,
Glorified by shepherds, who sang your praise,
And three great Arab kings who came,
Melchior, and Gaspar, and Balthasar,
Offering gold, and fragrant myrrh, and frankincense,
Which also was your wish.
You who saved Jonah, who fell in the sea,
You who protected Daniel in the den of lions,
And saved Saint Susannah from lecherous liars,
You who saved Saint Sebastian, in harsh old Rome—
For thirty-two years you walked and roamed
The earth, performing wonders we must remember:
The water you turned to wine, the bread you made of stones,
And Lazarus you raised from the grave, returned from the dead;
Allowing Jews to take you high on Calvary
And, at Golgotha, putting you on the cross,
Along with two thieves, on either side of you,
One of whom came to heaven, the other did not.
And even on the cross you worked your miracles:

diot' con la lança en el costado   dont ixió la sangre,
corrió por el astil ayuso,   las manos se ovo de untar,
alçólas arriba,   llególas a la faz,
abrió sos ojos,   cató a todas partes,
en ti crovo al ora,   por end es salvo de mal;
en el monumento rresucitest,   fust a los infiernos | como fue tu
    voluntad,
quebranteste las puertas   e saqueste los sanctos padres.
Tú eres rrey de los rreyes   e de tod' el mundo padre,
a ti adoro e creo   de toda voluntad
e rruego a San Peidro   que me ayude a rrogar
por Mio Cid el Campeador   que Dios le curie de mal;
quando oy nos partimos,   en vida nos faz juntar."
La oración fecha,   la missa acabada la an,
salieron de la eglesia,   ya quieren cavalgar.
El Cid a doña Ximena   ívala abraçar,
doña Ximena al Cid   la mánol' va besar,
llorando de los ojos   que non sabe qué se far,
e él a las niñas   tornólas a catar:
"A Dios vos acomiendo, fijas,   e al Padre spiritual,
agora nos partimos,   Dios sabe el ajuntar."
Llorando de los ojos   que non viestes atal,
assís' parten unos d'otros   como la uña de la carne.
Mio Cid con los sos vassallos   pensó de cavalgar,
a todos esperando,   la cabeça tornando va;
a tan grand sabor   fabló Minaya Álbar Fáñez:
"Cid, ¿dó son vuestros esfuerços?   En buen ora nasquiestes de
    madre;
pensemos de ir nuestra vía,   esto sea de vagar.
Aún todos estos duelos   en gozo se tornarán,
Dios que nos dio las almas   consejo nos dará."
Al abat don Sancho   tornan de castigar
cómo sirva a doña Ximena   e a la[s] fijas que ha
e a todas sus dueñas   que con ellas están;
bien sepa el abat   que buen galardón d'ello prendrá.
Tornado es don Sancho   e fabló Álbar Fáñez:
"Si viéredes yentes venir   por connusco ir, | abat,
dezildes que prendan el rrastro   e piessen de andar

Blind Longinus, who had no sight at all,
Pierced your side with his spear, your blood poured out,
And running down the shaft, anointed his hands:
He raised his bloodstained fingers to his face
And, opening his eyes, could see, and saw wherever he looked,
And then and there believed in you, and so was saved forever.
You rose from your grave, you willingly descended to hell,
Smashed its gates, and carried off our holy fathers.
You are King of all kings, Father of the whole world,
In whom I wholly believe, and whom I adore,
So may Saint Peter help me as I beg of you, O Lord,
To keep my Cid, this Warrior, free of harm.
We separate, today, but I beg you to bring us together once more."
    Her prayer was over, the mass was sung;
They left the church, ready, now, to ride.
My Cid went to Doña Jimena, and put his arms around her,
As she kissed his hands
And wept the tears she could not hold back.
The Warrior turned, looking at his daughters:
    "I leave you in the hands of our Lord, our holy Father.
Only God knows when we'll meet again."
    You'll never see such a flood of tears as he shed,
Their parting was like fingernails pulled from the flesh.
    He and his men prepared to ride,
But my Cid kept looking eagerly back,
Until Minaya Alvar Fáñez gave him this wise advice:
"Cid, where has your courage gone? You were born to your
      mother
In good fortune! What a waste of time! We need to ride.
All our sorrows can still be turned to delight;
The God who gave us souls can also give advice."
    Abbot Don Sancho was admonished, again,
To care for Doña Jimena and her daughters
And all her ladies as well.
The abbot knew he'd be richly rewarded.
As the priest was leaving, Alvar Fáñez said:
"Abbot, if more men come looking for us,
Tell them to follow our hoofprints, and hurry:

ca en yermo o en poblado   poder nos [han] alcançar."
Soltaron las rriendas,   piessan de andar,
cerca viene el plazo   por el rreino quitar.
Vino Mio Cid yazer   a Spinaz de Can,
grandes yentes se le acojen   essa noch de todas partes.
Otro día mañana   piensa de cavalgar,
ixiendos' va de tierra   el Canpeador leal,
de siniestro Sant Estevan,   una buena cipdad,
de diestro Alilón las torres   que moros las han,
passó por Alcobiella,   que de Castiella fin es ya,
la calçada de Quinea   ívala traspassar,
sobre Navas de Palos   el Duero va passar,
a la Figueruela   Mio Cid iva posar;
vánsele acogiendo   yentes de todas partes.

19

Í se echava Mio Cid   después que fue cenado,
un suéñol' priso dulce,   tan bien se adurmió;
el ángel Gabriel   a él vino en sueño:
"¡Cavalgad, Cid,   el buen Campeador!
Ca nunqua | en tan buen punto   cavalgó varón;
mientra que visquiéredes   bien se fará lo to."
Quando despertó el Cid,   la cara se sanctigó,
sinava la cara,   a Dios se acomendó,
mucho era pagado   del sueño que á soñado.

20

Otro día mañana   piensan de cavalgar,
és día á de plazo,   sepades que non más.
A la sierra de Miedes   ellos ivan posar.

They can catch up, out in these fields, or else in some town."
    Then they loosened the reins and rode off:
There was little left of my Cid's nine days.
He slept, that night, at Espinazo de Can—
Where many more men joined them, coming from all over.
They rode on, the next morning.
As my Cid was about to leave Castile, the homeland he loved,
San Esteban—a good-sized city—was on his left,
And on his right, the fortress walls of Moorish Ayllón.
He rode past Alcubilla, right on the borders of Castile,
Rode across Quinea, an ancient Roman road,
Crossing the Duero river at Navapalos,
Then stopped at Figueruela—and there more men
Came crowding into his army, coming from everywhere.

19

My Cid had his dinner, then lay down;
Falling deeply asleep, a sweet dream came to him,
In which the angel Gabriel appeared, and spoke:
"Go on, Cid, go on, you wonderful Warrior!
No man has ever come riding out at such a perfect moment:
For as long as you live, whatever you start will always end well."
When he awoke, my Cid traced a cross over his forehead,
Then silently framed a thankful prayer to the Lord,
Pleased and encouraged by what his dream had brought him.

20

The next morning, they rode rapidly on,
Well aware that this was the very last of my Cid's nine days.
They planned to stop at the high Sierra de Miedes,
Near the forts of Atienza, held by the Moors.

21

Aún era de día,   non era puesto el sol,
mandó ver sus yentes   Mio Cid el Campeador,
sin las peonadas   e omnes valientes que son,
notó trezientas lanças   que todas tienen pendones.

22

"Temprano dat cevada,   ¡sí el Criador vos salve!
El qui quisiere comer;   e qui no, cavalgue.
Passaremos la sierra   que fiera es e grand,
la tierra del rrey Alfonso   esta noch la podemos quitar;
después, qui nos buscare,   fallarnos podrá."
De noch passan la sierra,   vinida es la man
e por la loma ayuso   piensan de andar.
En medio d'una montaña   maravillosa e grand
fızo Mio Cid posar   e cevada dar,
díxoles a todos   cómo querié trasnochar;
vassallos tan buenos   por coraçón lo an,
mandado de so señor   todo lo han a far.
Ante que anochesca   piensan de cavalgar,
por tal lo faze Mio Cid   que no [l]o ventasse nadi,
andidieron de noch,   que vagar non se dan.
Ó dizen Castejón,   el que es sobre Fenares,
Mio Cid se echó en celada   con aquellos que él trae.
Toda la noche yaze en celada   el que en buen ora nasco
como los consejava   Minaya Álbar Fáñez.

23

"¡Ya Cid,   en buen ora cinxiestes espada!
Vós con *ciento*   de aquesta nuestra conpaña,
pues que a Castejón   sacaremos a celada . . ."

21

Night had not yet fallen, the sun still hung in the sky
When my Cid paused to review his growing army:
Not counting foot soldiers, fierce and courageous men,
He counted three hundred knights, each with a banner fluttering
    on his lance.

22

"Those who expect God to help us, get up early and feed your
    animals.
Whoever wants to eat, eat, and whoever doesn't, ride on.
We're crossing this wild mountain range, which reaches so high,
And when we come down on the other side, we'll be free of
    Castile.
Whoever looks to join us won't have much trouble."
They crossed the mountain that night, and as dawn broke
They began their downward descent.
Earlier, in the middle of a dense and wonderful wood,
My Cid had them stop, as before, to feed the horses,
And also to tell his men he meant to ride all night;
Soldiers as good as these knew he was right,
They would always accept his orders.
He meant to keep them out of sight,
So as it grew dark, they rode on again,
Not resting all through the long night.
But when they reached Castejón, and the river Henares,
He had them stop and hide, preparing an ambush.

23

They waited all night, and he who was born at a lucky hour
Lay listening to advice from Minaya Alvar Fáñez:
"Since you plan to lead the Castejón Moors into an ambush,

[*There is a brief gap in the manuscript; Cid speaks:*]
"Vós con los *dozientos*   idvos en algara,
allá vaya Álbar Á[*l*]barez | e Álbar Salvadórez sin falla,
e Galín García,   una fardida | lança,
cavalleros buenos   que aconpañen a Minaya;
a osadas corred,   que por miedo non dexedes nada,
Fita ayuso   e por Guadalfajara,
fata Alcalá   lleguen las alg[*aras*]
e bien acojan   todas las ganancias
que por miedo de los moros   non dexen nada;
e yo con lo[s] *ciento*   aquí fıncaré en la çaga,
terné yo Castejón   dón abremos grand enpara.
Si cueta vos fuere   alguna al algara,
fazedme mandado   muy privado a la çaga,
¡d'aqueste acorro   fablará toda España!"
Nonbrados son   los que irán en el algara
e los que con Mio Cid   fıcarán en la çaga.
Ya quiebran los albores   e vinié la mañana,
ixié el sol,   ¡Dios, qué fermoso apuntava!
En Castejón   todos se levantavan,
abren las puertas,   de fuera salto davan
por ver sus lavores   e todas sus heredades;
todos son exidos,   las puertas abiertas an dexadas
con pocas de gentes   que en Castejón fıncaron;
las yentes de fuera   todas son derramadas.
El Campeador   salió de la celada,
corre a Castejón   sin falla.
Moros e moras   aviénlos de ganancia
e essos gañados   quantos en derredor andan.
Mio Cid don Rrodrigo   a la puerta adeliñava,
los que la tienen,   quando vieron la rrebata,
ovieron miedo   e fue dese[*m*]parada.
Mio Cid Rruy Díaz   por las puertas entrava,
en mano trae   desnuda el espada,
quinze moros matava   de los que alcançava.
Gañó a Castejón   e el oro e la plata,
sos cavalleros   llegan con la ganancia,
déxanla a Mio Cid,   todo esto non precia[*n*] nada.

You ought to take a hundred of our men . . ."
[*There is a brief gap in the manuscript; Cid speaks:*]
"Go in advance, with two hundred men;
Take Alvar Alvarez, and Alvar Salvadórez, too,
And that brave knight, Galín García,
Good men to go with Minaya.
Ride like proud demons, afraid of nothing.
Go down along the Hita, right through Guadalajara,
As far as Alcalá, taking everything
You find, don't leave them a thing—
And pay no attention to the Moors: they're nothing to worry
    about.
I'll bring up the rear, with another hundred men,
Based in Castejón—a good defensive position.
If you're attacked and need assistance,
Send me word immediately:
You'll have the kind of help no one in Spain will ever forget!"
    Those who were in the raiding party were named,
And those who would stay with my Cid.
Daylight began to break through, and morning came,
And the sun with it. Lord, what a beautiful dawn!
People woke up, in Castejón,
Opened their doors and left their houses,
Going out to check on their fields and their workers,
Leaving almost no men in town.
Then the Warrior came out of hiding
And galloped straight into the place.
He captured Moorish men and Moorish women,
And all the cattle being herded out.
My Cid rode straight up to the gate,
And those who guarded it were terribly afraid,
Seeing him come; they ran for their lives.
My Cid rode right through, and into the town,
His sword held high and bare in his hand.
He killed fifteen Moors as they ran.
There was silver, there was gold,
And his knights kept coming to him with more,
Free and easy, piling treasure on his horde.

Afevos los *dozientos   e tres* en el algara
e sin dubda corren; . . . .
fasta Alcalá llegó   la seña de Minaya
e desí arriba   tórnanse con la ganancia,
Fenares arriba   e por Guadalfajara.
Tanto traen   las grandes gana[n]cias,
muchos gañados | de ovejas e de vacas,
e de rropas   e de otras rriquizas largas;
derecha viene   la seña de Minaya,
non osa ninguno   dar salto a la çaga.
Con aqueste aver   tórnanse essa conpaña,
fellos en Castejón   ó el Campeador estava;
el castiello dexó en so poder,   el Canpeador cavalga,
saliólos rrecebir   con esta su mesnada,
los braços abiertos   rrecibe a Minaya:
"¡Venides, Álbar Fáñez,   una fardida lança!
Dó yo vos enbiás   bien abría tal esperança;
esso con esto   sea ajuntado,
dovos la quinta,   si la quisiéredes, Minaya."

24

"Mucho vos lo gradesco,   Campeador contado;
d'aquesta quinta   que me avedes mand[ad]o
pagar se ía d'ella   Alfonso el castellano.
Yo vos la suelto   e avello quitado;
a Dios lo prometo,   a Aquel que está en alto,
fata que yo me pague   sobre mio buen cavallo
lidiando con moros   en el campo,
que enpleye la lança   e al espada meta mano
e por el cobdo ayuso   la sangre destellando
ante Rruy Díaz   el lidiador contado,
non prendré de vós   quanto vale un dinero malo.
Pues que por mí ganaredes   quesquier que sea d'algo,
todo lo otro   afelo en vuestra mano."

His two hundred and thirty men in the raiding party
Never slowed or stopped, sacking everywhere they went.
Minaya's banner was seen as far as Alcalá,
And from that point they turned back,
Following the Henares through Guadalajara,
Carrying great quantities of loot—oxen,
Sheep, cows, all kinds of clothing and other rich things.
Minaya's banner flew high, he went wherever he wanted;
No one dared to bother his rear guard.
And so they returned, richly burdened,
Right into Castejón, where they found my Cid.
He rode out from the castle he'd conquered,
He and his men, welcoming their comrades,
And the Warrior threw his arms around Minaya:
"Here you are, Alvar Fáñez, you daring knight!
Bringing back the kind of victory I always expect from you.
What we already have, together with what you bring,
Minaya, is one-fifth yours, if you want it."

24

"I am deeply grateful to you, famous Warrior,
And I am sure King Alfonso himself would be pleased
If he had this one-fifth share you have offered me.
But I hand it back to you, and there let it be.
I swear to God, to him who lives on high,
That until I prove myself—on this good horse of mine,
Fighting Moors on fields of battle,
Using my lance and this sword, here in my hand,
And blood comes dripping down to my elbow,
In the very presence of Ruy Díaz, greatest of Warriors—
Until then, I will not take a penny from you.
Until you're presented with something tremendous—
And not before then, by God!—everything is yours."

25

Estas ganancias   allí eran juntadas.
Comidiós' Mio Cid,   el que en buen ora fue nado,
el rrey Alfonso   que llegarién sus compañas,
quel' buscarié mal   con todas sus mesnadas.
Mandó partir   tod' aqueste aver,
sos quiñoneros   que ge los diessen por carta.
Sos cavalleros   í an arribança,
a cada uno d'ellos   caen *ciento* marcos de plata
e a los peones   la meatad sin falla,
toda la quinta   a Mio Cid fincava.
Aquí non lo puede vender   nin dar en presentaja,
nin cativos nin cativas   non quiso traer en su conpaña.
Fabló con los de Castejón   e envió a Fita e a Guadalfajara
esta quinta   por quánto serié conprada,
aun de lo que diessen   oviessen grand ganancia,
asmaron los moros   *tres* mill marcos de plata;
plogo a Mio Cid   d'aquesta presentaja,
a tercer día   dados fueron sin falla.
Asmó Mio Cid   con toda su conpaña
que en el castiello   non í avrié morada,
e que serié rretenedor   mas non í avrié agua:
"Moros en paz,   ca escripta es la carta,
buscar nos ie el rrey Alfonso   con toda su mesnada;
quitar quiero Castejón,   ¡oíd, escuelas e Minyaya!

26

"Lo que yo dixier   non lo tengades a mal,
en Castejón   non podriemos fincar,
cerca es el rrey Alfonso   e buscarnos verná.
Mas el castiello   non lo quiero ermar,
ciento moros e ciento moras   quiero las quitar
porque lo pris d'ellos   que de mí non digan mal.
Todos sodes pagados   e ninguno por pagar,

25

They made a heap of everything they'd won.
Then he who'd been born at just the right time, my Cid,
Began to wonder if King Alfonso might be getting closer,
He and his armies hunting them down.
So he ordered those whose job it was
To quickly distribute this treasure, keeping careful records.
Each of his knights was rewarded
With a full hundred marks,
And every foot soldier got half that much;
One-fifth of the total was reserved for my Cid.
But what could be sold or given away, there in the mountains?
—And he wanted no captives with him, no men, no women.
So he spoke to the people of Castejón, sent messengers to Hita
And Guadalajara, asking what his share would be worth,
Since anything they offered him would be pure profit.
The Moors said three thousand marks
And my Cid cheerfully accepted.
Three days later, they paid the bill in full.
It was not wise, my Cid believed,
To remain in the Castejón castle:
They could defend it, yes, but there would be no water.
"Let's leave these Moors in peace: we've taken their money,
They've paid every penny—and King Alfonso's army
Could be coming. Hear me, Minaya and all my men: let's leave!

26

"No one should misunderstand what I've said:
We simply cannot stay in Castejón.
King Alfonso's army can't be far away, he's looking for us.
Nor do I wish to damage or destroy this castle:
I'll set free a hundred Moorish men and a hundred Moorish
     women,
So they can't speak badly of my taking it from them.

cras a la mañana   pensemos de cavalgar,
con Alfonso mio señor   non querría lidiar."
Lo que dixo el Cid   a todos los otros plaz.
Del castiello que prisieron   todos rricos se parten,
los moros e las moras   bendiziéndol' están.
Vanse Fenares arriba   quanto pueden andar,
trocen las Alcarias   e ivan adelant,
por las Cuevas d'Anquita   ellos passando van,
passaron las aguas,   entraron al campo de Torancio,
por essas tierras ayuso   quanto pueden andar.
Entre Fariza e Cetina   Mio Cid iva albergar,
grandes son las ganancias   que priso por la tierra dó va.
Non lo saben los moros   el ardiment que an.
Otro día moviós'   Mio Cid el de Bivar
e passó a Alfama,   la Foz ayuso va,
passó a Bovierca   e a Teca que es adelant
e sobre Alcocer   Mio Cid iva posar
en un otero rredondo,   fuerte e grand,
acerca corre Salón,   agua nol' puedent vedar.
Mio Cid don Rrodrigo   Alcocer cueda ganar.

27

Bien puebla el otero,   firme prende las posadas,
los unos contra la sierra   e los otros contra la agua.
El buen Canpeador   que en buen ora nasco
derredor del otero   bien cerca del agua
a todos sos varones   mandó fazer una cárcava
que de día nin de noch   non les diessen arrebata,
que sopiessen que Mio Cid   allí avié fincança.

28

Por todas essas tierras   ivan los mandados
que el Campeador Mio Cid   allí avié poblado,
venido es a moros,   exido es de cristianos;

You've all been well paid, no one's purse is empty,
So tomorrow morning I want us to ride away.
Alfonso is still my king, I do not want to fight with him."
No one disagreed with my Cid.
They'd conquered the castle as poor men; they left it rich;
And Moorish men and women blessed them.
They rode rapidly along the river Henares,
Crossed the Alcarria, passed the Anquita caves,
Then crossed the Tajuña and went through Campo Taranz:
It was a downward path, and they kept galloping on.
Finally, between Ariza and Cetina, they pitched their camp,
Having taken immense amounts of loot along the way.
The Moors had no idea where they were going.
The next day, my Cid, the Warrior from Vivar, moved on,
Passing Alhama, then La Hoz,
Then Bubierca and even Ateca, further along,
Making camp, at last, on a round hill, which looked down,
High and imposing, on the city of Alcocer.
The river Jalón ran past; their water supply was endless.
My Cid, Don Rodrigo, decided to capture Alcocer.

27

He built a sturdy campsite, fortified the position,
Setting some of his men near the hill, others along the river.
Then the Warrior, born in a lucky hour,
Ordered his men to dig a deep ditch, starting near the water
And running all around the hill;
No one could attack them, now, by night or day.
The message was clear: my Cid had come to stay.

28

The news was known through all the lands around.
The Warrior, my Cid, had settled down
Near Alcocer, exiled by Christians, come to the Moors:

en la su vezindad   non se treven ganar tanto.
Aguardándose va Mio Cid   con todos sus vassallos,
el castiello de Alcocer   en paria va entrando.
Los de Alcocer a Mio Cid   yal' dan parias de grado

29

e los de Teca   e los de Ter*r*er la casa;
a los de Calataút,   sabet, ma[*l*] les pesava.
Allí yogo Mio Cid   complidas *quinze* semanas.
Quando vio Mio Cid   que Alcocer non se le dava,
él fizo un art   e non lo detardava:
dexa una tienda fita   e las otras levava,
cojó[*s*'] Salón ayuso,   la su seña alçada,
las lorigas vestidas   e cintas las espadas
a guisa de menbrado   por sacarlos a celada.
Veyénlo los de Alcocer,   ¡Dios, cómo se alabavan!
"Fallido á a Mio Cid   el pan e la cevada;
las otras abés lieva,   una tienda á dexada,
de guisa va Mio Cid   como si escapasse de arrancada.
Demos salto a él   e feremos grant ganancia
antes quel' prendan los de Ter*r*er,   si non, non nos darán dent
    nada;
la paria qu'él á presa   tornar nos la ha doblada."
Salieron de Alcocer   a una priessa much estraña,
Mio Cid, quando los vio fuera,   cogiós' como de arrancada,
cojós' Salón ayuso,   con los sos abuelta *anda*.
Dizen los de Alcocer: "¡Ya se nos va la ganancia!"
Los grandes e los chicos   fuera salto dan,
al sabor del prender   de lo ál non piensan nada,
abiertas dexan las puertas   que ninguno non las guarda.
El buen Campeador   la su cara tornava,
vio que entr'ellos e el castiello   mucho avié grand plaça,
mandó tornar la seña,   apriessa espoloneavan:
"¡Firidlos, cavalleros,   todos sines dubdança!
¡Con la merced del Criador   nuestra es la ganancia!"
Bueltos son con ellos   por medio de la llana.

Earning a living, with him close by, was hard,
He and all his men forever on guard.
And Alcocer was soon paying him tribute.

29

And the people of Teca, too, and also Terrer: all of them
Paid. And those in Calatayud, for sure, were worried sick.
    My Cid stayed there, waiting, for all of fifteen weeks,
But saw that Alcocer would not surrender.
He thought of a simple trick,
And quickly tried it, taking down the tents, all but one,
Then riding down along the Jalón, banners flying,
His men in armor, their swords close-sheathed.
He thought this plan would draw them out. And it did.
    All Alcocer watched—and God! how they rejoiced!
"Cid is running out of bread and fodder!
There's hardly a tent still standing—one out of ten—
Cid is running off, he sees he has no choice!
If we jump on him, now, we'll make ourselves rich,
But if we wait for the men of Terrer to attack, we won't get a bit.
We can get double what we've paid him!"
They fairly tumbled out their gates, running brainless.
My Cid saw them, and pretended to panic,
Galloping down the Jalón faster and faster.
The Moors shouted, "Look! Our gold is running away!"
Little and large, they came dashing through the gates,
Gold dust in their eyes and nothing else in their minds;
They left the wide-open gates, and no guards, behind them.
The great Warrior turned his head, looked back,
And saw how far from the fortress they'd run, to attack him.
He swung his banner around, ordered his knights to gallop at
    them:
"Charge! Let no one hesitate!
With God's good grace, we'll smash them!"
They reached the Moors right on the level plain.

¡Dios, qué bueno es el gozo   por aquesta mañana!
Mio Cid e Álbar Fáñez   adelant aguijavan,
tienen buenos cavallos,   sabet, a su guisa les andan,
entr'ellos e el castiello   en essora entravan.
Los vassallos de Mio Cid   sin piedad les davan,
en un ora e un poco de logar   *trezientos* moros matan.
Dando grandes alaridos   los que están en la celada,
dexando van los delant,   por el castiello se tornavan,
las espadas desnudas   a la puerta se paravan.
Luego llegavan los sos,   ca fecha es el arrancada.
Mio Cid gañó a Alcocer,   sabet, por esta maña.

30

Vino Pero Vermúez,   que la seña tiene en mano,
metióla en somo,   en todo lo más alto.
Fabló Mio Cid Rruy Díaz,   el que en buen ora fue nado:
"Grado a Dios del cielo   e a todos los sos sanctos,
ya mejoraremos posadas   a dueños e a cavallos.

31

"¡Oíd a mí, Álbar Fáñez   e todos los cavalleros!
En este castiello   grand aver avemos preso,
los moros yazen muertos,   de bivos pocos veo;
los moros e la[s] moras   vender non los podremos,
que los descabecemos   nada non ganaremos,
cojámoslos de dentro   ca el señorío tenemos,
posaremos en sus casas   e d'ellos nos serviremos."

32

Mio Cid con esta ganancia   en Alcocer está,
fizo enbiar por la tienda   que dexara allá.
Mucho pesa a los de Teca   e a los de Ter*rer* non plaze

God, what a gorgeous morning, what a wonderful day!
My Cid and Alvar Fáñez spurred their fine horses,
Which went, of course, as fast as anyone wanted,
And got between the Moors and the fortress.
My Cid's men showed no mercy,
Killing three hundred Moors in an hour, in that tiny space.
Those who were trapped were screaming away
As my Cid and his fast-riding men ran to the gates
And stood on guard, their sword blades naked.
The fighting was over, the others came to them.
And that, please understand, is how my Cid conquered Alcocer.

30

Pedro Bermúdez rode up, bearing the banner.
He planted it high above the walls.
Then my Cid, Ruy Díaz, born at a fortunate hour, declared:
"With the grace of God on high, and all his saints,
We've gotten better lodgings for both men and horses.

31

"Now listen to me, Alvar Fáñez and all you knights!
Winning this castle has earned us a very great prize.
Many of the Moors are dead, not many are still alive.
But how could we sell these captives, men or women?
How would we be better off if we killed them?
Let them come back, because we'll be in charge:
We'll live in their houses, and be their lords."

32

My Cid lived in Alcocer, rich as a lord.
But, still, he took down the last of his tents, and stored it.
The Moors of Ateca were deeply concerned; those of Terrer

e a los de Calatayut   non plaze;
al rrey de Valencia   enbiaron con mensaje
que a uno que dizién   Mio Cid Rruy Díaz de Bivar:
"Airólo el rrey Alfonso,   de tierra echado lo ha,
vino posar sobre Alcocer   en un tan fuerte logar,
sacólos a celada,   el castiello ganado á.
Si non das consejo,   a Teca e a Ter*rer* perderás,
perderás Calatayut,   que non puede escapar,
rribera de Salón   toda irá a mal,
assí ferá lo de Siloca,   que es del otra part."
Quando lo oyó el rrey Tamín   por cuer le pesó mal:
"Tres rreyes veo de moros   derredor de mí estar,
non lo detardedes,   los dos id pora allá,
tres mill moros levedes   con armas de lidiar,
con los de la frontera   que vos ayudarán
prendétmelo a vida,   aduzídmelo deland,
porque se me entró en mi tierra   derecho me avrá a dar."
Tres mill moros cavalgan   e piensan de andar,
ellos vinieron a la noch   en Sogorve posar.
Otro día mañana   piensan de cavalgar,
vinieron a la noch   a Celfa posar;
por los de la frontera   piensan de enviar,
non lo detienen,   vienen de todas partes.
Ixieron de Celfa,   la que dizen de Canal,
andidieron todo'l día   que vagar non se dan,
vinieron essa noche   en Calatayu[t] posar.
Por todas essas tierras   los pregones dan,
gentes se ajuntaron   sobejanas de grandes
con aquestos dos rreyes   que dizen Fáriz e Galve;
al bueno de Mio Cid   en Alcocer le van cercar.

33

Fincaron las tiendas   e prendend las posadas,
crecen estos virtos   ca yentes son sobejanas;
las arrobdas   que los moros sacan

Were angry, and those of Calatayud, too.
They sent a message to the King of Valencia, a Moor:
"Someone who calls himself Cid, Ruy Díaz, from Vivar,
Angered King Alfonso, who banished him from Castile.
He set up a fortified camp, in front of Alcocer,
Set a trap for our people, and captured the castle.
If you don't get involved and don't help us, you'll lose Ateca,
Terrer and Calatayud, too: there is no other way to stop this.
And then everywhere along the Jalón will be lost,
And after that the Jiloca, on the opposite side."
This message made King Tamín's heart feel heavy:
"Three Moorish kings are staying with me.
Two of you go, immediately,
With an army of three thousand, fully equipped.
Join with the Moors who have asked for our help.
Capture that man and bring him here, alive:
Invade my land, and you pay a price."
Three thousand Moors galloped along at a good pace,
Arriving in Segorvé that night.
They headed off, next morning,
And stopped that night at Celfa;
From there they called the local troops to join them,
As they promptly did, flocking from all adjoining
Lands. Leaving Celfa (known as the Canal),
They rode straight on, not pausing to rest,
And as darkness fell, reached Calatayud, where they stopped for
    the night.
Heralds were sent in all directions, calling for fighting
Men—who continued to come, assembling
A vast army for the two kings, Fáriz and Galvé,
Who quickly besieged my Cid, in Alcocer.

33

The Moors pitched their tents, taking up positions;
Their numbers increased to gigantic proportions.
They sent out patrols, by day and night,

de día | e de noch   enbueltos andan en armas;
muchas son las arrobdas   e grande es el almofalla,
a los de Mio Cid   ya les tuellen el agua.
Mesnadas de Mio Cid   exir querién a la batalla,
el que en buen ora nasco   firme ge lo vedava.
Toviérongela en cerca   complidas tres semanas.

34

A cabo de tres semanas,   la quarta querié e[n]trar,
Mio Cid con los sos   tornós' a acordar:
"El agua nos an vedada,   exir nos ha el pan,
que nos queramos ir de noch   no nos lo consintrán;
grandes son los poderes   por con ellos lidiar,
dezidme, cavalleros,   cómo vos plaze de far."
Primero fabló Minaya,   un cavallero de prestar:
"De Castiella la gentil   exidos somos acá,
si con moros non lidiáremos,   no nos darán del pan.
Bien somos nós *seis*cientos,   algunos ay de más,
en el no[m]bre del Criador,   que non passe por ál;
vayámoslos ferir   en aquel día de cras."
Dixo el Campeador: "A mi guisa fablastes;
ondrástesvos, Minaya,   ca aver vos lo iedes de far."
Todos los moros e las moras   de fuera los manda echar
que non sopiesse ninguno   esta su poridad;
el día e la noche   piénsanse de adobar.
Otro día mañana   el sol querié apuntar,
armado es Mio Cid   con quantos que él ha,
fablava Mio Cid   como odredes contar:
"Todos iscamos fuera   que nadi non rraste
sinon dos peones solos   por la puerta guardar,
si nós muriéremos en campo,   en castiello non entrarán,
si venciéremos la batalla,   creçremos en rrictad;
e vós, Pero Vermúez,   la mi seña tomad,
como sodes muy bueno,   tener la edes sin art,
mas non aguijedes con ella   si yo non vos lo mandar."
Al Cid besó la mano,   la seña va tomar.

Heavily armed, and ready to fight.
Their army had grown to tremendous might.
And then they managed to cut off my Cid's water supply.
His men were itching to open the gates and charge them,
But he who was born at a lucky time kept the gates barred.
The siege went on and on, for three whole weeks.

34

After three weeks, as the fourth began,
My Cid thought it was best to confer with his men:
"They've blocked our water supply; soon we'll be out of bread.
We can't sneak out at night;
They're terribly strong for us to fight them.
Tell me what you wish, my worthy knights."
Brave Minaya was the first to speak:
"We've left sweet Castile behind us.
If we don't fight the Moors, they surely won't feed us.
We are six hundred strong, and maybe more:
In the name of God, our only choice is war.
Let's go out and fight them tomorrow."
The Warrior replied: "I like what you've said.
Minaya, this honors you, and it's what I expected."
    Moorish men and women were ordered out of the city;
Their plans required secrecy,
And day and night they worked to make themselves ready.
The next day, before the morning light, just at dawn,
My Cid and his men were fully armed.
He addressed his men, and here are his words:
"We'll all go out, except for two foot soldiers, to guard
The gate. If we die in battle, they'll have it all.
But if we win, we'll earn ourselves far more.
And you, Pedro Bermúdez, will carry my banner to war—
A loyal follower, who deserves such honor.
But don't rush ahead, wait for my order."
He kissed my Cid's hand, and lifted the banner.
    They opened the gates and charged straight out.

Abrieron las puertas,   fuera un salto dan,
viéronlo las arrobdas de los moros,   al almofalla se van tornar.
¡Qué priessa va en los moros!   e tornáronse a armar,
ante rroído de atamores   la tierra querié quebrar;
veriedes armarse moros,   apriessa entrar en az.
De parte de los moros   dos señas ha cabdales,
e fizieron dos azes de peones mezclados,   ¿quí los podrié contar?
La[s] azes de los moros   yas' mueven adelant
por a Mio Cid e a los sos   a manos los tomar.
"Quedas sed, me[s]nadas,   aquí en este logar,
non derranche ninguno   fata que yo lo mande."
Aquel Pero Vermúez   non lo pudo endurar,
la seña tiene en mano,   conpeçó de espolonar:
"¡El Criador vos vala,   Cid, Campeador leal!
Vo meter la vuestra seña   en aquella mayor az;
los que el debdo avedes   veremos cómo la acorredes."
Dixo el Campeador: "¡Non sea, por caridad!"
Rrespuso Pero Vermúez: "¡Non rrastará por ál!"
Espolonó el cavallo   e metiól' en el mayor az.
Moros le rreciben   por la seña ganar,
danle grandes colpes   mas nol' pueden falsar.
Dixo el Campeador: "¡Valelde, por caridad!"

35

Enbraçan los escudos   delant los coraçones,
abaxan las lanças   abue*l*tas de los pendones,
enclinaron las caras   de suso de los arzones,
ívanlos ferir   de fuertes coraçones.
A grandes vozes llama   el que en buen ora nasco:
"¡Feridlos, cavalleros,   por amor de caridad!
¡Yo só Rruy Díaz de Bivar,   el Cid Campeador!"
Todos fieren en el az   dó está Pero Vermúez,
trezientas lanças son,   todas tienen pendones;
seños moros mataron,   todos de seños colpes;
a la tornada que fazen   otros tantos [*muertos*] son.

The Moors' patrol bands saw them, and quickly retreated.
How the Moors began to scurry, to get themselves armed!
Their drums were beating hard enough to split the world.
You could see their soldiers rushing into battle lines.
Having two kings, the Moors carried two banners,
They formed as if two armies—and who could count them all?
And then they began to move forward,
Ready to meet my Cid and his men, sword against sword.
"Let them come to us," said the Warrior. "Stay where you are.
No one take a single step until I order it."
They obeyed. But Pedro Bermúdez could not wait;
Lifting the banner high, he spurred his horse:
"God shield you, O Cid, loyal Warrior!
I'll set your banner in the thickest line of Moors,
And then we'll see how these men of ours fight for it!"
"No!" cried my Cid. "Don't! In the name of honor, stop!"
Pedro Bermúdez replied, "I can't stay here—"
And galloped his horse straight at the Moors.
They welcomed him, trying to take the banner,
Their weapons hitting him hard, but unable to break his armor.
"Help him!" called my Cid. "In the name of honor!"

35

They raised their shields in front of their breasts,
Lowered their lances, all covered with flags,
Bent their faces down toward their saddle horns,
And attacked, their hearts as bold as their swords.
And he who'd been born at just the right time shouted,
"At them, knights! In the name of honor!
I am Ruy Díaz, the Cid, the Warrior!"
They smashed into the Moors' front line, alongside Pedro
    Bermúdez,
Three hundred lances, the flags all fluttering,
And every blow brought death for a Moor.
They turned and charged once more, and more Moors died.

36

Veriedes tantas lanças   premer e alçar,
tanta adágara   foradar e passar,
tanta loriga   falsa[r] [e] desmanchar,
tantos pendones blancos   salir vermejos en sangre,
tantos buenos cavallos   sin sos dueños andar.
Los moros llaman Mafómat   e los cristianos Sancti Yagü[e];
cayén en un poco de logar   moros muertos mill e [trezientos ya].

37

¡Quál lidia bien   sobre exorado arzón
Mio Cid Rruy Díaz,   el buen lidiador!
Minaya Álbar Fáñez,   que Çorita mandó,
Martín Antolínez,   el burgalés de pro,
Muño Gustioz,   que fue so criado,
Martín Muñoz,   el que mandó a Mont Mayor,
Álbar Álbarez   e Álbar Salvadórez,
Galín García,   el bueno de Aragón,
Félez Muñoz,   so sobrino del Campeador.
Desí adelante,   quantos que í son
acorren la seña   e a Mio Cid el Canpeador.

38

A Minaya Álbar Fáñez   matáronle el cavallo,
bien lo acorren   mesnadas de cristianos.
La lança á quebrada,   al espada metió mano,
maguer de pie   buenos colpes va dando.
Violo Mio Cid   Rruy Díaz el castellano,
acostós' a un aguazil   que tenié buen cavallo,
diol' tal espadada   con el so diestro braço
cortól' por la cintura,   el medio echó en campo.

36

It was a sea of lances rising and falling,
Shields pierced through and broken open,
Body armor smashed,
Blood spattered all over white flags,
And many, many horses who had no rider.
The Moors cried, "Mohammad!" The Christians, "Saint James!"
In a moment, thirteen hundred Moors lay dead on the field.

37

How well he fought, bent over his gilded saddle horn,
My Cid, Ruy Díaz, that great Warrior!
And there was Minaya Alvar Fáñez, Zurita's lord,
And Martín Antolínez, that fine man from Burgos,
And Muño Gustioz, Cid's brother-in-law,
And Martín Muñoz, who ruled in Montemayor,
And Alvar Alvarez, Alvar Salvadórez,
Galín García, that good man from Aragon,
And Félix Muñoz, my Cid's nephew.
Everyone who was there, from that moment on,
Rushed toward the banner, and fought for my Cid, their great
    Warrior.

38

The Moors succeeded in killing Minaya's horse,
And at once Christians came rushing to help him.
His lance had been broken, but he drew his sword
And, staying on his feet, fought furiously on.
My Cid, Ruy Díaz, seeing his problem,
Headed for one of the Moors, who rode a first-rate horse,
And gave him such a savage blow with his sword

A Minaya Álbar Fáñez   íval' dar el cavallo:
"¡Cavalgad, Minaya,   vós sodes el mio diestro braço!
Oy en este día   de vós abré grand bando;
firme[s] son los moros,   aún nos' van del campo."
Cavalgó Minaya,   el espada en la mano,
por estas fuerças   fuertemientre lidiando,
a los que alcança   valos delibrando.
Mio Cid Rruy Díaz,   el que en buen ora nasco,
al rrey Fáriz   *tres* colpes le avié dado,
los dos le fallen   e el únol' ha tomado;
por la loriga ayuso   la sangre destella[n]do
bolvió la rrienda   por írsele del campo.
Por aquel colpe   rrancado es el fonsado.

39

Martín Antolínez   un colpe dio a Galve,
las carbonclas del yelmo   echógelas aparte,
cortól' el yelmo   que llegó a la carne;
sabet, el otro   non gel' osó esperar.
Arrancado es   el rrey Fáriz e Galve.
¡Tan buen día   por la cristiandad
ca fuyen los moros   de la part!
Los de Mio Cid   firiendo en alcaz,
el rrey Fáriz   en Ter*r*er se fue entrar
e a Galve   nol' cogieron allá,
para Calatayu*t*,   quanto puede, se va;
el Campeador   íval' en alcaz,
fata Calatayu*t*   duró el segudar.

That he cut him in half, at the waist; what was left of him fell to
    the ground.
Then he rode to Minaya, leading the horse:
"Ride him, Minaya, my good right hand!
I'll be leaning on you for some heavy work today:
The Moors are fighting back, they still might beat us."
Minaya galloped into action, swinging his sword,
Delivering heavy blows, driving through the Moorish horde;
Souls flew from the bodies of all who approached him.
My Cid, Ruy Díaz, born at a lucky hour,
Had swung at King Fáriz three times;
Twice he'd missed, but the third time he hit him,
And blood came gushing down the length of his mail shirt,
And the king swung his horse around, so he could run from the
    battle.
That single blow broke his army's resistance.

39

Martín Antolínez struck at Galvé, the other king,
Smashing apart his helmet, at the neck,
Cutting through right into his flesh.
Believe me, he did not wait to be hit again.
King Fáriz and King Galvé were beaten, both had fled.
What a magnificent day for the Christians,
Seeing the Moors turn and run!
My Cid's followers chased after them:
King Fáriz took shelter in Terrer,
But Galvé took a different direction,
Running as fast as he could, all the way to Calatayud.
And that was as far as the Warrior pursued him,
Not riding any farther than Calatayud.

40

A Minaya Álbar Fáñez   bien l'anda el cavallo,
d'aquestos moros   mató *treínta e quatro*,
espada tajador,   sangriento trae el braço,
por el cobdo ayuso   la sangre destellando.
Dize Minaya: "Agora só pagado,
que a Castiella   irán buenos mandados
que Mio Cid Rruy Díaz   lid campal á vencida."
Tantos moros yazen muertos   que pocos bivos á dexados
ca en alcaz   sin dubda les fueron dando.
Yas' tornan   los del que en buen ora nasco;
andava Mio Cid   sobre so buen cavallo,
la cofia fronzida,   ¡Dios, cómo es bien barbado!
Almófar a cuestas,   la espada en la mano,
vio los sos   cómos' van allegando:
"Grado a Dios,   [a] Aquel que está en alto,
quando tal batalla   avemos arrancado."
Esta albergada los de Mio Cid   luego la an rrobada
de escudos e de armas   e de otros averes largos;
de los moriscos,   quando son llegados,
fallaron   *quinientos e diez* cavallos.
Grand alegreya va   entre essos cristianos,
más de quinze de los sos   menos non fallaron.
Traen oro e plata   que non saben rrecabdo,
rrefechos son todos essos cristianos   con aquesta ganancia.
A so castiello a los moros   dentro los an tornados,
mandó Mio Cid aún   que les diessen algo.
Grant á el gozo Mio Cid   con todos sos vassallos,
dio a partir estos dineros   e estos averes largos;
en la su quinta al Cid   caen *ciento* cavallos.
¡Dios, qué bien pagó   a todos sus vassallos,
a los peones   e a los encavalgados!
Bien lo aguisa   el que en buen ora nasco,
quantos él trae   todos son pagados.
"¡Oíd, Minaya,   sodes mio diestro braço!
D'aquesta rriqueza   que el Criador nos á dado

40

The horse ran well for Minaya Alvar Fáñez:
His sharp sword caught thirty-four
Of these fleeing Moors; he was bloody all over,
His arm stained from hand to elbow.
And seeing that, he said: "I'm satisfied, now,
Because all Castile will soon know
That my Cid, Ruy Díaz, fought a battle and won it."
Many Moors lay dead, not many survived:
When they broke and ran, they were pursued and struck down.
Then he who was born at a lucky time swung around,
Riding high on his splendid horse,
His netted cap pushed back. That was a man with a beard,
By God! Chain-mail hood down on his shoulders,
Sword in hand, he watched his men returning:
"We thank our God, high in heaven,
That we have conquered, won in such a battle."
Then his men went up and down the field, collecting loot—
Swords, shields, whatever was worth the taking.
The fallen Moors had left behind them
Five hundred and ten horses.
These Christians were overjoyed, finding
That, of their three hundred, no more than fifteen were lost.
They collected more gold and silver than anyone could count:
All these Christians were enriched by what they'd won.
My Cid ordered that even the Alcocer Moors,
Returning to the castle, ought to be given something.
My Cid and all his men were wonderfully pleased,
As he had them distribute gold and other prizes;
His own share included a full hundred horses.
Dear God, how happy his men were,
Every knight and every foot soldier!
He who was born at just the right time did it just right,
And all were satisfied.
"Listen, Minaya," he said, "my good right arm,
Take whatever you like, this time,

a vuestra guisa   prended con vuestra mano.
Enbiarvos quiero   a Castiella con mandado
d'esta batalla   que avemos arrancada,
al rrey Alfonso   que me á airado
quiérol' e[n]biar en don   *treínta* cavallos,
todos con siellas   e muy bien enfrenados,
señas espadas   de los arzones colgadas."
Dixo Minaya Álbar Fáñez: "Esto faré yo de grado."

41

"Evades aquí   oro e plata,
una huesa llena, | que nada nol' mingua;
en Sancta María de Burgos   quitedes mill missas,
lo que rromaneciere   daldo a mi mugier e a mis fijas
que rrueguen por mí   las noches e los días;
si les yo visquier,   serán dueñas rricas."

42

Minaya Álbar Fáñez   d'esto es pagado;
por ir con él   omnes son [contados],
agora davan cevada,   ya la noch era entrada,
Mio Cid Rruy Díaz   con los sos se acordava.

43

"¡Ídesvos, Minaya,   a Castiella la gentil!
A nuestros amigos   bien les podedes dezir:
'Dios nos valió   e venciemos la lid.'
A la tornada,   si nos falláredes aquí;
si non, dó sopiéredes que somos,   indos conseguir.
Por la[n]ças e por espadas   avemos de guarir,
si non, en esta tierra angosta   non podriemos [bivir]."

Of these riches given us by God!
I want to send you to Castile, with word
Of this battle we have won,
And thirty horses—with saddles, bridles,
Everything, and a sword hanging from each saddlebow.
This will be a gift to King Alfonso,
My great lord, who sent me into exile."
"With pleasure," Minaya Alvar Fáñez said, in reply.

41

"Take this riding boot," said my Cid, "filled to the brim,
All of it gold and silver,
To pay for a thousand masses at Santa María, in Burgos.
Give my wife and daughters whatever's left over:
Ask them to pray for me, both day and night.
They'll be rich ladies, if I'm still alive."

42

Minaya Alvar Fáñez swore to comply
With every request; knights to ride with him were chosen;
They foddered their horses, as darkness fell;
And my Cid gave them some final words:

43

"Minaya, you're headed for sweet Castile.
And now you can tell our friends:
'By the grace of God we've conquered.'
When you return, perhaps we'll be here—
Perhaps not. Then find out where we've gone and join us.
Remaining in this barren land is neither joyful
Nor safe: we need to protect ourselves with lances and swords."

44

Ya es aguisado,   mañanas' fue Minaya
e el Campeador   [*fincó*] con su mesnada.
La tierra es angosta   e sobejana de mala,
todos los días   a Mio Cid aguardavan
moros de las fronteras   e unas yentes estrañas;
sanó el rrey Fáriz,   con él se consejavan.
Entre los de Teca   e los de Ter*r*er la casa
e los de Calatayut,   que es más ondrada,
assí lo an asmado   e metudo en carta,
vendido les á Alcocer   por tres mill marcos de plata.

45

Mio Cid Rruy Díaz   Alcocer á ven[*d*]ido,
¡qué bien pagó   a sus vassallos mismos!
A cavalleros e a peones   fechos los ha rricos,
en todos los sos   non fallariedes un mesquino;
qui a buen señor sirve   siempre bive en delicio.

46

Quando Mio Cid   el castiello quiso quitar,
moros e moras   tomáronse a quexar:
"¡Vaste, Mio Cid!   ¡Nuestras oraciones váyante delante!
Nós pagados fin*c*amos,   señor, de la tu part."
Quando quitó a Alcocer   Mio Cid el de Bivar,
moros e moras   compeçaron de llorar.
Alçó su seña,   el Campeador se va,
passó Salón ayuso,   aguijó cabadelant,
al exir de Salón   mucho ovo buenas aves.
Plogo a los de Terrer   e a los de Calatayut más;
pesó a los de Alcocer   ca pro les fazié grant.
Aguijó Mio Cid,   ivas' cabadelant,

44

No more needed saying. At dawn the next day,
Minaya departed; the Warrior and his men remained
In that arid place, extremely barren.
Moors from nearby lands and from other places
Were always on watch, day and night.
King Fáriz was healthy again, and they met with him.
But the people of Ateca, and those of Terrer,
Together with Calatayud, a town much larger,
Agreed with my Cid, and put in writing,
That they would buy Alcocer for three thousand silver marks.

45

And so my Cid sold them Alcocer—
And how happy this made all his men!
Knights and soldiers on foot, now all alike were rich:
You couldn't have found a poor man among them,
For those who serve a good master always live well.

46

The Moors who lived in Alcocer
Lamented his departure:
"My Cid, you're leaving us! Our prayers will always precede you!
We're deeply satisfied, our lord, with all you've done."
And when he left Alcocer, my Cid from Vivar,
Both men and women began to weep.
He raised his banner, and then he was gone,
Riding beside the Jalón, his horses galloping:
Turning away from the river, he saw many signs predicting good
    fortune.
Terrer was happy he was leaving; Calatayud was even happier;
But not Alcocer, which he had treated so well.

í fincó en un poyo   que es sobre Mont Rreal;
alto es el poyo,   maravilloso e grant;
non teme guerra,   sabet, a nulla part.
Metió en paria   a Doroca enantes,
desí a Molina,   que es del otra part,
la tercera Teruel,   que estava delant,
en su mano tenié   a Celfa la de Canal.

47

¡Mio Cid Rruy Díaz   de Dios aya su gracia!
Ido es a Castiella   Álbar Fáñez Minaya,
treínta cavallos   al rrey los enpresentava.
Violos el rrey,   fermoso sonrrisava:
"¿Quín' los dio éstos,   sí vos vala Dios, Minaya?"
"Mio Cid Rruy Díaz,   que en buen ora cinxo espada.
Venció dos rreyes de moros   en aquesta batalla;
sobejana es, señor,   la su gana[n]cia.
A vós, rrey ondrado,   enbía esta presentaja;
bésavos los pies   e las manos amas
quel' ay[a]des merced,   sí el Criador vos vala."
Dixo el rrey: "Mucho es mañana
omne airado   que de señor non ha gracia
por acogello   a cabo de tres semanas.
Mas después que de moros fue,   prendo esta presentaja;
aún me plaze de Mio Cid   que fizo tal ganancia.
Sobr'esto todo   a vós quito, Minaya,
honores e tierras   avellas condonadas,
id e venit,   d'aquí vos do mi gracia;
mas del Cid Campeador   yo non vos digo nada.
Sobre aquesto todo   dezirvos quiero, Minaya,

48

"de todo mio rreino   los que lo quisieren far,
buenos e valientes   pora Mio Cid huyar,

My Cid went galloping on, riding quickly
Until he reached a hill above Monreal—
A high hill, broad and beautiful,
Which could not be attacked, believe me, from any direction.
The first town to pay him tribute was Daroca,
And then Molina, on the other side of the hill,
And then Teruel, farther along.
He already held Celfa de Canal.

47

God grant his grace to my Cid, Ruy Díaz!
Alvar Fáñez Minaya arrived in Castile,
And presented thirty fine horses to the king:
He smiled with pleasure, seeing them.
"May God save you, Minaya, but who's given me such a gift?"
"My Cid, Ruy Díaz, knighted at just the right time.
He defeated two Moorish kings in battle,
Winning immense riches.
He sends you these horses, as his honored ruler,
And kisses your hands and your feet,
Asking for your forgiveness, in the name of our Lord."
The king said: "That cannot yet be done:
A man who's been exiled and disgraced
Cannot be pardoned three weeks later.
Still, the gift was won from the Moors, so I'll take it.
I am pleased that my Cid has done
So well. You stand here pardoned,
Minaya: your lands and honors are yours again.
Come and go as you please.
Yet as for the Cid, that Warrior, I've not decided.

48

"But still, Minaya, let me also say
That any strong, brave men who wish to prey

suéltoles los cuerpos   e quítoles las heredades."
Besóle las manos   Minaya Álbar Fáñez:
"Grado e gracias, rrey,   como a señor natural,
esto feches agora,   ál feredes adelant."

49

"Id por Castiella   e déxenvos andar, Minaya,
si[n] nulla dubda   id a Mio Cid buscar ganancia."
Quiero vos dezir   del que en buen ora nasco e cinxo espada.
Aquel poyo,   en él priso posada,
mientra que sea el pueblo de moros   e la yente cristiana
El Poyo de Mio Cid   assil' dirán por carta.
Estando allí,   mucha tierra preava,
el río de Martín   todo lo metió en paria.
A Saragoça   sus nuevas llegavan,
non plaze a los moros,   firmemientre les pesava,
allí sovo Mio Cid   conplidas quinze semanas.
Quando vio el caboso   que se tardava Minaya,
con todas sus yentes   fizo una trasnochada;
dexó El Poyo,   todo lo desenparava,
allén de Teruel   don Rrodrigo passava,
en el pinar de Tévar   don Rroy Díaz posava,
todas essas tierras   todas las preava,
a Saragoça   metuda la [á] en paria.
Quando esto fecho ovo,   a cabo de tres semanas
de Castiella   venido es Minaya,
dozientos con él,   que todos ciñen espadas,
non son en cuenta,   sabet, las peonadas.
Quando vio Mio Cid   asomar a Minaya,
el cavallo corriendo,   valo abraçar sin falla,
besóle la boca   e los ojos de la cara.
Todo ge lo dize,   que nol' encubre nada,
el Campeador   fermoso sonrrisava:

On the Moors with my Cid may go;
Neither their persons or property will suffer."
Kissing the king's hands, Minaya told him:
"I thank you most gladly, my king and lord,
For you'll do this now, and soon will do more."

49

"Cross Castile, Minaya, just as you please;
Rejoin my Cid and seek more treasure."
    Now I will speak of him, born and knighted at fortunate
Times: the hill he'd chosen for his camp
Will be called, by Christians and by Moors,
My Cid's Hill, for forever more.
From that base he conducted many raids;
Towns along the river Martín paid him.
Unwelcome news of this arrived in Saragossa,
Where the Moors were absolutely outraged.
My Cid stayed there a hundred days,
But seeing that Minaya had been delayed,
In the darkness of night he and his men went away,
Leaving the hill completely undefended.
They rode beyond Teruel and camped,
At last, in the pine woods of Tévar.
And there, too, he demanded tribute;
Even Saragossa made a contribution.
He raided for three full weeks
Before Minaya returned from Castile,
Followed by two hundred armed men
And more on foot, let me tell you, than could be counted.
My Cid came galloping toward them,
Then threw his arms around Minaya,
Kissing his mouth and also his eyes.
Minaya told him who had said what to whom, in great detail,
Omitting nothing. And the Warrior smiled.

"¡Grado a Dios   e a las sus vertudes sanctas,
mientra vós visquiéredes,   bien me irá a mí, Minaya!"

50

¡Dios, cómo fue alegre   todo aquel fonsado
que Minaya Álbar Fáñez   assí era llegado,
diziéndoles saludes   de primos e de ermanos
e de sus compañas,   aquellas que avién dexadas!

51

¡Dios, cómo es alegre   la barba vellida
que Álbar Fáñez   pagó las mill missas
e quel' dixo saludes   de su mugier e de sus fijas!
¡Dios, cómo fue el Cid pagado   e fızo grand alegría!
"¡Ya Álbar Fáñez,   bivades muchos días!"

52

Non lo tardó   el que en buen ora nasco,
tierras d'Alcañ[i]z   negras las va parando
e aderredor   todo lo va preando;
al tercer día   dón ixo, í es tornado.

53

Ya va el mandado   por las tierras todas,
pesando va a los de Monçón   e a los de Huesca;
porque dan parias   plaze a los de Saragoça,
de Mio Cid Rruy Díaz   que non temién ninguna fonta.

"I thank God and all his saints on high!
My life will go well, Minaya, as long as you're alive!"

50

O Lord, how everyone was smiling,
Seeing once again their comrade Minaya!
He carried messages from brothers and friends
And cousins they'd left behind them.

51

O Lord, how the bearded Warrior went on smiling,
Happy his thousand masses were paid for,
Delighted to hear from his daughters and his wife!
Dear God! How pleased he was, how he rejoiced!
"I wish you, Alvar Fáñez, a long long life!"

52

He could not wait, he who was born at a fortunate hour,
Riding out with his men to Alcañiz, and all around it,
Everywhere they went, they were paid;
They did not return for three entire days.

53

News of this new raid
Reached Monzón and Huesca, and deeply dismayed them.
But the people of Saragossa were not afraid,
For they'd paid tribute, and my Cid, Ruy Díaz, would never
   betray them.

54

Con estas ganancias   a la posada tornándose van,
todos son alegres,   ganancias traen grandes,
plogo a Mio Cid   e mucho a Álbar Fáñez.
Sonrrisós' el caboso,   que non lo pudo endurar:
"Ya cavalleros,   dezir vos he la verdad:
qui en un logar mora siempre,   lo so puede menguar;
cras a la mañana   pensemos de cavalgar,
dexat estas posadas   e iremos adelant."
Estonces se mudó el Cid   al puerto de Aluca[n]t,
dent corre Mio Cid   a Huesa e a Mont Alván;
en aquessa corrida   *diez* días ovieron a morar.
Fueron los mandados   a todas partes
que el salido de Castiella   assí los trae tan mal.
Los mandados son idos   a todas partes.

55

Llegaron las nuevas   al conde de Barcilona
que Mio Cid Rruy Díaz   quel' corrié la tierra toda;
ovo grand pesar   e tóvos'lo a grant fonta.

56

El conde es muy follón   e dixo una vanidat:
"Grandes tuertos me tiene   Mio Cid el de Bivar.
Dentro en mi cort   tuerto me tovo grand,
firióm' el sobrino   e non' lo enmendó más;
agora córrem' las tierras   que en mi enpara están.
Non lo desafié,   nil' torné enemistad,
mas quando él me lo busca,   ir ge lo he yo demandar."
Grandes son los poderes   e apriessa llegando se van,
entre moros e cristianos   gentes se le allegan grandes,

54

They made their return, smiling
From ear to ear, all happy with what they'd gotten;
My Cid was delighted; so too was Alvar Fáñez.
My Cid could not restrain his pleasure.
"And yet," he told his men, "I warn you: leisure
Is not for us. We're lost if we stay in one place.
Tomorrow morning we must leave this camp
And keep on riding, first here, then there."
He took them through Gallocanta Pass,
Which took them ten long days to cross,
Then on to Huesa and Montalbán, raiding
For ten more treasure-laden days.
The news of these devastating
Forays spread far and wide:
Castile's great exile had become a serious danger.

55

News that my Cid, Ruy Díaz, was ravaging far and wide
Came to the Count of Barcelona,
Who was deeply upset at such an attack on his pride.

56

The count was boastful, stuffed with conceit, and reckless:
"This Cid from Vivar is causing me trouble, he thinks I'm
    helpless.
Right here in my court he wounded one of my nephews,
And never apologized.
Now he's raiding lands lying in my protection.
I've never challenged him, or picked a quarrel—
But when he comes looking for me, I'll make him pay."
He quickly assembled a massive army,

adeliñan tras Mio Cid   el bueno de Bivar;
tres días e dos noches   pensaron de andar,
alcançaron a Mio Cid   en Tévar e el pinar;
assí viene esforçado el conde   que a manos se le cuidó tomar.
Mio Cid don Rrodrigo   ganancia trae grand,
dice de una sierra   e llegava a un val.
Del conde don Rremont   venídol' es mensaje,
Mio Cid, quando lo oyó,   enbió pora allá:
"Digades al conde   non lo tenga a mal,
de lo so non lievo nada,   déxem' ir en paz."
Rrespuso el conde: "¡Esto non será verdad!
Lo de antes e de agora   tódom' lo pechará;
¡sabrá el salido   a quién vino desondrar!"
Tornós' el mandadero   quanto pudo más;
essora lo connosce   Mio Cid el de Bivar
que a menos de batalla   nos' pueden dén quitar.

57

"Ya cavalleros,   apart fazed la ganancia,
apriessa vos guarnid   e metedos en las armas;
el conde don Rremont   dar nos ha grant batalla,
de moros e de cristianos   gentes trae sobejanas,
a menos de batalla   non nos dexarié por nada.
Pues adelant irán tras nós,   aquí sea la batalla;
apretad los cavallos   e bistades las armas.
Ellos vienen cuesta yuso   e todos trahen calças
e las siellas coceras   e las cinchas amojadas;
nós cavalgaremos siellas gallegas   e huesas sobre calças,
ciento cavalleros   devemos vencer aquellas mesnadas.
Antes que ellos lleguen a[l] llano,   presentémosles las lanças,
por uno que firgades,   tres siellas irán vazias;
¡verá Rremont Verenguel   tras quién vino en alcança
oy en este pinar de Tévar   por tollerme la ganancia!"

Moors and Christians gathered at his call
And followed the tracks of that good man from Vivar, my Cid,
And found him, in the pine woods of Tévar.
The count was sure his massive army would capture my Cid,
Who was coming down from the mountains,
Loaded with treasure he'd taken.
The count's messenger arrived,
My Cid listened, and quickly replied:
"Tell the count I have no quarrel with him;
I've taken nothing of his. He should let me continue in peace."
The count responded: "He's lying!
I'll make him pay for what he's done and is doing!
This exile will learn just who he's dishonored!"
The messenger ran back as fast as he could,
And then my Cid, he who came from Vivar, understood
That unless he fought this battle, he could not go on.

57

"All right, my knights, lay down your treasure:
First things first! Get ready to fight:
Count Ramón is about to attack us
With a great army of Moors and Christians.
If we try to escape, he'll stop us.
As long as they're advancing, let them come.
Tighten your saddle buckles, put on your armor:
They're riding downhill, not wearing boots or shoes;
Their saddles are light, and loose, and ours are heavy, and we've
    got boots.
Our hundred knights have to beat these hordes!
Before they reach the plain, we'll attack with lances—
Every thrust will empty three saddles.
Hah! Count Ramón will see just who he's met,
Here in these woods, trying to steal our treasure!"

58

Todos son adobados   quando Mio Cid esto ovo fablado,
las armas avién presas   e sedién sobre los cavallos,
vieron la cuesta yuso   la fuerça de los francos;
al fondón de la cuesta,   cerca es de[l] llano,
mandólos ferir Mio Cid,   el que en buen ora nasco.
Esto fazen los sos   de voluntad e de grado,
los pendones e las lanças   tan bien las van enpleando,
a los unos firiendo   e a los otros derrocando.
Vencido á esta batalla   el que en buen [ora] nasco;
al conde don Rremont   a presón le an tomado.

59

Í gañó a Colada,   que más vale de mill marcos de plata.
[Í benció] esta batalla   por ó ondró su barba.
Prísolo al conde,   pora su tienda lo levava,
a sos creenderos   guardarlo mandava.
De fuera de la tienda   un salto dava,
de todas partes   los sos se ajuntaron;
plogo a Mio Cid   ca grandes son las ganancias.
A Mio Cid don Rrodrigo   grant cozínal' adobavan;
el conde don Rremont   non ge lo precia nada,
adúzenle los comeres,   delant ge los paravan,
él non lo quiere comer,   a todos los sosañava:
"Non combré un bocado   por quanto ha en toda España,
antes perderé el cuerpo   e dexaré el alma,
pues que tales malcalçados   me vencieron de batalla."

58

When he stopped talking, they all were ready,
Armor on, seated on their horses.
They saw the count's Catalonian forces
Hurrying down the slopes, approaching
The plain. And then my Cid, born in a lucky hour,
Ordered his men to attack.
They'd been eagerly waiting, and gladly
Galloped into battle, making good use of their lances,
Striking some, tumbling others to the ground.
And just like that, it was over; he who'd been born
At a lucky hour had won the battle, and Count Ramón was his
    prisoner.

59

He'd also won Colada, a sword worth more than a thousand
Silver marks; the battle brought him still more in honor.
He took his noble captive to his tent
And left him there, under good guard.
And then my Cid strolled out,
And his men swarmed all around him,
Everyone happy at how much this victory had brought them.
My Cid had a huge banquet prepared for the count,
But Count Ramón did not give a damn,
Pushing away all the food brought in for him:
He would not eat, rejecting every dish.
"I won't put a thing in my mouth, not for all the gold in Spain.
Now that I've been beaten in battle by a band of nobodies,
I'd just as soon give up body and soul together."

60

"Mio Cid Rruy Díaz   odredes lo que dixo:
Comed, conde, d'este pan   e beved d'este vino;
si lo que digo fiziéredes,   saldredes de cativo,
si non, en todos vuestros días   non veredes cristianismo."

61

Dixo el conde don Rremont: . . . .
"Comede, don Rrodrigo,   e pensedes de fol[gar],
que yo dexar me [é] morir,   que non quiero comer."
Fasta tercer día   nol' pueden acordar;
ellos partiendo   estas ganancias grandes,
nol' pueden fazer comer   un muesso de pan.

62

Dixo Mio Cid: "Comed, conde, algo,
ca si non comedes   non veredes [cristianos];
e si vós comiéredes   dón yo sea pagado,
a vós   e [a] dos fijos d'algo
quitar vos he los cuerpos   e dar vos é de [mano]."
Quando esto oyó el conde,   yas' iva alegrando:
"Si lo fiziéredes, Cid,   lo que avedes fablado,
tanto quanto yo biva   seré dent maravillado."
"Pues comed, conde,   e quando fuéredes yantado,
a vós e a otros dos   dar vos he de mano;
mas quanto avedes perdido   e yo gané en canpo,
sabet, non vos daré   a vós un dinero malo,
ca huebos me lo he   e pora estos mios vassallos
que comigo   andan lazrados.
Prendiendo de vós e de otros   ir nos hemos pagando;
abremos esta vida   mientra ploguiere al Padre sancto,

60

Here's what my Cid, Ruy Díaz, told him:
"Eat, Count, eat this bread and drink this wine.
Do as I say, and you'll be a free man.
Don't, and you'll never see Christendom again."

61

Count Ramón replied: "You eat, Don Ruy, eat and relax,
Because I'd rather die than break bread with you."
For three whole days he stayed stubborn.
They were dividing all the riches they'd won,
And he wouldn't eat, not even a single crumb.

62

My Cid said: "Eat, Count. Take something,
Because unless you eat you'll never see another Christian,
And if you eat as I want you to,
You and two of your noblemen
Will be released, free to ride where you please."
Hearing these words, the count began to feel better:
"Cid, if you'll do what you say you will,
For the rest of my life I'll be bewildered."
"Then eat, Count, and when you've eaten your fill
You and the other two can go where you please.
But what you've lost, and what I've won in battle—
Hear me: I won't give back a wooden nickel,
Because I need it for these men of mine,
Who have, like me, no other way to find it.
We stay alive by taking from others, as we have with you.
And this will be our life for as long as God desires,

como que ira á de rrey   e de tierra es echado."
Alegre es el conde   e pidió agua a las manos
e tiénengelo delant   e diérongelo privado;
con los cavalleros   que el Cid le avié dados
comiendo va el conde,   ¡Dios, qué de buen grado!
Sobr'él sedié   el que en buen ora nasco:
"Si bien non comedes, conde,   dón yo sea pagado,
aquí feremos la morada,   no nos partiremos amos."
Aquí dixo el conde: "De voluntad e de grado."
Con estos dos cavalleros   apriessa va yantando;
pagado es Mio Cid,   que lo está aguardando,
porque el conde don Rremont   tan bien bolvié la[s] manos.
"Si vos ploguiere, Mio Cid,   de ir somos guisados,
mandad nos dar las bestias   e cavalgaremos privado;
del día que fue conde   non yanté tan de buen grado,
el sabor que de[n]d é   non será olbidado."
Danle tres palafrés   muy bien ensellados
e buenas vestiduras   de pelliçones e de mantos.
El conde don Rremont   entre los dos es entrado;
fata cabo del albergada   escurriólos el castellano:
"Ya vos ides, conde,   a guisa de muy franco,
en grado vos lo tengo   lo que me avedes dexado.
Si vos viniere emiente   que quisiéredes vengallo,
si me viniéredes buscar,   fallarme podredes;
e si non,   mandedes buscar:
o me dexaredes | de lo vuestro,   o de lo mío levaredes algo."
"Folguedes ya, Mio Cid,   sodes en vuestro salvo;
pagado vos he   por todo aqueste año,
de venir vos buscar   sól non será pensado."

Aguijava el conde   e pensava de andar,
tornando va la cabeça   e catandos' atrás;
miedo iva aviendo   que Mio Cid se rrepintrá;

Living as men must, when their king has thrown them into exile."
The happy count asked for water, to wash his hands;
It was brought at once, as he had asked,
And he and the two noblemen, as my Cid had agreed,
Began to eat. And eat. And eat!
He who was born in just the right time sat next to him:
"Remember, Count: you need to eat freely—
Or else we'll have to sit here forever, and never leave."
The count replied: "O, I agree, I agree!"
He and his two noblemen fairly attacked their food,
And my Cid was pleased, seeing
For himself how quickly the count was wielding
His hands.

     "At your pleasure, my Cid, we're ready to leave.
Have them bring our horses, and off we'll go.
In all my life as a count I've never eaten
Better. I'll never forget the delight of this meal."
They were given three palfreys, very well saddled,
And also fine clothes, fur-lined, and mantles.
Count Ramón rode between the two nobles,
With the exiled Castilian as their escort, beside them.
"So here you leave us, Count, and you ride
As a free Catalonian. I'm grateful for all you've left
Behind. If ever you feel the need to find me
Again, and revenge yourself, do let me know.
Or not: just come and find me,
And either I'll take something from you, or you from me."
"Ah, don't worry, my Cid, be at ease!
I've already paid you a year's assessment:
Returning for more is not my intention."

                              63

The count spurred his horse and rode right off,
But kept turning his head and looking behind him,
Afraid my Cid might change his mind

lo que non ferié el caboso   por quanto en el mundo ha,
una deslea[*l*]tança,   ca non la fızo alguandre.
Ido es el conde,   tornós' el de Bivar,
juntós' con sus mesnadas,   conpeçós' de *pa*gar
de la ganancia que an fecha   maravillosa e grand.

And retake them—a betrayal this untainted hero could never
   make:
In all his life he had never gone back on his word.
  The count had gone. The man from Vivar
Turned back and joined his men, still delighted
With the marvelous wealth they'd earned in that day's fighting.
His men were now so rich they couldn't count it!

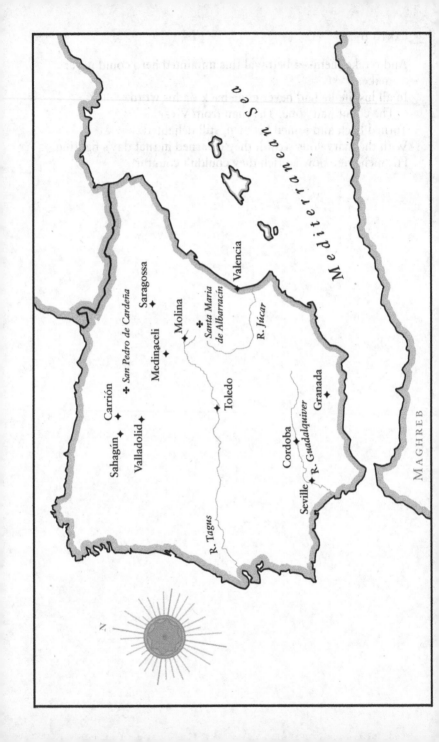

CANTO TWO

64

Aquís' conpieça la gesta   de Mio Cid el de Bivar.
Tan rricos son los sos   que non saben qué se an.
Poblado ha Mio Cid   el puerto de Alucant,
dexado á Saragoça   e las tierras ducá
e dexado á Huesa   e las tierras de Mont Alván.
Contra la mar salada   conpeçó de guerrear,
a orient exe el sol   e tornós' a essa part.
Mio Cid gañó a Xérica   e a Onda e [a] Almenar,
tierras de Borriana   todas conquistas las ha.

65

Ayudól' el Criador,   el Señor que es en cielo.
Él con todo esto   priso a Murviedro;
ya v[e]yé Mio Cid   que Dios le iva valiendo.
Dentro en Valencia   non es poco el miedo.

66

Pesa a los de Valencia,   sabet, non les plaze,
prisieron so consejo   quel' viniessen cercar;
trasnocharon de noch,   al alva de la man
acerca de Murviedro   tornan tiendas a fincar.
Violo Mio Cid,   tomós' a maravillar;
"¡Grado a ti,   Padre spiritual!
En sus tierras somos   e fémosles todo mal,

64

Here begin the true heroics of my Cid, from Vivar.
   He'd made his camp near the Olocau Pass,
Having left Saragossa and the duke's other lands,
Riding past Huesa and Montalbán.
Then he rode toward the sea, to fight down there—
As the sun rises in the east, that's where
He headed. He conquered Jérica, Onda, and Almenara,
And everything around Burriana, on the coast.

65

He was helped by God, the Lord of heaven on high.
And when he took Murviedro
He was convinced that God was on his side.
But to the south, in Moorish Valencia, people were afraid.

66

They were really concerned, God knows, not pleased at all.
Deciding to besiege him, there in the city he'd conquered,
They marched all night and, next morning, at break of dawn,
Their tents were set around Murviedro.
Seeing all this, my Cid was amazed:
"Our Father in heaven, thank you!
We've invaded their lands, we've wronged them over and over,

bevemos so vino   e comemos el so pan;
si nos cercar vienen,   con derecho lo fazen.
A menos de lid   aquesto nos' partirá;
vayan los mandados   por los que nos deven ayudar,
los unos a Xérica   e los otros a Alucad,
desí a Onda   e los otros a Almenar,
los de Borriana   luego vengan acá;
conpeçaremos   aquesta lid campal,
yo fío por Dios   que en nuestro pro eñadrán."
Al tercer día   todos juntados son,
el que en buen ora nasco   compeçó de fablar:
"¡Oíd, mesnadas,   sí el Criador vos salve!
Después que nos partiemos   de la linpia cristiandad,
non fue a nuestro grado   ni nós non pudiemos más,
grado a Dios,   lo nuestro fue adelant.
Los de Valencia   cercados nos han,
si en estas tierras   quisiéremos durar,
firmemientre son éstos   a escarmentar.

67

"Passe la noche   e venga la mañana,
aparejados me sed   a cavallos e armas,
iremos ver   aquella su almofalla;
como omnes exidos   de tierra estraña,
allí pareçrá   el que merece la soldada."

68

Oíd qué dixo   Minaya Álbar Fáñez:
"Campeador, fagamos   lo que a vós plaze.
A mí dedes *ciento* cavalleros,   que non vos pido más,
vós con los otros   firádeslos delant,
bien los ferredes,   que dubda non í avrá;
yo con los ciento   entraré del otra part,
como fío por Dios,   el campo nuestro será."

We've eaten their bread and drunk their wine,
Here they are to besiege us; surely, they have that right.
But unless they beat us in battle, we will not leave.
Messages must be sent to those who should shield us—
Some to Jérica, others to Olocau,
Then on to Onda, and others to Almenara.
Men from Burriana should come at once.
We'll begin the fighting out in the open,
I trust in God to help us."
It took three days for his troops to assemble;
Then he who was born in a lucky hour addressed them:
"Soldiers, listen to me! You who believe in our God!
Ever since we left Christian-clean lands—
By neither choice nor desire: there was no other way—
By God's great grace, we have prospered.
Valencia has now besieged us,
And if we want to linger where we've come,
We need to give these people a heavy-handed lesson.

67

"Let the night go by, but tomorrow at daybreak
I want to see you armed and already mounted,
So we can pay a visit to that army out there,
And I can see just who among you exiles from another land
Really deserves his soldier's wages!"

68

And then Minaya Alvar Fáñez spoke:
"O Warrior, we'll do what we're told to.
Let me have a hundred knights, I ask for no more.
You and all the others attack them straight on:
You'll hit them hard, I know you will.
And I with my hundred knights will strike from the side.
By my faith in God, the field will be ours!"

Como ge lo á dicho,   al Campeador mucho plaze.
Mañana era   e piénsanse de armar,
quis cada uno d'ellos   bien sabe lo que ha de far.
Con los alvores   Mio Cid ferirlos va:
"¡En el nombre del Criador   e del apóstol Sancti Yagüe,
feridlos, cavalleros,   d'amor e de grado e de grand voluntad,
ca yo só Rruy Díaz,   Mio Cid el de Bivar!"
Tanta cuerda de tienda   í veriedes quebrar,
arrancarse las estacas   e acostarse a todas partes los tendales.
[Los] moros son muchos,   ya quieren rreconbrar.
Del otra part   entróles Álbar Fáñez,
maguer les pesa,   oviéronse a dar e a arrancar,
de pies de cavallo   los ques' pudieron escapar.
Grand es el gozo   que va por és logar;
dos rreyes de moros   mataron en és alcanz,
fata Valencia   duró el segudar.
Grandes son las ganancias   que Mio Cid fechas ha,
rrobavan el campo   e piénsanse de tornar.
Prisieron Cebolla   e quanto que es í adelant,
entravan a Murviedro   con estas ganancias que traen grandes.
Las nuevas de Mio Cid,   sabet, sonando van,
miedo an en Valencia   que non saben qué se far.
Sonando van sus nuevas   allent parte del mar.

69

Alegre era el Cid   e todas sus compañas
que Dios le ayudara   e fiziera esta arrancada.
Davan sus corredores   e fazién las trasnochadas,
llegan a Gujera   e llegan a Xátiva,
aún más ayusso   a Deyna la casa;
cabo del mar tierra de moros   firme la quebranta,
ganaron Peña Cadiella,   las exidas e las entradas.

The Warrior was more than merely satisfied.
Morning came, and they put on their armor,
Each man in the army knew what he had to do.
My Cid attacked at dawn's first light:
"In the name of God and the apostle Saint James,
At them, knights, with zest, and pleasure, and delight!
Because I am Cid, Ruy Díaz from Vivar!"
You should have seen the tent ropes snap,
Their poles yanked from the ground, canvas flapping, sagging.
There were a lot of Moors, they tried to stand and fight.
Then Alvar Fáñez came at them, from the other side:
Not wanting to retreat, they had to run or ride (if they could) for
    their lives.
The battlefield became a happy place.
Two Moorish kings were killed, trying to escape;
The chase ran all the way to Valencia.
My Cid had won enormous booty.
They turned and took Cebolla and everything all around it,
Then stripped the field and rode back to Murviedro with their
    loot.
Word of what my Cid had done, believe me, spread like fire,
Valencia was at a loss, and terrified.
The news went traveling over the ocean, spread far and wide.

69

My Cid and his men were glad that God had helped them
And made this victory happen.
They sent out raiding parties, riding at night,
Reaching Cullera, and then Játiva,
Roaming south, even as far as Denia,
Harassing and burning Moorish towns along the coast
And capturing Benicadell, and all roads leading in and out.

70

Quando el Cid Campeador   ovo Peña Cadiella,
ma[l] les pesa en Xátiva   e dentro en Gujera,
non es con rrecabdo   el dolor de Valencia.

71

En tierra de moros   prendiendo e ganando
e durmiendo los días   e las noches tranochando,
en ganar aquellas villas   Mio Cid duró *tres* años.

72

A los de Valencia   escarmentados los ha,
non osan fueras exir   nin con él se ajuntar;
tajávales las huertas   e fazíales grand mal,
en cada uno d'estos años   Mio Cid les tollió el pan.
Mal se aquexan los de Valencia   que non sabent qués' far,
de ninguna part que sea   non les vinié pan;
nin da cossejo padre a fijo,   nin fijo a padre,
nin amigo a amigo   nos' pueden consolar.
Mala cueta es, señores,   aver mingua de pan,
fijos e mugieres   verlo[s] murir de fanbre.
Delante veyén so duelo,   non se pueden uviar,
por el rrey de Marruecos   ovieron a enbiar;
con el de los Montes Claros   avié guerra tan grand,
non les dixo cossejo   nin los vino uviar.
Sópolo Mio Cid,   de coraçón le plaz,
salió de Murviedro   una noch en trasnochada,
amaneció a Mio Cid   en tierras de Mon Rreal.
Por Aragón e por Navarra   pregón mandó echar,
a tierras de Castiella   enbió sus mensajes:
quien quiere perder cueta   e venir a rritad,

70

When my Cid, the Warrior, took Benicadell
The people of Cullera and Játiva were deeply concerned,
But in Valencia gloom was everywhere.

71

And so, for the next three years,
My Cid raided and robbed the Moors,
Sleeping by day, marching at night.

72

Valencia had learned its lesson:
People stayed inside the walls, no one confronted my Cid,
Who chopped down their fields and made their lives difficult,
For three long years taking away their food.
And how they grumbled, not knowing what else to do,
Unable to bring in food from anywhere—
Fathers not knowing what to say to sons, or sons to fathers,
Friends unable to comfort friends.
How hard it is, gentlemen, denied the food you need,
Watching your children, your wives, die of starvation!
Misery was their only future, they could not help
    themselves—
And the King of Morocco, to whom they appealed,
Was so caught up in war with the Atlas mountain king
He could not help them, could not so much as advise them.
Learning of this, my Cid's heart leaped,
And he rode all night, to the far northwest, and from there
Sent messengers all through Aragon, and Navarre,
And everywhere in Castile:
"Whoever wants to give up poverty and become rich,

viniesse a Mio Cid   que á sabor de cavalgar,
cercar quiere a Valencia   por a cristianos la dar:

73

"Quien quiere ir comigo   cercar a Valencia,
todos vengan de grado,   ninguno non ha premia;
tres días le speraré   en Canal de Celfa."

74

Esto dixo Mio Cid,   el que en buen ora nasco.
Tornavas' a Murviedro   ca él ganada se la á.
Andidieron los pregones,   sabet, a todas partes,
al sabor de la ganancia   non lo quiere[n] detardar,
grandes yentes se le acojen   de la buena cristiandad.
Creciendo va en rriqueza   Mio Cid el de Bivar,
quando vio Mio Cid las gentes juntadas,
        conpeçós' de pagar.
Mio Cid don Rrodrigo   non lo quiso detardar,
adeliñó pora Valencia   e sobr'ellas' va echar,
bien la cerca Mio Cid   que non í avía art,
viédales exir   e viédales entrar.
Sonando va[n] sus nuevas   todas a todas partes,
más le vienen a Mio Cid,   sabet, que nos' le van.
Metióla en plazo,   si les viniessen uviar;
nueve meses complidos,   sabet, sobr'ella yaz[e],
quando vino el dezeno   oviérongela a dar.
Grandes son los gozos   que van por és logar
quando Mio Cid gañó a Valencia   e entró en la cibdad.
Los que fueron de pie   cavalleros se fazen;
el oro e la plata   ¿quién vos lo podrié contar?
Todos eran rricos,   quantos que allí ha.
Mio Cid don Rrodrigo   la quinta mandó tomar,
en el aver monedado   *treínta* mill marcos le caen,
e los otros averes   ¿quién los podrié contar?

Come join my Cid, who's planning a siege
Of Valencia, to make it Christian once more!

73

"Come, whoever would like to join me.
Come, if you want to; I pressure no one.
I'll wait three days for you, down south at Celfa."

74

My Cid sent out these words, he who was born at the right time,
And then rode back to Murviedro, which was already his.
His messengers, let me tell you, went everywhere,
And anyone who could smell good prizes came running,
A great assembly of decent Christians.
My Cid from Vivar could see himself growing richer,
Observing these crowds of new men. How pleased he was!
Nor did he wait any longer, my Cid, Ruy Díaz:
He set out at once, and began the siege,
Made it so tight, no one could escape,
No one could enter, no one could leave.
News of this siege went everywhere,
And more men came, by God, than ever left him!
The city hoped for relief; he gave them a limit on waiting,
Then gave them the full nine months, believe me, perched at its
    gates.
When the tenth month came, they had no choice but surrender.
Valencia was shaken with their rejoicing
When my Cid and his men entered the city.
Now those who fought on foot had horses of their own,
And gold, and silver beyond description.
All his men were suddenly rich.
My Cid, Ruy Díaz, had his share of one-fifth,
Including thirty thousand marks in money—
But who could count the rest?

Alegre era el Campeador   con todos los que ha
quando su seña cabdal   sedié en somo del alcáçar.

75

Ya folgava Mio Cid   con todas sus conpañas.
[A] aquel rrey de Sevilla   el mandado llegava
que presa es Valencia,   que non ge la enparan;
vino los ver   con *treínta* mill de armas.
Après de la huerta   ovieron la batalla,
arrancólos Mio Cid,   el de la luenga barba.
Fata dentro en Xátiva   duró el arrancada,
en el passar de Xúcar   í veriedes barata,
moros en arruenço   amidos bever agua.
Aquel rrey de Marruecos   con tres colpes escapa.
Tornado es Mio Cid   con toda esta ganancia;
buena fue la de Valencia   quando ganaron la casa,
más mucho fue provechosa,   sabet, esta arrancada,
a todos los menores   cayeron *ciento* marcos de plata.
Las nuevas del cavallero   ya vedes dó llegavan.

76

Grand alegría es   entre todos essos cristianos
con Mio Cid Rruy Díaz,   el que en buen ora nasco.
Yal' crece la barba   e vále allongando,
dixo Mio Cid   de la su boca atanto:
"Por amor del rrey Alfonso   que de tierra me á echado,"
nin entrarié en ella tigera,   ni un pelo non avrié tajado
e que fablassen d'esto   moros e cristianos.
Mio Cid don Rrodrigo   en Valencia está folgando,
con él Minaya Álbar Fáñez   que nos' le parte de so braço.
Los que exieron de tierra   de rritad son abondados,
a todos les dio en Valencia casas,   e heredades | de que son
     pagados.
El amor de Mio Cid   ya lo ivan provando,

The Warrior, and every one of his men, cheered
When, at the soaring top of the fortress, his banner appeared.

75

My Cid and his men took time to rest.
But when the King of Morocco and lord of Seville was informed
Valencia had fallen, for lack of support,
He came to see for himself, with thirty thousand men.
My Cid, he of the long and flowing beard,
Came to meet him just beyond the orchards.
The king's defeated army fled, pursued as far as Játiva—
And what a desperate, floundering fight
The Moors then fought, against the fast-flowing Júcar!
They drank a lot more water than they wanted.
Three times wounded, the king escaped,
And my Cid took back more loot than when he'd taken Valencia,
So much, believe me, that every common soldier
Received a hundred silver marks.
It isn't hard to see how high his reputation rose.

76

All the Christians who'd come with my Cid, Ruy Díaz,
He who was born at just the right time, were delighted.
His beard kept growing, and he meant
To let it grow as long as it liked:
"Because of my love for King Alfonso, who sent me into exile,
No scissors will touch it, not a single hair will be cut.
And let this be told to Moors and Christians alike."
My Cid, Ruy Díaz, rested in Valencia,
Along with Minaya Alvar Fáñez, never more than an arm's
    length away.
Those who had left their homes were now tremendously rich,
They'd been given homes in Valencia, they had lucrative estates:
My Cid had proved his goodwill, and they were pleased,

los que fueron con él   e los de después todos son pagados;
véelo Mio Cid   que con los averes que avién tomados
que sis' pudiessen ir   fer lo ien de grado.
Esto mandó Mio Cid,   Minaya lo ovo consejado,
que ningún omne de los sos ques' le non spidiés,   o nol' besás la
    ma[no],
sil' pudiessen prender   o fuesse alcançado,
tomássenle el aver   e pusiéssenle en un palo.
Afevos todo aquesto   puesto en buen rrecabdo,
con Minaya Álbar Fáñez   él se va consejar:
"Si vós quisiéredes, Minaya,   quiero saber rrecabdo
de los que son aquí   e comigo ganaron algo;
meter los he en escripto   e todos sean contados,
que si algunos' furtare   o menos le fallaren,
el aver me avrá a tornar | [a] aquestos mios vassallos
que curian a Valencia   e andan arrobdando."
Allí dixo Minaya: "Consejo es aguisado."

77

Mandólos venir a la cort   e a todos los juntar,
quando los falló,   por cuenta fízolos nonbrar;
tres mill e seiscientos   avié Mio Cid el de Bivar,
alégras'le el coraçón   e tornós' a sonrrisar:
"¡Grado a Dios, Minaya,   e a Sancta María madre!
Con más pocos ixiemos   de la casa de Bivar;
agora avemos rriquiza,   más avremos adelant.
Si a vós ploguiere, Minaya,   e non vos caya en pesar,
enbiarvos quiero a Castiella,   dó avemos heredades,
al rrey Alfonso   mio señor natural;
d'estas mis ganancias   que avemos fechas acá
darle quiero *ciento* cavallos   e vós ídgelos levar.
Desí por mí besalde la mano   e firme ge lo rrogad
por mi mugier e mis fijas, ...
si fuere su merced, | quen' las dexe sacar;
enbiaré por ellas   e vós sabed el mensage:
'la mugier de Mio Cid   e sus fijas las infantes

Both those who'd come first, and those who'd come later.
My Cid could tell that some who were suddenly rich
Might slip away, if they were able.
On Minaya's advice, he ordered no one to leave
Without a farewell kiss of their leader's hand,
For he would come after them, and when he caught them
He would take back their wealth, and hang them.
Once this was properly made known,
He spoke to Minaya again:
"Minaya, I'd like you to keep a written record
Of those who came to us and earned a reward—
Set down how many came, and their names,
So if a man leaves us, or something is missing,
He'll give it back to me, and it will be given
To those who stay, guarding the city and patrolling
    around it."
Minaya said: "This is both wise and sensible."

77

His men were called to the courtyard, all of them together,
And once they'd assembled, he had them counted.
My Cid, from Vivar, was now followed by three thousand
    six hundred—
Which warmed his heart and made him smile:
"Minaya, our thanks to God, and Saint Mary, his holy mother!
There were not so many of us, when we left Vivar.
We are rich men, now, and will be much richer.
If you will, Minaya, and it isn't too much trouble,
I'd like to send you to Castile, where you can find my lord
Alfonso, and my estates.
A hundred of the horses we've won
Will go with you, for King Alfonso.
Kiss his hand for me, and beg him
To grant me, if he will, my wife and daughters.
I will send for them; give them this message:
'My Cid's wife and his two little daughters

de guisa irán por ellas   que a grand ondra vernán
a estas tierras estrañas   que nos pudiemos ganar.'"
Essora dixo Minaya: "De buena voluntad."
Pues esto an fablado,   piénsanse de adobar;
ciento omnes le dio   Mio Cid a Álbar Fáñez
por servirle en la carrer[a] . . . . . .
e mandó mill marcos de plata   a San Pero levar
e que los diesse   a don Sancho   [e]l abat.

78

En estas nuevas   todos se alegrando,
de parte de orient   vino un coronado,
el obispo don Jerónimo   so nombre es llamado,
bien entendido es de letras   e mucho acordado,
de pie e de cavallo   mucho era arreziado.
Las provezas de Mio Cid   andávalas demandando,
sospirando el obispo   ques' viesse con moros en el campo,
que sis' fartás lidiando   e firiendo con sus manos
a los días del sieglo   non le llorassen cristianos.
Quando lo oyó Mio Cid,   de aquesto fue pagado:
"¡Oíd, Minaya Álbar Fáñez,   por Aquel que está en alto!
Quando Dios prestar nos quiere,   nós bien ge lo gradescamos,
en tierras de Valencia   fer quiero obispado
e dárgelo   a este buen cristiano;
vós, quando ides a Castiella,   levaredes buenos mandados."

79

Plogo a Álbar Fáñez   de lo que dixo don Rrodrigo;
a este don Jerónimo   yal' otorgan por obispo,
diéronle en Valencia   ó bien puede estar rrico.
¡Dios, qué alegre era   todo cristianismo
que en tierras de Valencia   señor avié obispo!
Alegre fue Minaya   e spidiós' e vinos'.

Will be very happy, and received with great honor,
Here in these foreign lands which we have fought for
     and won.'"
Then Minaya said: "Gladly."
Plans for this journey were quickly made.
My Cid gave Alvar Fáñez a hundred men for the trip,
And asked him, if he would, to take with him
A thousand silver marks for the church at San Pedro,
And hand them to the abbot, Don Sancho.

78

Castile received Minaya's message with great applause.
A priest newly arrived from France—
Named Bishop Don Jerónimo,
Well-educated, sensible, and knowing,
An accomplished fighter, on foot or on a horse—
Was trying to learn as much as he could
Of my Cid's great deeds, yearning to fight with the Moors,
Saying he'd be more than satisfied to die in such warfare,
And no one would ever need to mourn him.
When my Cid heard this, he was delighted:
"Hear me, Minaya Alvar Fáñez! O blessèd God on high!
How grateful we should be, when the Lord himself helps us!
I want there to be a bishop here in Valencia
And this good Christian wearing that holy headdress.
On your next visit to Castile, you'll carry good news!"

79

Alvar Fáñez was pleased by these words of Don Rodrigo.
Valencia's bishop was to be this Don Jerónimo,
Who could live there like a king.
Lord, what happiness for all of Christendom,
Knowing Valencia would finally have a bishop!
Minaya was happy, said his farewells, and headed to Castile again.

80

Tierras de Valencia   rremanidas en paz,
adeliñó pora Castiella   Minaya Álbar Fáñez;
dexarévos las posadas,   non las quiero contar.
Demandó por Alfonso,   dó lo podrié fallar.
Fuera el rrey a San Fagunt   aún poco ha,
tornós' a Carrión,   í lo podrié fallar.
Alegre fue de aquesto   Minaya Álbar Fáñez,
con esta presenteja   adeliñó pora allá.

81

De missa era exido   essora el rrey Alfonso,
afé Minaya Álbar Fáñez   dó llega tan apuesto,
fincó sos inojos   ante tod' el pueblo,
a los pies del rrey Alfonso   cayó con grand duelo,
besávale las manos   e fabló tan apuesto:

82

"¡Merced, señor Alfonso,   por amor del Criador!
Besávavos las manos   Mio Cid lidiador,
los pies e las manos,   como a tan buen señor,
quel' ayades merced,   ¡sí vos vala el Criador!
Echástesle de tierra,   non ha la vuestra amor,
maguer en tierra agena   él bien faze lo so:
ganada [á] a Xérica   e a Onda por nombre,
priso a Almenar   e a Murviedro que es miyor,
assí fizo Cebolla   e adelant Castejón
e Peña Cadiella   que es una peña fuert;
con aquestas todas   de Valencia es señor,
obispo fizo de su mano   el buen Campeador
e fizo cinco lides campales   e todas las arrancó.
Grandes son las ganancias   quel' dio el Criador,

80

And while he was on his way
Valencia, and all around it, remained at peace.
I omit the places he stopped at; they have no interest for me.
He asked for Alfonso, and where he might find him;
The king had been in Sahagún, not long ago,
But now had come back to Carrión, he was told.
Minaya Alvar Fáñez was pleased to hear this;
With the gifts he was bringing, he hurried to Carrión.

81

Mass had just been said, and Alfonso was leaving church:
What a perfect moment for Minaya's arrival!
He went down on his knees in front of the king,
Where everyone could see him, bent with grief,
Kissed the king's hands, and spoke these noble words:

82

"Have mercy, Lord Alfonso, for the love of God, who made us all!
My Cid, the great Warrior, kisses your hands
And feet, as befits so excellent a master,
And begs for your grace—as you beg God for his!
You sent him into exile, he is still out of favor,
Yet in foreign lands he is doing wonderful things:
He has captured Jérica, and also Onda,
He took Almenara, and an even bigger prize, Murviedro;
He's taken Cebolla, Castejón, and that powerful fortress,
    Benicadell;
And on top of all this, the Warrior is lord of Valencia
And able, himself, to restore the bishopric there.
He has won five pitched battles against the Moors.
Our God has granted him rich rewards—

fevos aquí las señas,   verdad vos digo yo,
cient cavallos   gruessos e corredores,
de siellas e de frenos   todos guarnidos son,
bésavos las manos   que los prendades vós;
rrazonas' por vuestro vassallo   e a vós tiene por señor."
Alçó la mano diestra,   el rrey se sanctigó:
"De tan fieras ganancias   como á fechas el Campeador
¡sí me vala Sant Esidro!   plazme de coraçón
e plázem' de las nuevas   que faze el Campeador;
rrecibo estos cavallos   quem' enbía de don."
Maguer plogo al rrey,   mucho pesó a Garcí Ordóñez:
"Semeja que en tierra de moros   non á bivo omne
quando assí faze a su guisa   el Cid Campeador."
Dixo el rrey al conde: "Dexad essa rrazón,
que en todas guisas   mijor me sirve que vós."
Fablava Minaya í   a guisa de varón:
"Merced vos pide el Cid,   si vos cayesse en sabor,
por su mugier doña Ximena   e sus fijas amas a dos:
saldrién del monesterio   dó elle las dexó
e irién pora Valencia   al buen Campeador."
Essora dixo el rrey: "Plazme de coraçón;
yo les mandaré dar conducho   mientra que por mi tierra
    fueren,
de fonta e de mal   curial/as e de desonor;
quando en cabo de mi tierra   aquestas dueñas fueren,
catad cómo las sirvades   vós e el Campeador.
¡Oídme, escuelas   e toda la mi cort!
Non quiero que nada   pierda el Campeador:
a todas las escuelas   que a él dizen señor,
por que los deseredé,   todo ge lo suelto yo;
sírvanle[s] sus herdades   dó fuere el Campeador,
atrégoles los cuerpos   de mal e de ocasión,
por tal fago aquesto   que sirvan a so señor."
Minaya Álbar Fáñez   las manos le besó.
Sonrrisós' el rrey,   tan vellido fabló:
"Los que quisieren ir   se[r]vir al Campeador
de mí sean quitos   e vayan a la gracia del Criador.
Más ganaremos en esto   que en otra desonor."

And in proof of what he has won
I bring you a hundred strong horses,
Saddled, harnessed, and ready for riding:
He kisses your hands and hopes you will take them,
For he remains your servant and proclaims you his lord."
The king raised his right hand and made the sign of the cross:
"In the name of Saint Isidore, I declare my pleasure
At what he has won: it warms my heart,
As do all his wonderful triumphs.
I am glad to accept these gifts from his hands."

    The king was pleased; Count García Ordóñez, my Cid's enemy,
Was not: "I gather no men are left in Moorish lands,
Since our great Warrior, this Cid, can do as he pleases."
The king declared: "Enough of that,
Since in all things he does more for me than you ever do."
Then Minaya said, speaking strongly:
"My Cid begs, if it pleases you to grant this,
That his wife, Doña Jimena, and his two daughters
May leave the monastery where he left them,
And join him in Valencia, of which he is now master."
The king then said: "I grant that most gladly.
I will have them escorted until they leave my lands;
They need fear nothing, neither danger nor dishonor.
But once these ladies reach the borders of Castile,
They fall into your and the Warrior's hands.

    "Now hear me, everyone here in my court!
I wish the Warrior to be deprived of nothing—
Neither he nor those who have chosen to fight at his side:
I hereby give them back their former property rights.
Whatever may be earned, while they serve my Cid,
Is theirs, wherever they may be. Nor are they themselves
Subject to any kind of penalty."
Minaya then kissed the king's hands,
And the king, smiling, spoke most graciously:
"Those who wish to leave my service and join him
Are hereby freed to do so—and God go with them.
Castile is better thus served than by dishonor."

    The nobles of Carrión began to whisper together:

Aquí entraron en fabla   los iffantes de Carrión:
"Mucho crecen las nuevas   de Mio Cid el Campeador,
bien casariemos con sus fijas   pora huebos de pro;
non la osariemos   acometer nós esta rrazón,
Mio Cid es de Bivar   e nós de los condes de Carrión."
Non lo dizen a nadi   e fincó esta rrazón.
Minaya Álbar Fáñez   al buen rrey se espidió.
"¡Ya vos ides, Minaya,   id a la gracia del Criador!
Levedes un portero,   tengo que vos avrá pro;
si leváredes las dueñas,   sírvanlas a su sabor,
fata dentro en Medina   denles quanto huebos les fuer,
desí adelant   piense d'ellas el Campeador."
Espidiós' Minaya   e vasse de la cort.

83

Los iffantes de Carrión . . . .
dando ivan conpaña   a Minaya Álbar Fáñez:
"En todo sodes pro,   en esto assí lo fagades:
saludadnos a Mio Cid,   el de Bivar,
somos en so pro   quanto lo podemos far;
el Cid que bien nos quiera   nada non perderá."
Rrespuso Minaya: "Esto non me á por qué pesar."
Ido es Minaya,   tórnanse los iffantes.
Adeliñó pora San Pero   ó las dueñas están,
tan grand fue el gozo   quándol' vieron assomar.
Decido es Minaya,   a San Pero va rrogar,
quando acabó la oración,   a las dueñas se tornó:
"Omíllom', doña Ximena,   Dios vos curie de mal,
assí faga   a vuestras fijas amas.
Salúdavos Mio Cid   allá onde elle está;
sano lo dexé   e con tan grand rrictad.
El rrey por su merced   sueltas me vos ha
por levaros a Valencia   que avemos por heredad.
Si vos viesse el Cid   sanas e sin mal,
todo serié alegre,   que non avrié ningún pesar."
Dixo doña Ximena: "¡El Criador lo mande!"

"My Cid, the Warrior, is certainly standing very high:
Marriage with his daughters would do us very well—
If we could risk saying such a thing,
Since we are nobles of Carrión, and my Cid is just someone from
    Vivar."
So they said nothing, and as yet nothing was done.
    Minaya Alvar Fáñez said farewell to the good king.
"You're leaving us, Minaya? May the grace of God go with you!
Take a royal courier: I think he'll be helpful.
If you travel with the three ladies, serve them well,
Be sure they lack for nothing, until they're in Medinaceli,
After which the Warrior will see to their care."
    Then Minaya, having said farewell, departed.

83

The nobles of Carrión escorted Minaya Alvar Fáñez.
"Whatever you touch, Minaya, goes well. Do something for us.
Give our greetings to my Cid, he who comes from Vivar.
Tell him he has our support, in whatever we're able to do,
And he can lose nothing by smiling on us."
Minaya replied: "That won't cost me much."
So Minaya left, and the Carrión nobles
Rode back to San Pedro, to the three ladies,
Who smiled, and laughed, and wept to see him.
But he stopped, first, at the church,
And prayed, and then returned to the women.
"My humble greetings, Doña Jimena. May God keep you
From all evil—you and both your daughters!
My Cid greets you, far-off as he is;
I left him healthy and happy with his riches.
King Alfonso has graciously freed you, and I am permitted
To guide you to Valencia, which we now possess.
If my Cid sees you there, healthy, safe from all harm,
His happiness will be complete, his worries will be gone."
Doña Jimena replied: "May God bring that to pass!"
    Minaya Alvar Fáñez directed three knights

Dio tres cavalleros   Minaya Álbar Fáñez,
enviólos a Mio Cid   a Valencia dó está:
"Dezid al Canpeador,   que Dios le curie de mal,
que su mugier e sus fijas   el rrey sueltas me las ha,
mientra que fuéremos por sus tierras   conducho nos mandó dar.
De aquestos *quinze* días,   si Dios nos curiare de mal,
seremos [í] yo e su mugier   e sus fijas que él á
y todas las dueñas con ellas,   quantas buenas ellas han."
Idos son los cavalleros   e d'ello pensarán,
rremaneció en San Pero   Minaya Álbar Fáñez.
Veriedes cavalleros   venir de todas partes,
irse quiere[n] a Valencia   a Mio Cid el de Bivar;
que les toviesse pro   rrogavan a Álbar Fáñez,
diziendo esto Mianaya: "Esto feré de veluntad."
A Minaya *sessaenta [e] cinco* cavalleros   acrecídol' han
e él se tenié *ciento*   que aduxiera d'allá;
por ir con estas dueñas   buena conpaña se faze.
Los quinientos marcos   dio Minaya al abat,
de los otros quinientos   dezir vos he qué faze:
Minaya a doña Ximina   e a sus fijas que ha
e a las otras dueñas   que las sirven delant,
el bueno de Minaya   pensólas de adobar
de los mejores guarnimientos   que en Burgos pudo fallar,
palafrés e mulas,   que non parescan mal.
Quando estas dueñas   adobadas las ha,
el bueno de Minaya   pensar quiere de cavalgar,
afevos Rrachel e Vidas   a los pies le caen:
"¡Merced, Minaya,   cavallero de prestar!
Desfechos nos ha el Cid,   sabet, si no nos val;
soltariemos la ganancia,   que nos diesse el cabdal."
"Yo lo veré con el Cid,   si Dios me lieva allá;
por lo que avedes fecho   buen cosiment í avrá."
Dixo Rrachel e Vidas: "¡El Criador lo mande!
Si non, dexaremos Burgos,   ir lo hemos buscar."
Ido es pora San Pero   Minaya Álbar Fáñez,
muchas yentes se le acogen,   pensó de cavalgar,
grand duelo es   al partir del abat:
"¡Sí vos vala el Criador,   Minaya Álbar Fáñez!

To bring my Cid this message:
"Say to my Cid—may God keep him from all evil!—
That the king has released his wife and daughters, and I have
     them;
He is escorting us, well provided, to the borders of Castile.
In fifteen days—may God be willing!—
Your wife, your daughters, and all the ladies
Who care for them (and good ladies they are) will be with you."
The knights rode off, knowing what they had to do;
Minaya waited at San Pedro. And knights came
From everywhere, all over Spain,
Wanting to join my Cid, he of Vivar, in Valencia,
Begging Alvar Fáñez to give them his backing.
He told them: "I will be glad to."
So Minaya added sixty-five knights
To the hundred he came with, which gave him
A fine escort to accompany the ladies.
Minaya gave half the thousand silver marks to the abbot.
Here's what he did with the other five hundred:
In Burgos, he bought Doña Jimena and her daughters,
And all the good ladies who attended on them,
The most beautiful dresses he could find,
As well as the best palfreys and mules he could buy,
So their appearance would be grand and fine.
When everyone was dressed and ready,
And Minaya was about to start their ride,
Raguel and Vidas appeared, and fell at his feet:
"Mercy, Minaya, O worthy knight!
My Cid will destroy us, truly he will, if he doesn't pay on time.
We forgive him the interest, if he'll pay back the loan."
"I'll talk to my Cid, God willing that I get there.
You'll be well paid for the favor you did him."
"May God grant it!" said Raguel and Vidas.
"If not, we'll have to leave Burgos and hunt for him."
     Minaya left Burgos, returned to San Pedro;
Eager knights were still appearing, anxious to join him.
The farewell from the abbot was deeply moving:
"You'll be blessed by God, Minaya Alvar Fáñez,

Por mí al Campeador   las manos le besad,
aqueste monesterio   no lo quiera olbidar,
todos los días del sieglo   en levarlo adelant
el Cid   siempre valdrá más."
Rrespuso Minaya: "Fer lo he de veluntad."
Yas' espiden   e piensan de cavalgar,
el portero con ellos   que los ha de aguardar,
por la tierra del rrey   mucho conducho les dan.
De San Pero fasta Medina   en *cinco* días van,
felos en Medina   las dueñas e Álbar Fáñez.
Dirévos de los cavalleros   que levaron el mensaje,
al ora que lo sopo   Mio Cid el de Bivar,
plógol' de coraçón   e tornós' a alegrar,
de la su boca   conpeçó de fablar:
"Qui buen mandadero enbía   tal deve sperar.
Tú, Muño Gustioz,   e Pero Vermúez delant,
e Martín Antolínez,   un burgalés leal,
el obispo don Jerónimo,   coronado de prestar,
cavalguedes con ciento   guisados pora huebos de lidiar;
por Sancta María   vós vayades passar,
vayades a Molina   que yaze más adelant,
tiénela Ave[n]galvón,   mio amigo es de paz,
con otros ciento cavalleros   bien vos consigrá;
id pora Medina   quanto lo pudiéredes far,
mi mugier e mis fijas   con Minaya Álbar Fáñez,
as[s]í como a mí dixieron,   í los podredes fallar;
con grand ondra   aduzídmelas delant.
E yo fincaré en Valencia,   que mucho costádom' ha,
grand locura serié   si la desenparás;
yo fincaré en Valencia   ca la tengo por heredad."
Esto era dicho,   piensan de cavalgar
e quanto que pueden   non fincan de andar.
Trocieron a Sancta María   e vinieron albergar a Frontael
e el otro día vinieron   a Molina posar.
El moro Ave[n]galvón,   quando sopo el mensaje,
saliólos rrecebir   con grant gozo que faze:
"¡Venides, los vassallos   de mio amigo natural!
A mí non me pesa,   sabet, mucho me plaze."

If you'll kiss the Warrior's hands, on my behalf!
Don't let him forget this monastery:
He'll rise and go on rising forever,
If he always keeps us in mind."
Minaya answered: "I will certainly remind him."
   So at last they started off on their journey,
The royal courier still with them, and constantly helpful.
They were well escorted and cared for, the whole way to the
   border.
They arrived in Medinaceli in five days—
And we will leave them there, Alvar Fáñez and the ladies.
Now I'll turn to the knights, Minaya's messengers to my Cid.
The moment he, the man of Vivar, heard the words they brought
   him
He smiled, his heart flooded with warmth,
And from his mouth flowed these words:
"He who sends good news is entitled to a good welcome!
You two go on ahead, Muño Gustioz, and you, Pedro Bermúdez.
You, Martín Antolínez, loyal merchant of Burgos,
And you, Bishop Don Jerónimo, much-honored priest,
Ride off with a hundred men, armed as if for war,
And go to Santa María de Albarracín,
And then still farther, on to Molina,
Ruled by Abengalbón, the Moor. I've made peace with him,
And I know he'll join you, with another hundred men.
And then you dash to Medinaceli, just as fast as you can:
Minaya Alvar Fáñez is waiting there, along with my wife
And my daughters—you'll surely find them—
Bring them here in the highest honor and dignity.
I will set myself in Valencia, for which we fought so valiantly:
It would be sheer madness to leave it exposed and empty.
I will be in Valencia, which now belongs to me."
He finished speaking; they rode off the next minute,
Galloping as fast as their horses could go.
They rode through Santa María de Albarracín, rested at
   Bronchales,
Then reached Molina the next day.
Hearing they had come, the Moor, Abengalbón,

Fabló Muño Gustioz,   non speró a nadi:
"Mio Cid vos saludava   e mandólo rrecabdar
co[n] ciento cavalleros   que privádol' acorrades;
su mugier e sus fijas   en Medina están;
que vayades por ellas,   adugádesgelas acá
e fata en Valencia   d'ellas non vos partades."
Dixo Ave[n]galvón: "Fer lo he de veluntad."
Essa noch   conducho les dio grand,
a la mañana   piensan de cavalgar;
ciéntol' pidieron,   mas él con dozientos' va.
Passan las montañas   que son fieras e grandes,
passaron   Mata de Toranz
de tal guisa   que ningún miedo non han,
por el val de Arbuxedo   piensan a deprunar.
E en Medina   todo el rrecabdo está,
envió dos cavalleros   Minaya Álbar Fáñez
. . . .   que sopiesse la verdad;
esto non detard[an]   ca de coraçón lo han,
el uno fincó con ellos   e el otro tornó a Álbar Fáñez:
"Virtos del Campeador   a nós vienen buscar;
afevos aquí   Pero Vermúez
e Muño Gustioz,   que vos quieren sin art,
e Martín Antolínez,   el burgalés natural,
e el obispo don Jerónimo,   coranado leal,
e el alcayaz Ave[n]galvón   con sus fuerças que trahe
por sabor de Mio Cid   de grand óndral' dar,
todos vienen en uno,   agora llegarán."
Essora dixo Minaya: "Vay[a]mos cavalgar."
Esso fue apriessa fecho,   que nos' quieren detardar,
bien salieron dén ciento   que non parecen mal,
en buenos cavallos   a cuberturas de cendales
e petrales a cascaveles;   e escudos a los cuellos,
e en las manos lanças   que pendones traen,
que sopiessen los otros   de qué seso era Álbar Fáñez
o cuémo saliera de Castiella   con estas dueñas que trahe.
Los que ivan mesurando   e llegando delant
luego toman armas   e tómanse a deportar,
por cerca de Salón   tan grandes gozos van.

Hurried out to give them a joyous greeting:
"Welcome, you who live for my great friend!
I am delighted, truly, to see you here."
Muño Gustioz did not wait a second:
"My Cid greets you and asks that you help us,
With a hundred men, as fast as you can.
His wife and daughters are now in Medinaceli:
Ride to Valencia with us, so his women
Have your protection for the rest of their journey."
Abengalbón did not blink an eye. "Gladly," he said.
That night he gave them a great feast;
The next morning they started to ride—
And though they requested a hundred men,
He brought a full two hundred.
They rode over towering, wild-wooded mountains,
Stampeding across Campo Taranz, unconcerned, unmolested,
Then straight down into Arbujuelo valley.
Medinaceli was on high alert, and finding
So large a force approaching, Minaya sent two men to inquire.
Bravely, they galloped right out—then one remained,
The other rode back to Minaya:
"Men from our great Warrior, looking for us:
Pedro Bermúdez is with them,
And Muño Gustioz—both good friends—
And Martín Antolínez, that fine fellow from Burgos,
And Bishop Don Jerónimo, a faithful friend,
And Lord Abengalbón, the Moor, bringing two hundred men,
All to honor my Cid—they're all together.
And they're almost here already."
"We ride out to meet them!" cried Minaya,
And no one waited to be told twice:
A hundred knights who rode in great style,
Their horses draped with silken coverings, breast plates rich
With tiny bells; the warriors with shields hung on their backs,
Their lances dangling banners—
All meant to display Minaya's skill and good sense
And how well the ladies would be cared for, as they left Castile.
The scouts and those who first arrived

Dón llegan los otros,   a Minaya Álvar Fáñez se van homillar;
quando llegó Ave[n]galvón,   dont a ojo [lo] ha,
sonrrisándose de la boca   ívalo abraçar,
en el ombro lo saluda   ca tal es su usaje:
"¡Tan buen día convusco,   Minaya Álbar Fáñez!
Traedes estas dueñas   por ó valdremos más,
mugier del Cid lidiador   e sus fijas naturales.
Ondrar vos hemos todos   ca tal es la su auze,
maguer que mal le queramos,   non ge lo podremos fer,
en paz o en guerra   de lo nuestro abrá,
múchol' tengo por torpe   qui non conosce la verdad."
Sorrisós' de la boca   Minaya Álbar Fáñez:

84

"¡Y[a] Ave[n]galvón,   amígol' sodes sin falla!
Si Dios me llegare al Cid   e lo vea con el alma,
d'esto que avedes fecho   vós non perderedes nada.
Vayamos posar,   ca la cena es adobada."
Dixo Avengalvón: "Plazme d'esta presentaja,
antes d'este te[r]cer día   vos la daré doblada."
Entraron en Medina,   sirvíalos Minaya,
todos fueron alegres   del cervicio que tomaron;
el portero del rrey   quitarlo mandava,
ondrado es Mio Cid   en Valencia dó estava
de tan grand conducho   como en Medínal' sacaron;
el rrey lo pagó todo   e quito se va Minaya.
Passada es la noche,   venida es la mañana,
oída es la missa   e luego cavalgavan;
salieron de Medina   e Salón passavan,
Arbuxuelo arriba   privado aguijavan,
el campo de Torancio   luégol' atravessavan,
vinieron a Molina,   la que Ave[n]galvón mandava.
El obispo don Jerónimo,   buen cristiano sin falla,
las noches e los días   las dueñas aguardava,

Took up arms and began to have a good time,
Brave men playing at battle, along the banks of the river Jalón.
Others arrived, and Minaya Alvar Fáñez was properly greeted,
Then Albengalbón came, and as soon as he saw Minaya
Embraced him, smiling broadly and,
According to his custom, kissed him on the shoulder:
"How good to see you, Minaya Alvar Fáñez!
This is a great honor for us, your bringing
Warrior Cid's wife and his daughters,
To whom we show honor, one and all, as his fortune
Deserves—for no one can harm him; in peace or war
He is destined for triumph, whatever we do.
Only an idiot can keep himself from seeing the truth."
Minaya Alvar Fáñez smiled and said:

84

"Ah, Abengalbón, you're an ideal friend!
If God lets me see him again, as I so long to,
Nothing of what you've done will be forgotten.
But now we should rest, for a banquet is coming."
Abengalbón said: "Your hospitality is much appreciated:
Before three days have gone by, I will reciprocate."
They rode into Medinaceli as Minaya's guests,
And were very happy with the treatment they received.
The king's courtier said his farewells, and left them,
Honoring my Cid, far-off in Valencia,
With the king's order that everything in Medinaceli
Be charged to him, and nothing to Minaya.
Night passed, morning came,
They heard mass, and then rode away,
Crossing over the river Jalón
And riding down the banks of the Arbujuelo,
Through the fields of Campo Taranz,
And quickly approaching Molina, where Abengalbón governed.
The bishop, Don Jerónimo, always a good Christian,
Watched over the ladies, night and day,

e buen cavallo en diestro   que va ante sus armas;
entre él e Álbar Fáñez   ivan a una compaña,
entrados son a Molina,   buena e rrica casa,
el moro Ave[n]galvón   bien los sirvié sin falla,
de quanto que quisieron   non ovieron falla,
aun las ferraduras   quitárgelas mandava;
a Minaya e a las dueñas   ¡Dios, cómo las ondrava!
Otro día mañana   luego cavalgavan,
fata en Valencia   sirvíalos sin falla,
lo so despendié el moro,   que d'el[l]os non tomava nada.
Con estas alegrías   e nuevas tan ondradas
aprés son de Valencia   a tres leguas contadas.

85

A Mio Cid,   el que en buen ora nasco,
dentro a Valencia   liévanle el mandado.
Alegre fue Mio Cid   que nunqua más nin tanto
ca de lo que más amava   yal' viene el mandado.
Dozi[en]tos cavalleros   mandó exir privado
que rreciban a Minaya   e a las dueñas fijas d'algo;
él sedié en Valencia   curiando e guardando
ca bien sabe que Álbar Fáñez   trahe todo rrecabdo.

86

Afevos todos aquéstos   rreciben a Minaya
e a las dueñas e a las niñas   e a las otras conpañas.
Mandó Mio Cid   a los que ha en su casa
que guardassen el alcáçar   e las otras torres altas
e todas las puertas   e las exidas e las entradas
e aduxiéssenle a Bavieca,   poco avié quel' ganara,
aún non sabié Mio Cid,   el que en buen ora cinxo espada,
si serié corredor   o si abrié buena parada;
a la puerta de Valencia,   dó fuesse en so salvo,

His warhorse always on his right hand, his weapons on a horse
    behind him,
He and Alvar Fáñez, to his left, enjoying each other's company.
And then they reached Molina, that fine, rich town,
Where the Moor Abengalbón took very good care of them,
And everything they wanted he gave them—
Even paying for their horses' new shoes!
As for Minaya and the ladies, God! how warmly he honored them!
The next morning they rode on again,
But Abengalbón stayed at their side all the way
To Valencia, and whatever was spent was always by him.
And in such joy and pledges of mutual friendship
They came within half a dozen miles of Valencia.

85

My Cid, he who was born at such a good time,
Was told that they were arriving.
He had never been happier in all his life,
Hearing that those he loved best had come.
He had two hundred knights galloping out, at once,
In welcome for Minaya and all the noble ladies,
While he stayed in Valencia, waiting
And guarding his city: he knew Minaya could be trusted.

86

How everyone welcomed Minaya, and the ladies,
And the little girls, and everyone else besides!
My Cid had his household out on the ramparts,
And all the high towers, and gates, and exits, and entrances.
And he called for his horse, Babieca—won
Not long ago, for as yet my Cid (who took up his sword at just
    the right time)
Was unsure how good a horse this was, and how easily he
    handled.

delante su mugier e sus fijas   querié tener las armas.
Rrecebidas las dueñas   a una grant ondrança,
el obispo don Jerónimo   adelant se entrava,
í dexava el cavallo,   pora la capiella adeliñava;
con quantos que él puede,   que con oras se acordaran,
sobrepel[l]iças vestidas   e con cruzes de plata,
rrecibir salién [a] las dueñas   e al bueno de Minaya.
El que en buen ora nasco   non lo detardava,
vistiós' el sobregonel,   luenga trahe la barba;
ensiéllanle a Bavieca,   cuberturas le echavan,
Mio Cid salió sobr'él   e armas de fuste tomava.
Por nombre el cavallo   Bavieca cavalga,
fizo una corrida,   ésta fue tan estraña,
quando ovo corrido,   todos se maravillavan,
d'és día se preció Bavieca   en quant grant fue España.
En cabo del cosso   Mio Cid desca[va]lgava,
adeliñó a su mugier   e a sus fijas amas;
quando lo vio doña Ximena,   a pies se le echava:
"¡Merced, Campeador,   en buen ora cinxiestes espada!
Sacada me avedes   de muchas vergüenças malas;
afeme aquí, señor,   yo e vuestras fijas amas;
con Dios e convusco   buenas son e criadas."
A la madre e a las fijas   bien las abraçava,
del gozo que avién   de los sos ojos lloravan.
Todas las sus mesnadas   en grant deleite estavan,
armas teniendo   e tablados quebrantando.
Oíd lo que dixo   el que en buen ora nasco:
"Vós, querida mugier   e ondrada
e amas mis fijas, | mi coraçón e mi alma,
entrad comigo   en Valencia la casa,
en esta heredad   que vos yo he ganada."
Madre e fijas   las manos le besavan,
a tan grand ondra   ellas a Valencia entravan.

At Valencia's gates, where he knew it was safe,
He thought he'd show off a bit, for his daughters and his wife.
The ladies had already been welcomed, with all due honor.
Bishop Don Jerónimo rode on ahead, dismounted,
And entered the chapel, where he and other priests,
Wearing surplices and bearing crosses made of silver,
Celebrated morning rites and prayers, then went
To receive the ladies and that good friend of them all, Minaya.
My Cid, he who was born at a fortunate hour,
Mounted Babieca the moment the horse was ready,
Carrying a wooden sword and shield
And wearing a flowing tunic, his long beard floating behind him.
And Babieca galloped,
And galloped—so fast that people gasped
And wondered at his speed and quick responses.
From that day on, Babieca was famous all over Spain.
When he'd finished this fabulous race, my Cid dismounted
And strode toward his wife and daughters.
Doña Jimena knelt at his feet:
"Bless you, Warrior, you who raised your sword at just the right
    time!
How many shameful moments I have escaped, because of you.
I'm here, my husband, my lord, and my two daughters with me:
God be thanked, they're good girls, and well behaved."
He embraced the girls and their mother,
The three of whom wept for joy.
My Cid's men were moved, and delighted;
They whirled their weapons, smashing wooden targets.
Then he who was born in a blessèd hour said:
"My dearest and deeply honored wife,
And my daughters—my heart, my soul—
Come with me to our home, in Valencia,
The joy and prosperity I have won for you."
His daughters and their mother kissed his hands,
And they made a grand and honorable entrance to Valencia.

87

Adeliñó Mio Cid   con ellas al alcáçar,
allá las subié   en el más alto logar.
Ojos vellidos   catan a todas partes,
miran Valencia   cómo yaze la cibdad
e del otra parte   a ojo han el mar,
miran la huerta,   espessa es e grand;
alçan las manos   por a Dios rrogar
d'esta ganancia   cómo es buena e grand.
Mio Cid e sus compañas   tan a grand sabor están.
El ivierno es exido,   que el março quiere entrar.
Dezirvos quiero nuevas   de allent partes del mar,
de aquel rrey Yúcef   que en Marruecos está.

88

Pesól' al rrey de Marruecos   de Mio Cid don Rrodrigo:
"Que en mis heredades   fuertemie[n]tre es metido
e él non ge lo gradece   sinon a Jesu Cristo."
Aquel rrey de Marruecos   ajuntava sus virtos,
con *cinquaenta* vezes mill de armas   todos fueron conplidos,
entraron sobre mar,   en las barcas son metidos,
van buscar a Valencia   a Mio Cid don Rrodrigo;
arribado an las naves,   fuera eran exidos.

89

Llegaron a Valencia,   la que Mio Cid á conquista,
fincaron las tiendas   e posan las yentes descreídas.
Estas nuevas   a Mio Cid eran venidas:

87

My Cid took them to the fortress,
And they followed him to the very top,
From which their lovely eyes could see everything,
The whole city spread out,
On one side the sea, and on the other
Fields and orchards, lush and green.
They raised their hands in prayer,
Thanking God for the immense goodness he had granted them.
My Cid and those who were with him lived in great gladness.
Winter was over, March and springtime were coming.
   Now let me take you across the sea,
To King Yusuf, King of Morocco.

88

The King of Morocco was angry at my Cid, Don Ruy Díaz:
"He's swept like a storm over my lands,
Believing Jesus Christ puts strength in his hands!"
The King of Morocco gathered his forces,
Fifty thousand men in all,
And put them in ships and sent them to sea,
Sailing to Valencia, hunting my Cid, Don Ruy Díaz.
The ships reached Spain and the soldiers landed.

89

They marched to Valencia, conquered by my Cid,
And then these dishonored soldiers pitched their tents.
When my Cid was told, he said:

90

"¡Grado al Criador   e a[l] padre espirital!
Todo el bien que yo he,   todo lo tengo delant;
con afán gané a Valencia   e éla por heredad,
a menos de muert   no la puedo dexar;
grado al Criador   e a Sancta María madre,
mis fijas e mi mugier   que las tengo acá.
Venídom' es delicio   de tierras d'allent mar,
entraré en las armas,   non lo podré dexar,
mis fijas e mi mugier   ver me an lidiar,
en estas tierras agenas   verán las moradas cómo se fazen,
afarto verán por los ojos   cómo se gana el pan."
Su mugier e sus fijas   subiólas al alcáçar,
alçavan los ojos,   tiendas vieron fincadas:
"¿Qu'es esto, Cid?   ¡sí el Criador vos salve!"
"¡Ya mugier ondrada,   non ayades pesar!
Rriqueza es que nos acrece   maravillosa e grand,
a poco que viniestes,   presend vos quieren dar,
por casar son vuestras fijas,   adúzenvos axuvar."
"A vós grado, Cid,   e al padre spiritual."
"Mugier, sed en este palacio,   e si quisiéredes, en el alcáçar,
non ayades pavor   porque me veades lidiar;
con la merced de Dios   e de Sancta María madre,
crécem' el coraçón   porque estades delant;
con Dios aquesta lid   yo la he de arrancar."

91

Fincadas son las tiendas   e parecen los alvores,
a una grand priessa   tañién los atamores;
alegravas' Mio Cid   e dixo: "¡Tan buen día es oy!"
Miedo á su mugier   e quiérel' quebrar el coraçón,
assí fazié a las dueñas   e a sus fijas amas a dos,
del día que nasquieran   non vieran tal tremor.

90

"Father in heaven, gracious Creator, I thank you!
Everything I have is here in front of me.
I fought for Valencia, it is my own:
Only death can take me from it.
And I thank you, Creator of the world, and your mother, Saint
    Mary,
That my daughters and my wife are here with me!
A wonderful gift has come from across the sea:
I cannot win it except by fighting.
My wife and daughters will see me waging war,
They'll see how we make our homes, in these strange lands,
See with their own eyes how we earn our bread!"
He took his wife and his daughters to the top of the fortress,
They looked down, they saw the forest of tents.
"What is this, Cid? May God help us!"
"Ha, my honored wife, don't let it worry you!
These are great and wonderful riches they've come to bring us!
Look, you've just arrived, and they've already sent you presents!
This is your daughters' dowry, it will pay for their weddings!"
"My thanks, gracious Cid! And to our Father in heaven!"
"Wife, stay in this castle—in the tower, if you like.
Don't be frightened, seeing me fighting:
With God's good grace, and by holy Mother Mary,
My heart surges, knowing you're here!
With God's blessing this battle will be mine!"

91

The sun began to rise over the forest of tents,
Moorish drums started to thunder,
And my Cid was happy: "What a great day this is!"
His wife was afraid her heart would burst in incredible fright,
A fear the ladies in waiting shared, as did her daughters:
Never in all their lives had they been so terrified.

Prisos' a la barba   el buen Cid Campeador:
"Non ayades miedo,   ca todo es vuestra pro;
antes d'estos *quinze* días,   si ploguiere a[*l*] Criador,
. . . .   aquellos atamores
a vós los pondrán delant   e veredes quáles son,
desí an a ser   del obispo don Jerónimo,
colgar los han en Sancta María   madre del Criador."
Vocación es que fizo   el Cid Campeador.
Alegre[*s*] son las dueñas,   perdiendo van el pavor.
Los moros de Marruecos   cavalgan a vigor,
por las huertas adentro   *ent*[*r*]*an* sines pavor.

92

Violo el atalaya   e tanxo el esquila,
prestas son las mesnadas   de las yentes cristianas,
adóbanse de coraçón   e dan salto de la villa;
dós' fallan con los moros   cometiénlos tan aína,
sácanlos de las huertas   mucho a fea guisa,
quinientos mataron d'ellos   conplidos en és día.

93

Bien fata las tiendas   dura aqueste alcaz,
mucho avién fecho,   piessan de cavalgar;
Álbar Salvadórez   preso fincó allá.
Tornados son a Mio Cid   los que comién so pan,
él se lo vio con los ojos,   cuéntangelo delant,
alegre es Mio Cid   por quanto fecho han:
"¡Oídme, cavalleros,   non rrastará por ál!
Oy es día bueno   e mejor será cras:
por la mañana prieta   todos armados seades,
dezir nos ha la missa   e pensad de cavalgar,
el obispo do Jerónimo   soltura nos dará,
ir los hemos ferir   . . . .
en el nombre del Criador   e del apóstol Sancti Yagüe;

My Cid tugged at his beard and told them: "Don't be afraid,
This is all for you. If God so wills, in less than two weeks those
    drums
Will be ours, and I'll set them in front of you, and you'll see
    what they really are.
Then they'll belong to Bishop Don Jerónimo,
And he'll hang them in Saint Mary's, to honor God's mother."
This was what my Cid, mighty Warrior, promised he would do.
The ladies grew less afraid, and began to stop trembling.
The Moroccan Moors galloped fast and hard, fearless,
Dashing straight across the fields and vineyards.

92

The castle watchman saw them, and sounded the alarm;
The Christian knights were ready and waiting.
Their hearts high, they came out of the castle.
When they met the Moors, they attacked at once
And hitting hard, they drove the Moroccans back,
Killing five hundred before the end of the day.

93

They pushed the Moors all the way
To their tents, and then they returned,
Except for Alvar Salvadórez, who'd been made a prisoner.
When those who ate my Cid's bread came to their lord,
They told him all they'd accomplished, though he'd seen them
    do it,
And he was happy with how much they'd done:
"Listen, my knights! We aren't stopping at this.
Today was a good day and tomorrow will be still better.
I want you armored and ready for battle well before dawn.
Bishop Don Jerónimo will have us all fully absolved,
We'll hear a mass, and then we'll ride.
We attack in the name of God and the apostle Saint James!

más vale que nós los vezcamos   que ellos cojan el [p]an."
Essora dixieron todos: "D'amor e de voluntad."
Fablava Minaya,   non lo quiso detardar:
"Pues esso queredes, Cid,   a mí mandedes ál,
dadme *ciento* [e] *treínta* cavalleros   pora huebos de lidiar,
quando vós los fuéredes ferir,   entraré yo del otra part;
o de amas o del una   Dios nos valdrá."
Essora dixo el Cid: "De buena voluntad."

94

És día es salido   e la noch es entrada,
nos' detardan de adobasse   essas yentes cristianas.
A los mediados gallos,   antes de la mañana,
el obispo don Jerónimo   la missa les cantava;
la missa dicha,   grant sultura les dava:
"El que aquí muriere   lidiando de cara
préndol' yo los pecados   e Dios le abrá el alma.
A vós, Cid don Rrodrigo,   en buen ora cinxiestes espada,
yo vos canté la missa   por aquesta mañana;
pídovos un don   e séam' presentado,
las feridas primeras   que las aya yo otorgadas."
Dixo el Campeador: "Desaquí vos sean mandadas."

95

Salidos son todos armados   por las torres de Va[le]ncia,
Mio Cid a los sos vassallos   tan bien los acordando;
dexan a las puertas   omnes de grant rrecabdo.
Dio salto Mio Cid   en Bavieca el so cavallo,
de todas guarnizones   muy bien es adobado.
La seña sacan fuera,   de Valencia dieron salto,
quatro mill menos *treínta*   con Mio Cid van a cabo,
a los cinquaenta mill   van los ferir de grado;

I like defeating them better than letting them steal our bread!"
His men all said: "With all our will and all our heart!"
Unable to hold back, Minaya declared:
"Since this is what you want, Cid, let me ask for something:
Give me a hundred and thirty knights, ready for a fight.
When you attack from one side, I'll come in from the other,
And God will reward one of us, or both."
Then my Cid answered: "Gladly."

94

Daylight left, night settled down.
We can't say these Christians were lazy, getting ready for
    tomorrow!
Not long before dawn,
Bishop Don Jerónimo sang a mass,
Then offered the very fullest of absolutions:
"Those of you who die, fighting face to face,
I forgive you your sins and God will accept your souls.
To you, my Cid, Don Ruy Díaz—who took up arms at so good
    an hour—
I've said mass for you, this morning:
Allow me to strike the first blows."
The Warrior said: "I grant you that privilege."
Armed and ready, they left the fortress of Valencia.

95

As they poured through the gates, my Cid
Was giving final instructions.
Then he mounted his horse, Babieca,
All wrapped in its splendid armor and ready for battle.
Their banner came first, as they left Valencia—
Just thirty less than four thousand, in all, and my Cid their
    leader,
Happy to be attacking fifty thousand Moors.

Álvar Álvarez   e Álvar Salvadórez
e Minaya Álvar Fáñez | entráronles del otro cabo.
Plogo al Criador   e ovieron de arrancarlos.
Mio Cid enpleó la lança,   al espada metió mano,
atantos mata de moros   que non fueron contados,
por el cobdo ayuso   la sangre destellando.
Al rrey Yúcef   tres colpes le ovo dados,
saliós'le de so'l espada   ca múchol' andido el cavallo,
metiós'le en Gujera,   un castiello palaciano,
Mio Cid el de Bivar   fasta allí llegó en alcaz
con otros quel' consiguen   de sus buenos vassallos.
Desd' allí se tornó   el que en buen ora nasco,
mucho era alegre   de lo que an caçado.
Allí preció a Bavieca   de la cabeça fasta a cabo.
Toda esta ganancia   en su mano á rrastado.
Los *cinquaenta* mill   por cuenta fuero[n] notados,
non escaparon   más de ciento e quatro.
Mesnadas de Mio Cid   rrobado an el canpo,
entre oro e plata   fallaron tres mill marcos,
las otras ganancias   non avía rrecabdo.
Alegre era Mio Cid   e todos sos vassallos
que Dios les ovo merced   que vencieron el campo.
Quando al rrey de Marruecos   assí lo an arrancado,
dexó [a] Álbar Fáñez   por saber todo rrecabdo;
con *ciento* cavalleros   a Valencia es entrado,
fronzida trahe la cara,   que era desarmado,
assí entró sobre Bavieca,   el espada en la mano.
Rrecibiénlo las dueñas   que lo están esperando;
Mio Cid fincó ant'ellas,   tovo la rrienda al cavallo:
"A vós me omillo, dueñas,   grant prez vos he gañado,
vós teniendo Valencia   e yo vencí el campo;
esto Dios se lo quiso   con todos los sos santos
quando en vuestra venida   tal ganancia nos an dada.
¿Vedes el espada sangrienta   e sudiento el cavallo?
—con tal cum esto   se vencen moros del campo.
Rrogand al Criador   que vos biva algunt año,
entraredes en prez   e besarán vuestras manos."
Esto dixo Mio Cid,   diciendo del cavallo.

Alvar Alvarez and Minaya Alvar Fáñez
Galloped in from the other side
—And thanks to God, the Moors were defeated.
My Cid used his lance, then drew his sword,
Killing so many Moors that no one could count them;
Their blood ran to his elbow, all down
His arm. He struck at King Yusuf three times,
But the king's horse was faster than my Cid's sharp blade,
And a hurried escape was made to the fort of Cullera,
My Cid and others galloping after, but in vain.
He who was born at a lucky hour turned back,
Well satisfied with the chase,
And with Babieca, fine from head to tail.
He had won everything; it was all in his hands.
Of the fifty thousand Moors
Only a hundred and four had escaped.
His men went up and down the battlefield,
Collecting three thousand marks, in gold and silver,
Plus more riches than had yet been counted.
My Cid was delighted, as were all his men,
That God's great grace had carried the day.
The King of Morocco now thoroughly routed,
My Cid put Alvar Fáñez in charge of the counting
And, with a hundred knights, rode back to Valencia;
His helmet was off, his hood was rolled down,
And sword in hand he came, riding Babieca.
He was welcomed by the ladies, who were waiting for him;
He reined in his horse, and stopped in front of them:
"My humble greetings, ladies! I've won you great rewards:
You took care of Valencia, and I conquered on the battlefield.
God and all his saints wanted exactly this
From the moment you arrived, and they gave us all we
    wished for.
Look at my bloody sword and my horse dripping sweat:
This is how you beat the Moors, in war!
Pray for God to give me more years,
And you'll all be rich, with everyone kissing your hands!"
My Cid said these words as he dismounted,

Quándol' vieron de pie,   que era descavalgado,
las dueñas e las fijas   e la mugier que vale algo
delant el Campeador   los inojos fincaron:
"Somos en vuestra merced   e ¡bivades muchos años!"
En buelta con él   entraron al palacio
e ivan posar con él   en unos preciosos escaños.
"Ya mugier daña Ximena,   ¿nom' lo aviedes rrogado?
Estas dueñas que aduxiestes,   que vos sirven tanto,
quiero las casar   con de aquestos mios vassallos;
a cada una d'ellas   doles *dozientos* marcos de plata,
que lo sepan en Castiella   a quién sirvieron tanto.
Lo de vuestras fijas   venir se á más por espacio."
Levantáronse todas   e besáronle las manos,
grant fue el alegría   que fue por el palacio;
como lo dixo el Cid   assí lo han acabado.
Minaya Álbar Fáñez   fuera era en el campo
con todas estas yentes   escriviendo e contando,
entre tiendas e armas   e vestidos preciados
tanto fallan d'esto   que es cosa sobejana.
Quiero vos dezir   lo que es más granado,
non pudieron ellos saber   la cuenta de todos los cavallos
que andan arrad[í]os   e non ha qui tomallos,
los moros de las tierras   ganado se an í algo;
maguer de todo esto,   *a*l Campeador contado
de los buenos e otorgados   cayéronle mill e *quinientos*
    cavallos;
quando a Mio Cid   cayeron tantos
los otros bien pueden   fincar pagados.
¡Tanta tienda preciada   e tanto tendal obrado
que á ganado Mio Cid   con todos sus vassallos!
La tienda del rrey de Marruecos,   que de las otras es cabo,
dos tendales la sufren,   con oro son labrados,
mandó Mio Cid Rruy Díaz   . . . .
que fita soviesse la tienda | e non la tolliesse dent cristiano:
"Tal tienda como ésta,   que de Marruecos es passada,
enbiarla quiero   a Alfonso el castellano,"
que croviesse sos nuevas   de Mio Cid que avié algo.
Con aquestas rriquezas tantas   a Valencia son entrados.

And when they saw him on his own two feet
All the women—ladies in waiting, the two girls, and his
    wonderful wife—
Knelt in front of the Warrior:
"We all depend on you! Live for many, many years!"
Then he and the ladies went into the palace,
Where they seated themselves on finely made couches.
"Now! Doña Jimena, my wife! Isn't this what you wanted
    from me?
I'd like your ladies in waiting, who have served you so well,
To marry some of my knights.
I'll give each and every bride two hundred silver marks,
So people in Castile will know how well they served, and whom.
We'll talk about your daughters later on."
The ladies rose and kissed his hands,
The palace rang with happy laughter,
And what my Cid had said was what was done!
Minaya Alvar Fáñez was still on the battlefield,
He and all his men counting and making a record.
The tents held weapons and armor and costly clothes,
All in great abundance.
But I must tell you the best of all:
They could not even begin to count the horses
Jogging up and down, none with riders.
The Moors who lived nearby got a few,
But in spite of them the Warrior ended with fifteen
Hundred magnificent, well-trained steeds—
And when his share was so large,
Certainly, none of the others were left in need!
How many gorgeous tents and embroidery-covered tent poles
My Cid had won, he and his men!
The King of Morocco's was the best of them all,
With poles covered with gold:
My Cid ordered it left exactly as it was,
No Christian allowed to take it away:
"A tent like this, come all the way
From Morocco, I ought to send to King Alfonso:
Let him see for himself how much I have won."

El obispo don Jerónimo,   caboso coronado,
quando es farto de lidiar   con amas las sus manos,
non tiene en cuenta   los moros que ha matados;
lo que cayé a él   mucho era sobejano,
Mio Cid don Rrodrigo,   el que en buen ora nasco,
de toda la su quinta   el diezmo l'á mandado.

96

Alegres son por Valencia   las yentes cristianas,
tantos avién de averes,   de cavallos e de armas;
alegre es doña Ximena   e sus fijas amas
e todas la[s] otras dueñas   que[s'] tienen por casadas.
El bueno de Mio Cid   non lo tardó por nada:
"¿Dó sodes, caboso?   Venid acá, Minaya;
de lo que a vós cayó   vós non gradecedes nada;
d'esta mi quinta,   dígovos sin falla,
prended lo que quisiéredes,   lo otro rremanga;
e cras a la mañana   ir vos hedes sin falla
con cavallos d'esta quinta   que yo he ganada,
con siellas e con frenos   e con señas espadas;
por amor de mi mugier   e de mis fijas amas,
porque assí las enbió   dond ellas son pagadas,
estos dozientos cavallos   irán en presentajas
que non diga mal el rrey Alfonso   del que Valencia manda."
Mandó a Pero Vermúez   que fuesse con Minaya.
Otro día mañana   privado cavalgavan
e dozientos omnes   lievan en su conpaña
con saludes del Cid   que las manos le besava:
d'esta lid   que ha arrancada
dozientos cavallos   le enbiava en presentaja,
"E servir lo he sienpre,"   mientra que ovisse el alma.

Indeed, they carried immense riches into Valencia.
Bishop Don Jerónimo, as good a priest as could be,
Swung weapons with both hands: when he'd finished fighting
He could no longer count the Moors he had killed.
Nor did he do badly, when it came to booty,
For my Cid, Ruy Díaz, born at a lucky hour,
Gave him a tenth of what he himself had earned.

96

The Christians of Valencia were exceedingly happy
With their new riches, and weapons and armor, and horses.
Doña Jimena was happy, too, and so were her daughters,
And the ladies in waiting, who felt as good as married.
My Cid's gifts never stopped:
"Where are you, my fine Minaya? Come here:
You've earned every bit of your share,
And more, so take what you want from mine—
Just do it, be quiet!—and leave me what's left.
Tomorrow morning, bright and early,
Take two hundred of my new horses,
Saddled and bridled, each one with a sword,
And since King Alfonso has sent me my family,
For love of my wife and daughters take these presents to him,
So he will think well of the man who now rules Valencia."
Pedro Bermúdez was sent with him.
The next day, they galloped off
With two hundred men, the entire company
Bearing my Cid's greetings, and to kiss the king's hands for him.
My Cid, Ruy Díaz, had won these horses, and much more;
He sent them to his royal master with a message:
"I will serve you forever, as long as I live!"

97

Salidos son de Valencia   e piensan de andar,
tales ganancias traen   que son a aguardar.
Andan los días e las noches   . . . . . .
e passada han la sierra | que las otras tierras parte.
Por el rrey don Alfonso   tómanse a preguntar.

98

Passando van las sierras   e los montes e las aguas,
llegan a Valladolid   dó el rrey Alfonso estava;
enviávanle mandado   Per Vermúez e Minaya
que mandasse rrecebir   a esta conpaña;
Mio Cid el de Valencia   enbía su presentaja.

99

Alegre fue el rrey,   non viestes atanto,
mandó cavalgar apriessa   todos sos fijos d'algo,
í en los primeros   el rrey fuera dio salto
a ver estos mensajes   del que en buen ora nasco.
Los ifantes de Carrión,   sabet, ís' acertaron,
[e] el conde don García,   so enemigo malo.
A los unos plaze   e a los otros va pesando.
A ojo lo[s] avién   los del que en buen ora nasco,
cuédanse que es almofalla   ca non vienen con mandado,
el rrey don Alfonso   seíse sanctiguando.
Minaya e Per Vermúez   adelante son llegados,
firiéronse a tierra,   decendieron de los cavallos,
ante'l rrey Alfonso,   los inojos fincados,
besan la tierra   e los pies amos:
"¡Merced, rrey Alfonso,   sodes tan ondrado!
Por Mio Cid el Campeador   todo esto vos besamos,
a vós llama por señor   e tienes' por vuestro vassallo,

97

When they left Valencia, they traveled hard,
Carefully guarding the wealth placed in their charge.
They rode day and night, not stopping to rest,
And crossed the great mountains between the two regions.
They arrived, and asked where the king could be found.

98

There were more mountains to cross, and rivers,
Before they reached Valladolid, where Alfonso was staying.
Pedro Bermúdez and Minaya sent him a message,
Asking if he would like to see this company,
Sent by my Cid, in Valencia, with presents for the king.

99

The king was delighted, happier than he'd ever been seen.
He ordered his courtiers to gallop out and meet
These messengers from the man born at a fortunate hour—
And riding in front was the king himself.
The nobles of Carrión, please understand, were among them,
As was Count Don García, who hated my Cid.
Some of these noblemen were pleased, and some were not.
But when they saw the company sent by my Cid,
They thought this might be an enemy army,
And King Alfonso crossed himself, as if heading into battle.
Minaya and Pedro Bermúdez came closer,
Quickly dismounted and knelt
In front of the king, kissing
His feet and the ground he stood on.
"Your mercy, King Alfonso! All honor to you!
We kiss you on behalf of my Cid, the Warrior—
He who knows you as his lord, and who is truly your servant.

mucho precia la ondra el Cid   quel' avedes dado.
Pocos días ha, rrey,   que una lid á arrancado;
a aquel rrey de Marruecos,   Yúcef por nombrado,
con cinquaenta mill   arrancólos del campo.
Las ganancias que fızo   mucho son sobejanas,
rricos son venidos   todos los sos vassallos
e embíavos dozientos cavallos   e bésavos las manos."
Dixo el rrey don Alfonso: "Rrecíbolos de grado;
gradéscolo a Mio Cid   que tal don me ha enbiado,
aún vea [el] ora   que de mí sea pagado."
Esto plogo a muchos   e besáronle las manos.
Pesó al conde don García   e mal era irado,
con *diez* de sus parientes   aparte davan salto:
"¡Maravilla es del Cid   que su ondra crece tanto!
En la ondra que él ha   nós seremos abiltados;
por tan biltadamientre   vencer rreyes del campo,
como si los fallasse muertos   aduzirse los cavallos,
por esto que él faze   nós abremos enbargo."

                              100

Fabló el rrey don Alfonso   e dixo esta rrazón:
"Grado al Criador   e al señor Sant Esidro el de León
estos dozientos cavallos   quem' enbía Mio Cid.
Mio rreino adelant   mejor me podrá servir.
A vós, Minaya Álbar Fáñez,   e a Pero Vermúez aquí
mándovos los cuerpos   ondradamientre servir e vestir
e guarnirvos de todas armas,   como vós dixiéredes aquí,
que bien parescades   ante Rruy Díaz Mio Cid;
dovos *tres* cavallos   e prendedlos aquí.
Assí como semeja   e la veluntad me lo diz,
todas estas nuevas   a bien abrán de venir."

He is honored by what you have given him.
Just a few days ago, good King, he won a battle
Against Yusuf, King of Morocco,
Who brought an army of fifty thousand men.
My Cid won immense treasure;
All his men have suddenly become wealthy.
So he sends you two hundred horses, and kisses your hands."
King Alfonso answered: "I accept this most gladly.
I am deeply grateful to my Cid for sending these gifts.
May the time come when I can return the favor."
Many were pleased, and kissed his hands,
But Count Don García was angry,
And walked away a little, with some of his family:
"This Cid is doing wonders, his honor grows and grows,
But the higher his, the lower ours is going.
If he continues, easily beating kings in battle, taking horses
As if these royal armies were corpses,
He'll make a host of problems for us!"

100

King Alfonso then made a declaration:
"I thank the Lord God and Saint Isidore of Léon
For these two hundred horses, sent by my Cid.
He's likely to do still more for me, in time to come.
Now you, Minaya Alvar Fáñez, and you too, Pedro Bermúdez,
I want both of you properly clothed, as loyal servants,
With whatever armor and weapons you choose:
Let Ruy Díaz, my Cid, see you as I wish you to be viewed.
And I give you three horses; take them right away.
I see this turn of things, today,
Bringing all kinds of blessings this way."

101

Besáronle las manos   e entraron a posar;
bien los mandó servir   de quanto huebos han.
De los iffantes de Carrión   yo vos quiero contar,
fablando en su consejo,   aviendo su poridad:
"Las nuevas del Cid   mucho van adelant,
demandemos sus fijas   pora con ellas casar,
creçremos en nuestra ondra   e iremos adelant."
Vinién al rrey Alfonso   con esta poridad:
"¡Merced vos pidimos   como a rrey e señor natural!

102

"Con vuestro consejo   lo queremos fer nós
que nos demandedes   fijas del Campeador;
casar queremos con ellas   a su ondra e a nuestra pro."
Una grant ora el rrey   pensó e comidió:
"Yo eché de tierra   al buen Campeador,
e faziendo yo a él mal   e él a mí grand pro,
del casamiento non sé   sis' abrá sabor,
mas pues bós lo queredes   entremos en la rrazón."
A Minaya Álbar Fáñez   e a Pero Vermúez
el rrey don Alfonso   essora los llamó,
a una quadra   ele los apartó:
"Oídme, Minaya   e vós, Per Vermúez,
sírvem' Mio Cid   el Campeador,
él lo merece | e de mí abrá perdón,
viniéssem' a vistas,   si oviesse dent sabor.
Otros mandados ha   en esta mi cort:
Diego e Ferrando,   los iffantes de Carrión,
sabor han de casar   con sus fijas amas a dos.
Sed buenos mensageros   e rruégovoslo yo
que ge lo digades   al buen Campeador:
abrá í ondra   e creçrá en onor
por consagrar   con los iffantes de Carrión."

101

They kissed his hands, and went to lie down;
His servants would give them whatever they wanted.
But the Carrión nobles, you need to know,
Had met in secret, and a plan was formed:
"Cid's fame continues its rapid growth;
Let's ask for his daughters,
So our honor, too, and our wealth, can grow."
They went to King Alfonso.

102

"We come to ask our lord and sovereign king
For his help! We would like
To marry the Warrior's daughters.
Their honor, and ours, can grow as one."
The king did not speak at once; they could see him thinking.
"I sent this fine Warrior off into exile.
I did not help him, but he has helped me.
How can I say what he will decide?
But now that you ask, I will speak to him, and we'll see."
Then King Alfonso summoned Minaya Alvar Fáñez
And Pedro Bermúdez, and spoke to them
Alone, the three of them in one room.
"Hear me, Minaya, and you, Pedro Bermúdez.
My Cid has served me well,
He deserves to be pardoned, and he will be.
If he so chooses, let him visit me.
Still other matters arise, here in my court:
Diego and Fernando, the two young Carrión lords,
Would like to marry the Warrior's daughters.
Please make yourselves my messengers
And let my Cid be fully informed.
It would do him honor, and his reputation no harm,

Fabló Minaya   e plogo a Per Vermúez:
"Rrogar ge lo emos   lo que dezides vós;
después faga el Cid   lo que oviere sabor."
"Dezid a Rruy Díaz,   el que en buen ora nasco,
quel' iré a vistas   dó fuere aguisado,
dó él dixiere   í sea el mojón.
Andarle quiero   a Mio Cid en toda pro."
Espidiénse al rrey,   con esto tornados son,
van pora Valencia   ellos e todos los sos.
Quando lo sopo   el buen Campeador,
apriessa cavalga,   a rrecebirlos salió,
sonrrisós' Mio Cid   e bien los abraçó:
"¡Venides, Minaya   e vós, Pero Vermúez!
En pocas tierras   á tales dos varones.
¿Cómo son las saludes   de Alfonso mio señor?
¿Si es pagado   o rrecibió el don?"
Dixo Minaya: "D'alma e de coraçón
es pagado   e davos su amor."
Dixo Mio Cid: "¡Grado al Criador!"
Esto diziendo,   conpieçan la rrazón,
lo quel' rrogava   Alfonso el de León
de dar sus fijas   a los ifantes de Carrión,
quel' connoscié í ondra   e creç[r]ié en onor,
que ge lo consejava   d'alma e de coraçón.
Quando lo oyó Mio Cid   el buen Campeador,
una grand ora   pensó e comidió:
"Esto gradesco   a Christus el mio señor.
Echado fu de tierra,   é tollida la onor,
con grand afán gané   lo que he yo.
A Dios lo gradesco   que del rrey he su gracia
e pídenme mis fijas   pora los ifantes de Carrión.
Ellos son mucho urgullosos   e an part en la cort,
d'este casamiento   non avría sabor,
mas pues lo conseja   el que más vale que nós,
fablemos en ello,   en la poridad seamos nós.
Afé Dios del cielo   que nos acuerde en lo mijor."
"Con todo esto   a vós dixo Alfonso
que vos vernié a vistas   dó oviéssedes sabor;

To accept this proposal of marriage."
Minaya spoke for them both:
"Indeed, he will surely be told.
And then my Cid will let us all know."
"Tell Ruy Díaz, born at such a fortunate hour,
That I will visit him, at whatever place he chooses.
Ask him to let me know.
I wish to honor him in whatever I do."
The king left them, and they hurried off,
With all their men, back to Valencia.
Hearing that they were coming, the good Warrior
Galloped out to meet them, embracing them both,
Smiling with happiness and warmth:
"So here you are, Minaya, and you, Pedro Bermúdez?
Not many countries can show two such men!
How did my lord, King Alfonso, welcome you both?
Was he pleased? Did he like my gift?"
Minaya said: "He was pleased in heart and soul;
He was very pleased, and greets you warmly."
My Cid said: "May God be praised!"
And then they began to tell him
What Alfonso of León proposed:
Marriage of his daughters to the heirs of Carrión,
An honor for them and also for him.
The king had strongly approved the plan.
My Cid was silent for a very long time,
The good Warrior reflecting on what he had heard.
"I owe everything to my Lord, Jesus Christ!
I was thrown out of my country, my honor taken away;
I have struggled hard and long for what I now have.
By the grace of God, the king grants me his favor
And asks me to marry my daughters to the Carrión heirs.
They are very haughty people, active courtiers.
This is not a marriage I would have chosen.
But since it has been suggested by him who is far above us,
Let's talk about it, quietly, among ourselves—
And in the end, may God in heaven show us the right way!"
"There's more," said Minaya. "Alfonso says

querer vos ie ver   e darvos su amor,
acordar vos iedes después   a todo lo mejor."
Essora dixo el Cid: "Plazme de coraçón."
"Estas vistas   ó las ayades vós,"
dixo Minaya,   "vós sed sabidor."
"Non era maravilla   si quisiesse el rrey Alfonso;
fasta dó lo fallássemos   buscarlo ir[i]emos nós,
por darle grand ondra   como a rrey de tierra.
Mas lo que él quisiere   esso queramos nós.
Sobre Tajo,   que es una agua cabdal,
ayamos vistas   quando lo quiere mio señor."
Escrivién cartas,   bien las selló,
con dos cavalleros   luego las enbió:
"Lo que el rrey quisiere   esso ferá el Campeador."

                                      103

Al rrey ondrado   delant le echaron las cartas;
quando las vio,   de coraçón se paga:
"Saludadme a Mio Cid,   el que en buen ora cinxo espada,
sean las vistas   d'estas *tres* semanas;
s[i] yo bivo só,   allí iré sin falla."
Non lo detardan,   a Mio Cid se tornavan.
D'ella part e d'ella   pora la[s] vistas se adobavan;
¿quién vio por Castiella   tanta mula preciada
e tanto palafré   que bien anda,
cavallos gruessos   e corredores sin falla,
tanto buen pendón   meter en buenas astas,
escudos boclados   con oro e con plata,
mantos e pielles   e buenos cendales d'A[n]dria?
Conduchos largos   el rrey enbiar mandava
a las aguas de Tajo   ó las vistas son aparejadas.
Con el rrey   atantas buenas conpañas;
los iffantes de Carrió[n]   mucho alegres andan,
lo uno adebdan   e lo otro pagavan,
como ellos tenién,   crecer les ía la gana[n]cia,

He'll come to meet you; you can choose the place.
He wants to see you, and show you his favor,
And then everything can be settled for the best."
Then my Cid said: "That warms my heart!"
"But you," said Minaya, "must choose where to meet him.
He leaves that decision entirely in your hands."
"I wouldn't have been surprised, had King Alfonso
Summoned us to come wherever he is holding court,
Commanding us as our king and lord.
But his mere wish is our command.
I like the banks of our great Tagus;
We will meet him there, whenever he wants us."
Letters were written, my Cid sealed them,
And two of his knights took them to the king.
Whatever the king wanted, the Warrior would do.

103

These letters reached the honored king,
Who was deeply pleased to receive them:
"Greet my Cid for me, he who took up his sword at a lucky hour.
Let our visits take place in exactly three weeks:
If I'm still among the living, I will be there without fail."
There was no hesitation, bringing this answer back.
Both sides made themselves ready:
When had Castile seen so many priceless mules,
So many fine palfreys, with dainty hooves,
So many full-bodied horses, sure-footed and fast,
So many costly banners dangling from spears,
Strong shields plated with silver and gold,
So many cloaks and rich furs, such splendid silk from Andros?
The king had ordered enormous supplies of food
To await them, along the banks of the Tagus.
Courtiers galore, and ladies, would come with the king.
The Carrión nobles were happy,
Buying things on credit, and sometimes paying money,
As if my Cid's vast fortune was already theirs,

quantos quisiessen   averes d'oro o de plata.
El rrey don Alfonso   apriessa cavalgava,
cuendes e podestades   e muy grandes mesnadas.
Los ifantes de Carrión   lievan grandes conpañas.
Con el rrey van leoneses   e mesnadas galizianas,
non son en cuenta,   sabet, las castellanas.
Sueltan las rriendas,   a las vistas se van adeliñadas.

104

Dentro en Valencia   Mio Cid el Campeador
non lo detarda,   pora las vistas se adobó.
Tanta gruessa mula   e tanto palafré de sazón,
tanta buena arma   e tanto buen cavallo corredor,
tanta buena capa   e mantos e pelliçones,
chicos e grandes   vestidos son de colores.
Minaya Álbar Fáñez   e aquel Pero Vermúez,
Martín Muñoz   . . . .
e Martín Antolínez,   el burgalés de pro,
el obispo don Jerónimo,   coranado mejor,
Álvar Álvarez   e Álvar Sa[l]vadórez,
Muño Gustioz,   el cavallero de pro,
Galind Garcíaz,   el que fue de Aragón,
éstos se adoban   por ir con el Campeador
e todos los otros   que í son.
[A] Álbar Salvadórez   e Galind Garcíaz el de Aragón
a aquestos dos   mandó el Campeador
que curien a Valencia | d'alma e de coraçón
e todos los [otros]   que en poder d'éssos fossen;
las puertas del alcáçar   . . . .
que non se abriessen   de día nin de noch;
dentro es su mugier   e sus fijas amas a dos,
en que tiene su alma   e su coraçón,
e otras dueñas   que las sirven a su sabor;
rrecabdado ha,   como tan buen varón,
que del alcáçar   una salir non puede
fata ques' torne   el que en buen ora nasco.

All the silver and gold they could ever desire.
King Alfonso galloped quickly,
Riding with counts and grand, important people in authority;
The Carrión nobles rode in their own great company.
Men from León and Galicia were with the king,
But, believe me, many more Castilians.
They all gave their horses the rein, and galloped on.

104

In Valencia, meanwhile, my Cid, great Warrior,
Made sure everything was readied for the meeting:
So many fat mules, so many first-rate palfreys,
So much fine armor, so many swift horses,
So many beautiful clothes, and capes, and fur-lined mantles!
Nobles and nobodies, all dressed to the hilt!
Minaya Alvar Fáñez, and Pedro Bermúdez,
Martín Muñoz, and Martín Antolínez from Burgos,
Bishop Don Jerónimo, worthiest of priests,
Alvar Alvarez, and Alvar Salvadórez,
Muño Gustioz, a first-class knight,
Galín García, who came from Aragon—
And all the many others who were coming.
But Alvar Alvarez and Galín García from Aragon
Were ordered by my Cid to stay at home
In Valencia, guarding with their hearts and souls
All those who stayed inside its gates—
Closed, the Warrior ordered, both night and day—
Among them his wife and his daughters,
Who were heart and soul to him,
And also their ladies in waiting.
Locked into Valencia, this way,
As he of lucky birth desired, they could not leave.
Cid and his men left Valencia, spurring their horses—
So many handsome steeds, strong and fast,
Which my Cid had won: the Moors had not been giving out
    gifts.

Salién de Valencia,   aguijan e espolonavan,
tantos cavallos en diestro,   gruessos e corredores,
Mio Cid se los gañara,   que non ge los dieran en don;
yas' va pora las vistas   que con el rrey paró.
De un día es llegado antes   el rrey don Alfonso;
quando vieron que vinié   el buen Campeador
rrecebirlo salen   con tan grand onor.
Dón lo ovo a ojo   el que en buen ora nasco,
a todos los sos   estar los mandó
sinon a estos cavalleros   que querié de coraçó[n];
con unos *quinze*   a tierras' firió,
como lo comidía   el que en buen ora nació,
los inojos e las manos   en tierra los fincó,
las yerbas del campo   a dientes las tomó,
llorando de los ojos   tanto avié el gozo mayor;
assí sabe dar omildança   a Alfonso so señor.
De aquesta guisa   a los pies le cayó;
tan grand pesar ovo   el rrey don Alfonso:
"Levantados en pie,   ya Cid Campeador,
besad las manos   ca los pies no[n];
si esto non feches,   non avredes mi amor."
Inojos fitos   sedié el Campeador:
"Merced vos pido a vós,   mio natural señor,
assí estando,   dédesme vuestra amor,
que lo oyan   quantos aquí son."
Dixo el rrey: "Esto feré d'alma e de coraçón;
aquí vos perdono   e dovos mi amor
[e] en todo mio rreino   parte desde oy."
Fabló Mio Cid   e dixo:
"¡Merced! Yo lo rrecibo,   Alfonso mio señor;
gradéscolo a Dios del cielo   e después a vós
e a estas mesnadas   que están aderredor."
Inojos fitos   las manos le besó,
levós' en pie   e en la bócal' saludó.
Todos los demás   d'esto avién sabor;
pesó a Álbar Díaz   e a Garcí Ordóñez.
Fabló Mio Cid   e dixo esta rrazón:
"Esto gradesco   al Criador

This was how they made their journey to meet with the king,
Who had arrived at the Tagus the day before.
When Alfonso saw the worthy Warrior approaching,
He went out to greet him with the honor my Cid deserved,
And when he who had been born lucky saw him,
He ordered everyone to stop, except for fifteen,
Who dismounted with him, as he had planned.
And then my Cid went down on his hands and knees
And with his teeth pulled up grass,
So overjoyed he could not keep from weeping,
For this was how he gave his homage to the king,
Falling at his feet.
But the king was deeply upset.
"Stand up, my Cid, my Warrior! Stand up!
You may kiss my hands, yes, but not my feet!
Stand up, or I cannot grant you my favor!"
My Cid remained on his knees.
"I must ask you, my noble lord,
To show me your favor, exactly as I am now,
So everyone here will know it from your words!"
The king declared: "With all my heart and soul,
I grant it! You are forgiven, I give you my love,
And—from this day—the complete freedom of Castile."
My Cid replied, and here is what he said:
"I thank you. I accept your pardon: you are my lord.
I thank God in heaven, and I thank you,
And I thank all these men who surround me here!"
Before he rose, my Cid kissed the king's hands;
When he rose, he kissed the king on the mouth.
And everyone watching was deeply pleased—
Except Alvar Díaz and García Ordóñez.
And then my Cid spoke once more:
"I thank our Father in heaven
For this grace I've been given by my lord:
May God be with me by both day and night!
Allow me to be your host, good King Alfonso."
"Of course," the king replied, "but not today.
We've been here since last night; you've only just arrived.

quando he la gracia   de don Alfonso mio señor;
valer me á Dios   de día e de noch.
Fuéssedes mi huésped,   si vos ploguiesse, señor."
Dixo el rrey: "Non es aguisado oy,
vós agora llegastes   e nós viniemos anoch;
mio huésped seredes,   Cid Campeador,
e cras feremos   lo que ploguiere a vós."
Besóle la mano,   Mio Cid lo otorgó.
Essora se le omillan   los iffantes de Carrión:
"¡Omillámosnos, Cid,   en buen ora nasquiestes vós!
En quanto podemos   andamos en vuestro pro."
Rrespuso Mio Cid: "¡Assí lo mande el Criador!"
Mio Cid Rruy Díaz   que en ora buena nasco,
en aquel día   del rrey so huésped fue;
non se puede fartar d'él,   tántol' querié de coraçón,
catándol' sedié la barba,   que tan aínal' creciera.
Maravíllanse de Mio Cid   quantos que í son.
És día es passado   e entrada es la noch;
otro día mañana   claro salié el sol,
el Campeador   a los sos lo mandó
que adobassen cozina   pora quantos que í son.
De tal guisa los paga   Mio Cid el Campeador,
todos eran alegres   e acuerdan en una rrazón:
passado avié *tres* años   no comieran mejor.
Al otro día mañana,   assí como salió el sol,
el obispo don Jerónimo   la missa cantó.
Al salir de la missa   todos juntados son,
non lo tardó el rrey,   la rrazón conpeçó:
"¡Oídme, las escuelas,   cuendes e ifançones!
Cometer quiero un rruego   a Mio Cid el Campeador,
assí lo mande Christus   que sea a so pro.
Vuestras fijas vos pido,   don Elvira e doña Sol,
que las dedes por mugieres   a los ifantes de Carrión.
Seméjam' el casamiento   ondrado e con grant pro,
ellos vos las piden   e mándovoslo yo.
D'ella e d'ella parte   quantos que aquí son,
los míos e los vuestros   que sean rrogadores;
¡dándoslas, Mio Cid,   sí vos vala el Criador!"

You'll be my guest right now, good Cid, my Warrior,
And I will be yours, tomorrow."
My Cid kissed the king's hand, and it was settled.
Just then the nobles of Carrión came up, bowing:
"We offer our respects, O Cid, born at a fortunate time!
If there are things to be done for you, they will be done."
My Cid replied: "May God so decree!"
Thus, that day, my Cid, born at a blessèd hour,
Became the king's guest, favored incessantly;
Even his beard, grown long, had Alfonso's attention.
Everyone there was struck by my Cid's presence.
The day rolled down and turned to night;
The sun came up, next morning, clear and bright.
My Cid ordered his men to prepare
An enormous feast for that night,
And people were so delighted they cried:
It was three full years since they had eaten so well!
As the sun rose up, the third morning,
Bishop Don Jerónimo said mass,
And after that, when they were all together,
The king immediately spoke, at his pleasure:
"Hear me, my subjects, you counts, and all my nobles!
I have a request to make of the Warrior, my Cid:
May he respond with favor, in the name of God!
I ask for your daughters, Doña Elvira and Doña Sol,
To be given in marriage to the Carrión heirs.
These seem to me honorable, splendid unions;
The Carrións have asked for your daughters, and I approve.
Let intermediaries be chosen from the best of your men
And the best of mine, among those present here.
Agree, my Cid, as you hope for God's support!"
"I have no daughters ready for marriage," replied the
    Warrior.
"They're still little girls, and very young.
The Carrións come from a noble family,
Fine for my daughters, fine for better-born girls.
I gave them life, and you have fed and schooled them:
This father, these daughters, live at your command,

"Non abría fijas de casar," rrespuso el Campeador,
"ca non han grant edad   e de días pequeñas son.
De grandes nuevas son   los ifantes de Carrión,
pertenecen pora mis fijas   e aun pora mejores.
Yo las engendré amas   e criásteslas vós,
entre yo y ellas   en vuestra merced somos nós;
afellas en vuestra mano   don Elvira e doña Sol,
dadlas a qui quisiéredes yós,   ca yo pagado só."
"Gracias," dixo el rrey,   "a vós e a tod' esta cort."
Luego se levantaron   los iffantes de Carrión,
ban besar las manos   al que en ora buena nació,
camearon las espadas   ant'el rrey don Alfonso.
Fabló el rrey don Alfonso   como tan buen señor:
"Grado e gracias, Cid, como tan bueno   e primero al Criador
quem' dades vuestras fijas   pora los ifantes de Carrión.
D'aquí las prendo por mis manos   don Elvira e doña Sol
e dolas por veladas   a los ifantes de Carrión.
Yo las caso a vuestras fijas   con vuestro amor,
al Criador plega   que ayades ende sabor.
Afellos en vuestras manos   los ifantes de Carrión,
ellos vayan convusco,   ca d'aquén me torno yo.
Trezientos marcos de plata   en ayuda les do yo
que metan en sus bodas   o dó quisiéredes vós;
pues fueren en vuestro poder   en Valencia la mayor,
los yernos e las fijas   todos vuestros fijos son;
lo que vos ploguiere   d'ellos fet, Campeador."
Mio Cid ge los rrecibe,   las manos le besó:
"Mucho vos lo gradesco,   como a rrey e a señor.
Vós casades mis fijas   ca non ge las do yo."
Las palabras son puestas . . . .
que otro día mañana, | quando salies[s]e el sol,
ques' tornasse cada uno   dón salidos son.
Aquís' metió en nuevas   Mio Cid el Campeador:
tanta gruessa mula   e tanto palafré de sazón,
tantas buenas vestiduras   que d'alfaya son,
conpeçó Mio Cid a dar   a quien quiere prender so don;
cada uno lo que pide   nadi nol' dize de no.
Mio Cid de los cavallos   *sessaenta* dio en don.

So I put these girls in your grace's hands.
Give them to the men you choose, and I will be pleased."
"My thanks," said the king, "to you and to all in this court."
The noble Carrións rose and kissed the hands
Of the man who'd been born at the right time, and as the king
    watched,
They sealed the union by exchanging swords with my Cid,
To whom the king spoke, as his sovereign lord:
"I am pleased and thankful, Cid, that you, so blessed
    by God,
Have consigned your daughters to me, for this Carrión
    marriage.
And I give them as wives to these noble lords:
I hereby sanction this marriage, with your approval.
May God reward you with his grace!
The Carrión nobles, now joined to your family,
Will go with you; I go in a different direction.
I give them three hundred silver marks,
To spend on their wedding, or whatever you think best.
They will all be your subjects, in Valencia,
Your daughters and your new sons.
Do with them as you think fit!"
My Cid welcomed them, kissing the king's hands:
"You have been very good to me, my king and my lord!
It's you who have made this marriage, not me."
    The pledges having been made, at dawn the next day
The parties were to go their different ways.
My Cid, great Warrior, attracted great attention,
Giving fat mules and fine palfreys away
To everyone who wanted something,
As well as much beautiful, well-made clothing.
Each got what he chose, no one refused the offer,
And my Cid gave away sixty horses, all told.
    It grew late, and people wanted to leave.
The king took the Carrións by the hand
And brought them to my Cid, the great Warrior.
"Here are your sons, your new sons-in-law,
Who from this day are subject to your orders."

Todos son pagados de las vistas,   quantos que í son;
partirse quieren   que entrada era la noch.
El rrey a los ifantes   a las manos les tomó,
metiólos en poder   de Mio Cid el Campeador:
"Evad aquí vuestros fijos,   quando vuestros yernos son;
oy de más sabed   qué fer d'ellos, Campeador."
"Gradéscolo, rrey,   e prendo vuestro don;
Dios que está en cielo   dém' dent buen galardón."
Sobr'el so cavallo Bavieca   Mio Cid salto dava:
"Aquí lo digo   ante mio señor el rrey Alfonso:
qui quiere ir a las bodas   o rrecebir mi don,
d'aquend vaya comigo,   cuedo quel' avrá pro.

105

"Yo vos pido merced   a vós, rrey natural:
pues que casades mis fijas   assí como a vós plaz,
dad manero a qui las dé,   quando vós las tomades;
non ge las daré yo con mi mano,   nin de[n]d non se alabarán."
Rrespondió el rrey: "Afé aquí Álbar Fáñez,
prendellas con vuestras manos   e daldas a los ifantes,
assí como yo las prendo d'aquent,   como si fosse delant,
sed padrino d'ellas   a tod' el velar;
quando vos juntáredes comigo,   quem' digades la verdat."
Dixo Álbar Fáñez: "Señor, afé que me plaz."

106

Tod' esto es puesto,   sabed, en grant rrecabdo.
"Ya rrey don Alfonso,   señor tan ondrado,
d'estas vistas que oviemos,   de mí tomedes algo.
Tráyovos *veínte* palafrés,   éstos bien adobados,
e *treínta* cavallos corredores,   éstos bien ensellados;
tomad aquesto   e beso vuestras manos."
Dixo el rrey don Alfonso: "Mucho me avedes enbargado;
rrecibo este don   que me avedes mandado;

"Thank you, my king; I accept this gift.
May God on high be pleased with what I've done!"
My Cid mounted Babieca, and then spoke:
"Let me announce, in the presence of my lord and king:
Those who wish to attend the weddings,
And have gifts from me, can follow me now. They'll be glad
    they did.

105

"But I beg a favor from you, my lord and king:
Since you have married my daughters as you think best,
I ask that you name someone you think fit
To replace me in the ceremony, giving my daughters away."
The king replied: "Who better than Alvar Fáñez?
Minaya, take them by the hands and give them to the Carrións,
Just as I have taken them—without their presence—from Cid.
You will be in charge of them till the wedding night.
When you see me next, tell me exactly what happens."
Alvar Fáñez said: "My lord, I am glad to accept."

106

So this was how, as you see, it was all arranged.
"Ah, King Alfonso," said Cid, "my honored lord!
You too must take something of mine with you.
I've brought you twenty palfreys, saddles and reins and all,
And thirty racing horses, nicely saddled.
Take them, as I kiss your hand in farewell."
The king replied: "You give too much, I'm afraid!
But I will accept this offer, now that you've made it.

plega al Criador   con todos los sos sanctos
este plazer | quem' feches   que bien sea galardonado.
Mio Cid Rruy Díaz,   mucho me avedes ondrado,
de vós bien só servido   e tengon' por pagado,
aún bivo seyendo   de mí ayades algo.
A Dios vos acomiendo,   d'estas vistas me parto.
¡Afé Dios del cielo   que lo ponga en buen logar!"

107

Yas' espidió Mio Cid   de so señor Alfonso,
non quiere quel' escurra,   quitól' dessí luego.
Veriedes cavalleros   que bien andantes son
besar las manos   [e] espedirse del rrey Alfonso:
"Merced vos sea   e fazednos este perdón:
iremos en poder de Mio Cid   a Valencia la mayor,
seremos a las bodas   de los ifantes de Carrión
e de las fijas de Mio Cid,   de don Elvira e doña Sol."
Esto plogo al rrey   e a todos los soltó,
la conpaña del Cid crece   e la del rrey mengó,
grandes son las yentes   que van con el Canpeador,
adeliñan pora Valencia,   la que en buen punto ganó.
E a don Fernando e a don Diego   aguardarlos mandó
a Pero Vermúez   e Muño Gustioz,
en casa de Mio Cid   non á dos mejores,
que sopiessen sos mañas   de los ifantes de Carrión.
E va í A[s]sur Gonçález,   que era bullidor,
que es largo de lengua   mas en lo ál non es tan pro.
Grant ondra les dan   a los ifantes de Carrión.
Afelos en Valencia,   la que Mio Cid gañó,
quando a ella assomaron   los gozos son mayores.
Dixo Mio Cid a don Pero   e a Muño Gustioz:
"Dadles un rreyal   a los ifantes de Carrión,
[e] vós con ellos sed,   que assí vos lo mando yo.
Quando viniére la mañana,   que apuntare el sol,
verán a sus esposas,   a don Elvira e a doña Sol."

May God and all his saints
Reward you for the many, many pleasures
You've given me! I've been much honored, my Cid, Ruy Díaz.
You've served me well, I leave here happy.
May I live to do as well by you!
I commend you to God, as I ride away:
May God in heaven, in time, make all of us glad!"

107

At last, my Cid left his lord Alfonso,
Swiftly, discouraging a farewell escort.
Many knights, believe me, rode up to the king,
Kissing his hands, begging for permission
To ride with my Cid: "Permit it, Lord Alfonso!
We wish to be in great Valencia
For the weddings of noble Carrións
To the daughters of our even greater Cid."
The king was pleased, and off they rode—
So many, the king's company shrank as my Cid's swelled:
The Warrior left, surrounded by many, many men.
On the way to Valencia, which he'd fought for, and won,
He asked Pedro Bermúdez and Muño Gustioz
(There were no better men in his service)
To watch Don Fernando and Don Diego,
Observing how these two behaved.
Ansur González, their brother, rode with them;
His tongue was very long, his reputation small.
These Carrión heirs were treated very well,
And when they reached Valencia, my Cid's great prize,
Their welcome was suitably noisy.
My Cid told Don Pedro and Muño Gustioz:
"Arrange some proper lodging,
And stay with them: that's an order.
Tomorrow morning, when the sun has risen,
They'll see their wives, Doña Elvira and Doña Sol."

108

Todos essa noch   fueron a sus posadas,
Mio Cid el Campeador   al alcáçar entrava,
rrecibiólo doña Ximena   e sus fıjas amas:
"¡Venides, Campeador,   en buena ora cinxiestes espada!
¡Muchos días vos veamos   con los ojos de las caras!"
"¡Grado al Criador,   vengo, mugier ondrada!
Yernos vos adugo   de que avremos ondrança;
¡gradídmelo, mis fıjas,   ca bien vos he casadas!"
Besáronle las manos   la mugier e las fıjas amas
e todas las dueñas   que las sirven:

109

"¡Grado al Criador   e a vós, Cid, barba vellida!
Todo lo que vós feches   es de buena guisa;
non serán menguadas   en todos vuestros días."
"Quando vós nos casáredes   bien seremos rricas."

110

"Mugier doña Ximena,   ¡grado al Criador!
A vós digo, mis fıjas,   don Elvira e doña Sol:
d'este vu[e]stro casamiento   creçremos en onor,
mas bien sabed verdad   que non lo levanté yo;
pedidas vos ha e rrogadas   el mio señor Alfonso
atan fırmemientre   e de todo coraçón
que yo nulla cosa   nol' sope dezir de no.
Metívos en sus manos,   fıjas amas a dos,
bien me lo creades   que él vos casa, ca non yo."

108

That night, everyone went to their rooms.
My Cid, the Warrior, came to the palace,
Welcomed by Doña Jimena and their daughters:
"You've come, my Warrior, knighted at so fortunate an hour!
May we see you day after day, with these eyes of ours!"
"Thank God I'm here, I've come, my honored wife!
I give you two sons-in-law, who will honor us all.
Be grateful, my daughters, I've married you so well."
His wife and daughters kissed his hands,
As did the ladies in waiting:

109

"We thank the Lord God, and you, my Cid, with your splendid
     beard!
Everything you do is always done right.
For the rest of our days, we'll never lack for a thing."
"You'll marry us off and make us rich brides."

110

"Doña Jimena, my wife, thanks indeed to the Lord!
But though I tell you, my daughters,
These marriages will bring us honor,
I must also tell you, to speak the plain truth,
This wasn't my idea, but the king's; he wanted it done,
And pressed me so hard I could not say no,
There was nothing else to do.
I put you in his hands, my daughters;
He will give you away, instead of your father."

III

Pensaron de adobar   essora el palacio,
por el suelo e suso   tan bien encortinado,
tanta pórpola e tanto xamed   e tanto paño preciado.
Sabor abriedes de ser   e de comer en el palacio.
Todos sus cavalleros   apriessa son juntados;
por los iffantes de Carrión   essora enbiaron,
cavalgan los iffantes,   adelant adeliñavan al palacio
con buenas vestiduras   e fuertemientre adobados,
de pie e a sabor,   ¡Dios, qué quedos entraron!
Rrecibiólos Mio Cid   con todos sus vas[s]allos;
a él e a su mugier   delant se le[s] omillaron
e ivan posar   en un precioso escaño.
Todos los de Mio Cid   tan bien son acordados,
están parando mientes   al que en buen ora nasco.
El Campeador   en pie es levantado:
"Pues que a fazer lo avemos,   ¿por qué lo imos tardando?
¡Venit acá, Álbar Fáñez,   el que yo quiero e amo!
Afé amas mis fijas,   métolas en vuestra mano,
sabedes que al rrey   assí ge lo he mandado,
no lo quiero fallir por nada   de quanto á í parado,
a los ifantes de Carrión   dadlas con vuestra mano
e prendan bendiciones   e vayamos rrecabdando."
Esto[n]z dixo Minaya: "Esto faré yo de grado."
Levántanse derechas   e metiógelas en mano;
a los ifantes de Carrión   Minaya va fablando:
"Afevos delant Minaya,   amos sodes ermanos,
por mano del rrey Alfonso   que a mí lo ovo mandado
dovos estas dueñas,   amas son fijas d'algo,
que las tomássedes por mugieres   a ondra e a rrecabdo."
Amos las rreciben   d'amor e de grado,
a Mio Cid e a su mugier   van besar la mano.
Quando ovieron aquesto fecho,   salieron del palacio,
pora Sancta María   apriessa adeliñando;
el obispo don Jerónimo   vistiós' tan privado,
a la puerta de la eclegia   sediéllos sperando;

I I I

They began to make the palace ready,
With tapestries hung on walls, rugs unrolled on floors—
Red and purple silks and wool were everywhere.
My Cid's brave knights came rushing;
The noble Carrión heirs were summoned:
They rode to the palace, dismounted—
Handsomely dressed, beautifully groomed
And elegant—how quietly they entered!
My Cid and his knights gave them good welcome;
They bowed to the Warrior, and to his wife,
Then seated themselves on a well-carved bench.
Those who followed my Cid listened as one,
Attentive, as the Warrior, he who was born at a fortunate hour,
Rose and began to address them:
"This ceremony awaits us: why keep it waiting?
Come here, Alvar Fáñez, for whom I feel great love!
Here are my two daughters, I put them in your hands,
Exactly as my king commanded:
Nothing I promised will be left undone.
Let the noble Carrións have what I've given you;
There'll be a blessing; we'll do it all as it should be done."
To which Minaya replied: "Gladly!"
The girls stood up, Minaya took them by the hands
And spoke to the two Carrión heirs:
"Here in front of you stands Minaya.
King Alfonso has given me, and I give you,
These two noble ladies, sisters to each other,
As lawful, proper wives to you two brothers."
The Carrións took them with warmth and pleasure,
And dutifully kissed both my Cid's hands and his wife's.
When this was done, they left the palace,
Going straight to Saint Mary's church,
Where Bishop Don Jerónimo, quickly donning his vestments,
Awaited them at the door,
Blessed them all, and sang a mass.

dioles bendictiones,   la missa á cantado.
Al salir de la eclesia   cavalgaron tan privado,
a la glera de Valencia   fuera dieron salto;
¡Dios, qué bien tovieron armas   el Cid e sus vassallos!
Tres cavallos cameó   el que en buen ora nasco.
Mio Cid de lo que veyé   mucho era pagado,
los ifantes de Carrión   bien an cavalgado.
Tórnanse con las dueñas,   a Valencia an entrado,
rricas fueron las bodas   en el alcáçar ondrado,
e al otro día fızo Mio Cid   fincar *siete* tablados;
antes que entrassen a yantar   todos los quebrantaron.
Quinze días conplidos   en las bodas duraron,
cerca de los *quinze* días   yas' van los fıjos d'algo.
Mio Cid don Rrodrigo,   el que en buen ora nasco,
entre palafrés e mulas   e corredores cavallos,
en bestias sines ál   *ciento á* mandados;
mantos e pelliçones   e otros vestidos largos;
non fueron en cuenta   los averes monedados.
Los vassallos de Mio Cid   assí son acordados,
cada uno por sí   sos dones avién dados.
Qui aver quiere prender   bien era abastado;
rricos' tornan a Castiella   los que a las bodas llegaron.
Yas' ivan partiendo   aquestos ospedados,
espidiendos' de Rruy Díaz,   el que en buen ora nasco,
e a todas las dueñas   e a los fıjos d'algo;
por pagados se parten   de Mio Cid e de sus vassallos,
grant bien dizen d'ellos,   ca será aguisado.
Mucho eran alegres   Diego e Fernando,
estos fueron fıjos   del conde don Gonçalo.
Venidos son a Castiella   aquestos ospedados,
el Cid e sos yernos   en Valencia son rrastados.
Í moran los ifantes   bien cerca de dos años,
los amores que les fazen   mucho eran sobejanos.
Alegre era el Cid   e todos sus vassallos.
¡Plega a Sancta María   e al Padre sancto
ques' pague d'és casamiento Mio Cid   o el que lo [ovo *a* algo]!
Las coplas d'este cantar   aquís' van acabando.
¡El Criador vos vala   con todos los sos sanctos!

After church, they galloped to the arena,
Where they played at war games—
God! My Cid and his men knew how to fight!
He who was born at a lucky time changed horses three times,
And was absolutely delighted with what he saw:
The Carrión brothers truly knew how to ride.
Then they took the ladies back to the city,
And celebrated this wedding in the Warrior's castle.
The next day, my Cid had seven wooden targets set out;
Before they touched their food, all seven were knocked apart.
The celebration went on for fifteen days,
And it was fifteen days before guests began to leave.
My Cid, Ruy Díaz, born at a lucky time,
Distributed palfreys and mules and good fast horses—
A full hundred animals in all—
Plus cloaks and fur-lined coats, and all kinds of other clothing.
No one could count the gold and silver he gave away.
And my Cid's good men gave too, with open hands:
Whoever asked, got what he wanted,
Whoever took, surely got a lot.
The guests from Castile were rich when they rode home.
So the visitors left, one by one,
Saying farewell to Ruy Díaz, he who was born at a lucky hour,
And to all the ladies and noble gentlemen;
And they left exceedingly happy they had come,
Praising their hosts, which was certainly proper.
The Carrión heirs, Diego and Fernando, sons
Of Count Gonzalo, were delighted.
After the guests had gone home
To Castile, my Cid and his sons-in-law
Lived on in Valencia for about two years,
And the Carrións were treated with very great warmth.
My Cid and all his men were pleased.
Pray that Saint Mary and our sacred Father
Make this marriage a good one, for my Cid and the king who
    made it!
And now this Canto has been completed:
May God's blessings fall on you, with those of all his saints!

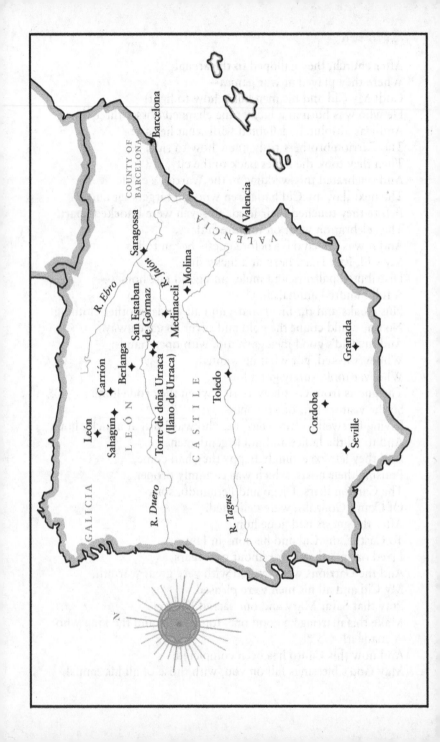

CANTO THREE

En Valencia seí Mio Cid   con todos sus vassallos,
con él amos sus yernos   los ifantes de Carrión.
Yaziés' en un escaño,   durmié el Campeador,
mala sobrevienta,   sabed, que les cuntió:
saliós' de la rred   e desatós' el león.
En grant miedo se vieron   por medio de la cort;
enbraçan los mantos   los del Campeador
e cercan el escaño   e fincan sobre so señor.
Ferrán Gonçález ....
non vio allí dós' alçasse,   nin cámara abierta nin torre,
metiós' so'l escaño,   tanto ovo el pavor.
Diego Gonçález   por la puerta salió,
diziendo de la boca: "¡Non veré Carrión!"
Tras una viga lagar   metiós' con grant pavor,
el manto e el brial   todo suzio lo sacó.
En esto despertó   el que en buen ora nació,
vio cercado el escaño   de sus buenos varones:
"¿Qué's esto, mesnadas,   o qué queredes vós?"
"Ya señor ondrado,   rrebata nos dio el león."
Mio Cid fincó el cobdo,   en pie se levantó,
el manto trae al cuello   e adeliñó pora' [l] león.
El león, quando lo vio,   assí envergonçó,
ante Mio Cid la cabeça premió   e el rrostro fincó.
Mio Cid don Rrodrigo   al cuello lo tomó
e liévalo adestrando,   en la rred le metió.
A maravilla lo han   quantos que í son
e tornáronse al palacio   pora la cort.

112

My Cid was in Valencia, with all his men
And both his sons-in-law, the Carrións.
The Warrior was lying on a couch, asleep—
When, suddenly, a serious problem arose:
Their lion was out of his cage, and walking free.
Terror spread through the palace;
My Cid's men belted their cloaks
And made a circle around their sleeping lord.
Fernando, my Cid's son-in-law, could see no place to hide
And, shaking with fear, went crawling under the couch;
His brother, Diego, ran straight for the door,
Screaming, "I'll never see my home again!"
Trembling, he squeezed himself behind a beam in the wine press,
His cloak and shirt grimy with sweat.
Then the man born at the right time awoke,
And saw the backs of his men around him.
"Good men, what's this, what's going on?"
"O honored lord, our lion's free!"
My Cid leaned up on his elbow, rose to his feet,
And with his cloak on his shoulder went walking toward the
    beast.
The lion was so afraid, at the sight of him,
That he stopped and bent his head,
And my Cid, Don Ruy Díaz, took hold of his mane
And walked him back to his cage.
Everyone there was amazed,
And all came back to the court.

Mio Cid por sos yernos demandó e no los falló,
maguer los están llamando, ninguno non rresponde.
Quando los fallaron, assí vinieron sin color,
non viestes tal juego como iva por la cort;
mandó lo vedar Mio Cid el Campeador.
Muchos' tovieron por enbaídos los ifantes de Carrión,
fiera cosa les pesa d'esto que les cuntió.

113

Ellos en esto estando, dón avién grant pesar,
fuerças de Marruecos Valencia vienen cercar,
cinquaenta mill tiendas fincadas ha de las cabdales,
aquéste era el rrey Búcar, sil' ouyestes contar.

114

Alegravas' el Cid e todos sus varones
que les crece la ganancia, grado al Criador;
mas, sabed, de cuer les pesa a los ifantes de Carrión
ca veyén tantas tiendas de moros de que non avié[n] sabor.
Amos ermanos apart salidos son:
"Catamos la ganancia e la pérdida no,
ya en esta batalla a entrar abremos nós,
esto es aguisado por non ver Carrión,
bibdas rremandrán fijas del Campeador."
Oyó la poridad aquel Muño Gustioz,
vino con estas nuevas a Mio Cid Rruy Díaz el Canpeador:
"Evades qué pavor han vuestros yernos tan osados,
por entrar en batalla desean Carrión.
Idlos conortar, sí vos vala el Criador,
que sean en paz e non ayan í rración.
Nós convusco la vençremos e valer nos ha el Criador."
Mio Cid don Rrodrigo sonrrisando salió:
"Dios vos salve, yernos, ifantes de Carrión.
En braços tenedes mis fijas tan blancas como el sol.

My Cid asked for the Carrións, who couldn't be found,
And though they called out names, no one answered.
Then they saw them, pale as ghosts—
And O! the giggling and chuckling around the court!
My Cid, the Warrior, commanded them to stop.
But the Carrións felt disgraced and scorned,
And never got over their flood of shame.

113

And while they were still boiling with anger,
Moroccan armies suddenly surrounded Valencia;
Fifty thousand huge tents sprouted right in front of them.
This was King Búcar, of whom you may have heard.

114

My Cid and all his men were delighted,
Already counting up their loot—may God be praised!
But, in fact, the Carrións were terrified at the sight
Of so many Moorish tents, which they did not like.
They conferred, in private:
"We calculated our gains and expected no losses:
We'll have to ride out and face those forces!
We'll never see Carrión again!
And Cid's daughters will both be widows!"
Muño Gustioz happened to overhear this,
And informed my Cid, Ruy Díaz, the Warrior:
"Your sons-in-law are shaking with fear: fighting is
Not on their minds—only running for home!
For God's sake, go calm them down!
Let them stay here and not lift a hand:
God will give us victory, with you in command!"
My Cid, Ruy Díaz, went to them, smiling:
"May God bless you, my sons-in-law, you Carrión heirs!
Your arms are holding my daughters, bright and fair!

Yo desseo lides   e vós a Carrión,
en Valencia folgad   a todo vuestro sabor
ca d'aquellos moros   yo só sabidor,
arrancar me los trevo   con la merced del Criador."

115

[*There is a full page missing from the manuscript, perhaps
fifty lines; we know from the chronicles that the first speaker,
below, is one of the Carrións, who had proposed to join the
fighting but turned and ran when a Moor attacked; Pedro
Bermúdez kills the Moor and brings the man's horse to the
Carrión, so he can claim to have won it in battle.*]

"aún vea el ora   que vos meresca dos tanto."
En una conpaña   tornados son amos,
assí lo otorga don Pero   cuemo se alaba Ferrando;
plogo a Mio Cid   e a todos sos vassallos:
"Aún, si Dios quisiere   e el Padre que está en alto,
amos los mios yernos   buenos serán en ca[m]po."
Esto van diziendo   e las yentes se allegando,
en la hueste de los moros   los atamores sonando,
a marav[i]lla lo avién   muchos d'essos cristianos
ca nunqua lo vieran,   ca nuevos son llegados.
Más se maravillan   entre Diego e Ferrando,
por la su voluntad   non serién allí llegados.
Oíd lo que fabló   el que en buen ora nasco:
"¡Ala, Pero Vermúez,   el mio sobrino caro!
Cúriesme a [don] Diego   e cúriesme a don Fernando,
mios yernos amos a dos,   la cosa que mucho amo,
ca los moros, con Dios,   non fincarán en canpo."

116

"Yo vos digo, Cid,   por toda caridad,
que oy los ifantes   a mí por amo non abrán;

We others long for a battle, and you for your home,
So enjoy yourself, here in Valencia,
While my men and I go after the Moors:
With God's own blessing, we'll make them run!"

115

*[There is a full page missing from the manuscript, perhaps
fifty lines; we know from the chronicles that the first speaker,
below, is one of the Carrións, who had proposed to join the
fighting but turned and ran when a Moor attacked; Pedro
Bermúdez kills the Moor and brings the man's horse to the
Carrión, so he can claim to have won it in battle.]*

". . . May I be able, some day, to pay you back twice over!"
Then they rode back like a pair of warriors,
And Pedro confirmed the Carrión's boasting.
This story pleased my Cid and all his men:
"May God, our Father on high,
Make my sons-in-law good fighters!"
As they spoke, the soldiers took their formations,
And from the Moorish host the great drums sounded,
Which many Christians new to their ways
Had never heard. They were amazed.
But the Carrión brothers were simply afraid
And wished they could be someplace else.
He who was born at just the right time heard them:
"Ah, Pedro Bermúdez, my dear good nephew!
Do something for me. Take care of my sons-in-law,
Because I'm very fond of them.
As for the Moors, well, we'll all take good care of them!"

116

"Now let me tell you, Cid, straight from the heart,
I don't want to coddle Carrións anymore.

cúrielos qui quier,   ca d'ellos poco m'incal.
Yo con los míos   ferir quiero delant,
vós con los vuestros   firmemientre a la çaga tengades,
si cueta fuere,   bien me podredes uviar."
Aquí llegó   Minaya Álbar Fáñez:
"¡Oíd, ya Cid,   Canpeador leal!
Esta batalla   el Criador la ferá
e vós tan dinno   que con él avedes part.
Mandadno' los ferir   de quál part vos semejar,
el debdo que á cada uno   a conplir será.
Ver lo hemos con Dios   e con la vuestra auze."
Dixo Mio Cid: "Ayamos más de vagar."
Afevos el obispo don Jerónimo   muy bien armado,
paravas' delant al Campeador   siempre con la buen auze:
"Oy vos dix la missa   de Sancta Trinidade;
por esso salí de mi tierra   e vin vos buscar
por sabor que avía   de algún moro matar;
mi orden e mis manos   querría las ondrar
e a estas feridas   yo quiero ir delant.
Pendón trayo a corças   e armas de señal,
si ploguiesse a Dios   querríalas ensayar,
mio coraçón   que pudiesse folgar
e vós, Mio Cid,   de mí más vos pagar.
Si este amor non' feches,   yo de vós me quiero quitar."
Essora dixo Mio Cid: "Lo que vós queredes plazme.
Afé los moros a ojo,   idlos ensayar.
Nós d'aquent veremos   cómo lidia el abat."

117

El obispo don Jerónimo   priso a espolonada
e ívalos ferir   a cabo del albergada.
Por la su ventura   e Dios quel' amava
a los primeros colpes   dos moros matava de la lanç[a];
el astil á quebrado   e metió mano al espada,
ensayavas' el obispo,   ¡Dios, qué bien lidiava!

Let someone who wants it have that job: I don't give a damn!
I want to take my men and attack these front lines,
While you and yours pin down the Moors in back.
That way you'll help me, if I go too far."
Then Minaya Alvar Fáñez joined them:
"Listen, O Cid, noble Warrior!
God will decide who wins this battle,
And no one's worthier for a warrior's role than you.
Order an attack wherever you want:
We know our duty, we'll do our part.
Your destiny and God are on our side!"
"Stay calm," said my Cid. "Don't get excited."
Then Bishop Don Jerónimo, well armored, arrived,
And stood in front of the Warrior who was blessed with good
    fortune:
"This day, I've said a Holy Trinity mass for you.
I left my country and sought for you
Because I was hungry for killing Moors.
My sacred vows and itching hands demand
That I be placed in front, wherever you attack.
I carry a holy banner, as well as a lance,
And—may it please God!—I want to use them,
As my heart passionately wishes,
For your pleasure as well as mine.
If you are displeased, I'll turn away and leave you."
My Cid said: "I'm pleased to grant your wish.
You can see the Moors, right there. Attack them!
We'll watch you from here, and see how a bishop fights!"

                              117

Bishop Don Jerónimo spurred his horse
And rode straight at the Moorish forces.
Because God loved him, and he was lucky,
He killed two Moors with his first few strokes.
The haft of his lance broke, so he drew his sword,
And knew how to use it. Lord, how well he fought!

Dos mató con lança   e *cinco* con el espada;
los moros son muchos,   derredor le cercavan,
dávanle grandes colpes   mas nol' falsan las armas.
El que en buen ora nasco   los ojos le fincava,
enbraçó el escudo   e abaxó el asta,
aguijó a Bavieca,   el cavallo que bien anda,
ívalos ferir   de coraçón e de alma.
En las azes primeras   el Campeador entrava,
abatió a *siete*   e a *quatro* matava.
Plogo a Dios,   aquésta fue el arrancada.
Mio Cid con los suyos   cae en alcança,
veriedes quebrar tantas cuerdas   e arrancarse las estacas
e acostarse los tendales,   con huebras eran tantas.
Los de Mio Cid a los de Búcar   de las tiendas los sacan.

118

Sácanlos de las tiendas,   cáenlos en alcaz,
tanto braço con loriga   veriedes caer apart,
tantas cabeças con yelmos   que por el campo caen,
cavallos sin dueños   salir a todas partes;
siete migeros conplidos   duró el segudar.
Mio Cid al rrey Búcar   cayól' en alcaz:
"¡Acá torna, Búcar!   Venist d'allent mar,
ver te as con el Cid,   el de la barba grant,
saludar nos hemos amos   e tajaremos amista*d*."
Rrespuso Búcar al Cid: "¡Cofonda Dios tal amistad!
El espada tienes desnuda en la mano   e véot' aguijar,
assí como semeja,   en mí la quieres ensayar;
mas si el cavallo non estropieça   o comigo non caye,
non te juntarás comigo   fata dentro en la mar."
Aquí rrespuso Mio Cid: "¡Esto non será verdad!"
Buen cavallo tiene Búcar   e grandes saltos faz,
mas Bavieca el de Mio Cid   alcançándolo va.
Alcançólo el Cid a Búcar   a tres braças del mar,
arriba alçó Colada,   un grant colpe dádol' ha,
las carbonclas del yelmo   tollidas ge la[s] ha,

His lance had killed two, now his sword killed five.
It was a huge army, and Moors crowded around him,
Swinging hard, but unable to pierce his armor.
He who was born at a lucky hour watched for a while,
Then took up his shield; raised his sword;
Then spurred Babieca; the horse galloped hard,
And my Cid fought with all his heart,
Smashing into the Moors' front ranks,
Driving seven out of their saddles and killing four.
God wanted the Christians to win.
My Cid and his men made the Moors run.
You should have seen the tent ropes snap, and the stakes crack,
The poles yanked out, gilted and carved and fine.
My Cid's men made Búcar's army run for their lives.

118

Having routed the Moors, they began to pursue them.
Arms wearing mail shirts lay lonely on the ground;
Heads wearing helmets had fallen down, too;
Horses that had no riders were everywhere.
They carried the chase for a full seven miles.
Galloping up behind King Búcar, my Cid called out:
"Turn back, Búcar, from across the sea!
Come to terms with long-bearded Cid, who is me!
We ought to greet each other, and talk like friends."
Búcar replied: "The devil with that kind of friendship!
You're trying to catch me, my death's
What you want: that blade is bare, and swift.
But if my horse keeps going, by God,
I'll reach the sea before you catch up!"
My Cid declared: "That isn't going to happen!"
Búcar's horse was fast, with a long, loose stride,
But Babieca gained, and finally, six lengths from the sea, ran
    alongside.
My Cid struck the king's helmet:
Pearls and other gems were scattered,

cortól' el yelmo   e, librado todo lo ál,
fata la cintura   el espada llegado ha.
Mató a Búcar,   al rrey de allén mar,
e ganó a Tizón   que mill marcos d'oro val.
Venció la batalla   maravillosa e grant,
aquís' ondró Mio Cid   e quantos con él son.

119

Con estas ganancias   yas' ivan tornando,
sabet, todos de firme   rrobavan el campo.
A las tiendas eran llegados   dó estava | el que en buen ora
    nasco.
Mio Cid Rruy Díaz   el Campeador contado
con dos espadas   que él preciava algo
por la matança   vinía tan privado,
la cara fronzida   e almófar soltado,
cofia sobre los pelos   fronzida d'ella yaquanto.
Algo v[e]yé Mio Cid   de lo que era pagado,
alçó sos ojos,   esteva adelant catando
e vio venir a Diego   e a Fernando;
amos son fijos   del conde don Go[n]çalo.
Alegrós' Mio Cid,   fermoso sonrrisando:
"¡Venides, mios yernos,   mios fijos sodes amos!
Sé que de lidiar   bien sodes pagados,
a Carrión de vós   irán buenos mandados
cómo al rrey Búcar   avemos arrancado.
Como yo fío por Dios   e en todos los sos sanctos,
d'esta arrancada   nós iremos pagados."
De todas partes   sos vassallos van llegando,
Minaya Álbar Fáñez   essora es llegado,
el escudo trae al cuello   e todo espad[ad]o,
de los colpes de las lanças   non avié rrecabdo,
aquellos que ge los dieran   non ge lo avién logrado.
Por el cobdo ayuso   la sangre destellando,
de veínte arriba   ha moros matado:
"Grado a Dios   e al padre que está en alto

Colada went through the head and neck
And all the way to the waist.
He'd killed Búcar, and won his sword,
Tizón, worth a thousand golden marks.
It had been a marvelous battle, my Cid had won it:
He and all his men earned great honor.

119

Pursuit ended, everyone returned,
By God, loaded down with loot.
Reaching the tents, they found
Him who was born at the right time,
With a pair of swords, both worth a great deal,
Dashing across the battlefield,
Hood and helmet off, face all bare,
Cap askew on his hair.
And then something pleasant occurred:
Riding toward him he saw
Diego and Fernando,
Both of them sons of Don Gonzalo.
This made Cid happy, he smiled like the sun:
"So here you are, my sons-in-law, now become
My sons! I'm pleased at how you fought;
There'll be word of the honor you gained,
Defeating King Búcar, and Carrión will know.
By God and all his saints, this victory
Is nothing we'll be ashamed of!"
Cid's men were returning from around the field.
Then Minaya Alvar Fáñez arrived,
His battered shield, pierced in places, hung from his neck,
Marked by scattered lance thrusts,
Not one of which had touched him—
Nor had they helped those who'd made them.
Blood from the twenty Moors he'd killed
Still trickled down his arm:
"Thanks to God, and our Father on high,

e a vós, Cid,   que en buen ora fuestes nado.
Matastes a Búcar   e arrancamos el canpo.
Todos estos bienes de vós son   e de vuestros vassallos,
e vuestros yernos   aquí son ensayados,
fartos de lidiar   con moros en el campo."
Dixo Mio Cid: "Yo d'esto só pagado,
quando agora son buenos,   adelant serán preciados."
Por bien lo dixo el Cid,   mas ellos lo tovieron a mal.
Todas las ganancias   a Valencia son llegadas,
alegre es Mio Cid   con todas sus conpañas
que a la rración caye   seiscientos marcos de plata.
Los yernos de Mio Cid   quando este aver tomaron
d'esta arrancada,   que lo tenién en so salvo,
cuidaron que en sus días   nunqua serién minguados,
fueron en Valencia   muy bien arreados,
conduchos a sazones,   buenas pieles e buenos mantos.
Mucho son alegres   Mio Cid e sus vassallos.

120

Grant fue el día   [por] la cort del Campeador
después que esta batalla vencieron   e al rrey Búcar mató,
alçó la mano,   a la barba se tomó:
"Grado a Christus,   que del mundo es señor,
quando veo   lo que avía sabor
que lidiaran comigo en campo   mios yernos amos a dos;
mandados buenos irán   d'ellos a Carrión
cómo son ondrados   e aver vos [an] grant pro.

121

"Sobejanas son las ganancias   que todos an ganadas,
lo uno es nuestro,   lo otro han en salvo."

And to you, Cid, born at just the right time!
You killed Búcar, we've swept the field.
All this wealth is yours and ours.
And your sons-in-law have fought hard,
Like all the rest of our fighting men."
My Cid said: "I'm pleased. I'll say it again.
A start this fine will lead them to finer."
He meant these words, but the brothers thought he despised
    them.

They carried their loot into Valencia.
My Cid was happy, and so were his warriors,
Each of whom earned six hundred silver marks.

Between them, the Carrión brothers thought,
This was surely riches enough
To last the rest of their lives.
They returned to Valencia with their purses loaded,
From which they bought themselves fine furs and clothing.
My Cid and all his men were delighted.

120

It was a wonderful day at the Warrior's court,
With the battle won and King Búcar dead.
My Cid raised his hand and tugged on his beard:
"Thanks to Christ, great Lord of this world,
For letting me see what I've longed for—
My new sons beside me, fighting our war!
Good news will travel to Carrión: honor
For my sons, and the promise of much, much more.

121

"The spoils of this war are rich, and properly shared.
I take mine, and you take yours—but save some!"

Mandó Mio Cid,   el que en buen ora nasco,
d'esta batalla   que han arrancado
que todos prisiessen   so derecho contado
e la su quinta   non fuesse olbidado.
Assí lo fazen todos,   ca eran acordados,
cayéronle en quinta   al Cid seixcientos cavallos
e otras azémilas   e camellos largos,
tantos son de muchos   que non serién contados.

122

Todas estas ganancias   fızo el Canpeador:
"¡Grado a Dios   que del mundo es señor!
Antes fu minguado,   agora rrico só,
que he aver e tierra   e oro e onor
e son mios yernos   ifantes de Carrión.
Arranco las lides   como plaze al Criador,
moros e cristianos   de mí han grant pavor;
allá dentro en Marruecos,   ó las mezquitas son,
que abrán de mí salto   quiçab alguna noch;
ellos lo temen,   ca non lo piesso yo.
No los iré buscar,   en Valencia seré yo,
ellos me darán parias,   con ayuda del Criador,
que paguen a mí   o a qui yo ovier sabor."
Grandes son los gozos en Valencia   con Mio Cid el Canpeado[r]
de todas sus conpañas   e de todos sus vassallos;
grandes son los gozos   de sus yernos amos a dos:
d'aquesta arrancada   que lidiaron de coraçón
valía de cinco mill marcos   ganaron amos a dos;
muchos' tienen por rricos   los ifantes de Carrión;
ellos con los otros   vinieron a la cort.
Aquí está con Mio Cid   el obispo do Jerónimo,
el bueno de Álbar Fáñez,   cavallero lidiador,
e otros muchos   que crió el Campeador;
quando entraron   los ifantes de Carrión,
rrecibiólos Minaya   por Mio Cid el Campeador:
"Acá venid, cuñados,   que más valemos por vós."

My Cid, he who was born at the right hour, was heard
And obeyed. They counted out accurate sums,
My Cid's great share among them,
And everything quietly, calmly done:
The Warrior's share was six hundred horses,
Plus many mules and camels—
Far too much for this song to tell!

122

But that was how much the Warrior won:
"I thank you, Lord, ruler of this world!
I began poor, and now I have earned
So much—land, and gold, and honor,
And the Carrión heirs have become my sons.
My victories, Lord, come
At your pleasure: Moors and Christians fear me.
In far-off Morocco, inside their mosques, they hear me
Coming in the darkness, and they tremble,
Though conquering them is not my plan.
I'm not on the hunt: right here is where I am,
In my Valencia. Morocco may pay me tribute,
Lord, if that is what you
Want—me, or anyone else I tell them to pay."

How they were celebrating, in great Valencia,
All his men and himself, my Cid, the Warrior!
The Carrión pair were just as delighted,
Their spirits fairly soaring as they learned
How much they had won, how much they were worth:
Five thousand marks. They were rich; they had earned it!
They came to court, these Carrión brothers,
Along with all the others:
Alvar Fáñez, Bishop Don Jerónimo,
And everyone who regularly attended there.
The Carrións were welcomed by Minaya, on behalf

Assí como llegaron,   pagós' el Campeador:
"Evades aquí, yernos,   la mi mugier de pro
e amas la[s] mis fijas,   don Elvira e doña Sol;
bien vos abracen   e sírvanvos de coraçón.
Venciemos moros en campo   e matamos
a aquel rrey Búcar,   provado traidor.
Grado a Sancta María,   madre del nuestro señor Dios,
d'estos nuestros casamientos   vós abredes honor.
Buenos mandados irán   a tierras de Carrión."

123

A estas palabras   fabló Ferrán Gonçález:
"Grado al Criador   e a vós, Cid ondrado,
tantos avemos de averes   que no son contados,
por vós avemos ondra   e avemos lidiado;
pensad de lo otro,   que lo nuestro tenémoslo en salvo."
Vassallos de Mio Cid   seyénse sonrrisando:
quien lidiara mejor   o quien fuera en alcanço,
mas non fallavan í   a Diego ni a Ferrando.
Por aquestos juegos   que ivan levantando
e las noches e los días   tan mal los escarmentando,
tan mal se consejaron   estos iffantes amos.
Amos saliero[n] apart,   veramientre son ermanos,
d'esto que ellos fablaron   nós parte non ayamos:
"Vayamos pora Carrión,   aquí mucho detardamos;
los averes que tenemos   grandes son e sobejanos,
mientra que visquiéremos   despender no lo podremos.

124

"Pidamos nuestras mugieres   al Cid Campeador,
digamos que las levaremos   a tierras de Carrión
[e] enseñar las hemos   dó las heredades son.

Of my Cid, the great Warrior:
"Come in, kinsmen; we're proud to have you!"
And my Cid, the Warrior, was also pleased:
"Come here, my sons! Let my dignified wife
And my daughters, Doña Elvira and Doña Sol,
Embrace you and serve you from the bottom of their hearts.
Thanks to Saint Mary, mother of our Lord!
Your weddings have brought you honor;
Good news of you will go to Carrión."

123

Fernando answered for them both:
"Thanks to God, and to you, honored Cid!
We've gained uncountable wealth.
Our honor depends on you, and for you we have fought,
Defeating the Moors in battle, and killing that King Búcar,
Truly a proven traitor.
Our thoughts now turn from fighting, with our fortune secure."
But my Cid's soldiers were smiling,
For they'd been right there, in battle and final chase,
Not seeing Diego or Fernando in any of those places.
They joked about this, and laughed, again and again,
Rubbing it in, over and over, all night, every day;
They made wicked fun of both Carrións.
The brothers sneaked out—what a fine pair!—
And began to plan what we're not supposed to know:
"We've stayed here too long; let's head for home.
We're wealthier than wealthy, now:
In the rest of our lives we couldn't spend it all!

124

"Let's ask the Cid to let us take our wives
And show them the world at Carrión,
And all the land we own.

Sacar las hemos de Valencia   de poder del Campeador,
después en la carrera   feremos nuestro sabor,
ante que nos rretrayan   lo que cuntió del león;
nós de natura somos   de condes de Carrión.
Averes levaremos grandes   que valen grant valor,
escarniremos   las fijas del Canpeador."
"D'aquestos averes   sienpre seremos rricos omnes,
podremos casar con fijas   de rreyes o de enperadores,
ca de natura somos   de condes de Carrión.
Assí las escarniremos   a las fijas del Campeador,
antes que nos rretrayan   lo que fue del león."
Con aqueste consejo   amos tornados son,
fabló Ferrán Gonçález   e fizo callar la cort:
"¡Sí vos vala el Criador,   Cid Campeador!
Que plega a doña Ximena   e primero a vós
e a Minaya Álbar Fáñez   e a quantos aquí son:
dadnos nuestras mugieres   que avemos a bendiciones,
levar las hemos   a nuestras tierras de Carrión,
meter las hemos   en las villas
que les diemos por arras   e por onores,
verán vuestras fijas   lo que avemos nós,
los fijos que oviéremos   en qué avrán partición."
Nos' curiava de ser afontado   el Cid | Campeador:
"Dar vos he mis fijas   e algo de lo mío;
vós les diestes villas por arras   en tierras de Carrión,
yo quiero les dar axuvar   *tres* mill marcos de plata;
dar vos é mulas e palafrés   muy gruessos de sazón,
cavallos pora en diestro,   fuertes e corredores,
e muchas vestiduras   de paños de ciclatones;
dar vos he dos espadas,   a Colada e a Tizón,
bien lo sabedes vós   que las gané a guisa de varón.
Mios fijos sodes amos   quando mis fijas vos do,
allá me levades   las telas del coraçón.
Que lo sepan en Gallizia   e en Castiella e en León
con qué rriqueza enbío   mios yernos amos a dos.
A mis fijas sirvades,   que vuestras mugieres son,
si bien las servides   yo vos rrendré buen galardón."
Atorgado lo han esto   los iffantes de Carrión,

Once we've got them away from Valencia, and their powerful
    father,
And we're out of his reach, we can do what we like—
Instead of staying here, teased by the tale of that lion!
We're heirs of the grand counts of Carrión!
We'll carry our riches with us,
We'll massacre these daughters of our great Warrior!"
"We've got gold enough to be rich forever!
We could marry the daughters of kings or emperors—
Because we're heirs of the counts of Carrión!
We'll beat them to a bloody pulp, these Warrior's daughters,
And never hear another word about that lion!"
Their minds made up, they returned to court.
Asking for silence, Fernando said:
"With the Lord's blessing, Warrior Cid!
If Doña Jimena agrees, and you, too,
As well as Minaya Alvar Fáñez, and many others here,
Let us have our wives, as we have already been granted them,
So we can bring them to our Carrión home
And give them, in person, the lands we owe them,
In all honor, as bridal presents,
And so your daughters can see what we own
And what our children will inherit, when they are born."
The Warrior said: "You will have my daughters, and something
    more."
My Cid had no suspicion of possible shame or injury.
"You gave them villas, as marriage gifts,
And I will add three thousand marks,
And give you mules and sleek and sturdy palfreys,
And strong, fast warhorses,
And quantities of wool and fine silk clothing.
And two swords, Colada and Tizón—
Which as you know I won in wars.
When I gave you my daughters, you became my sons—
Though parting with them is like pulling my heartstrings.
Let them know in Galicia, and in Castile and León,
That both my new sons have been richly endowed!
Be good to my daughters, who are now your wives:

aquí rreciben   las fijas del Campeador,
conpieçan a rrecebir   lo que el Cid mandó;
quando son pagados   a todo so sabor,
ya mandavan cargar   iffantes de Carrión.
Grandes son las nuevas   por Valencia la mayor,
todos prenden armas   e cavalgan a vigor
porque escurren sus fijas del Campeador   a tierras de Carrión.
Ya quieren cavalgar,   en espidimiento son;
amas ermanas   don Elvira e doña Sol
fincaron los inojos   ant'el Cid Campeador:
"¡Merced vos pedimos, padre,   sí vos vala el Criador!
Vós nos engendrastes,   nuestra madre nos parió;
delant sodes amos,   señora e señor.
Agora nos enviades   a tierras de Carrión,
debdo nos es a cunplir   lo que mandáredes vós.
Assí vos pedimos merced   nós amas a dos
que ayades vuestros mensajes   en tierras de Carrión."
Abraçólas Mio Cid   e saludólas amas a dos.

125

Él fizo aquesto,   la madre lo doblava:
"Andad, fijas, d'aquí   el Criador vos vala,
de mí e de vuestro padre   bien avedes nuestra gracia.
Id a Carrión   dó sodes heredadas,
assí como yo tengo,   bien vos he casadas."
Al padre e a la madre   las manos les besavan;
amos las bendixieron   e diéronles su gracia.
Mio Cid e los otros   de cavalgar pensavan
a grandes guarnimientos,   a cavallos e armas.
Ya salién los ifantes   de Valencia la clara
espi[di]endos' de las dueñas   e de todas sus compañas.
Por la huerta de Valencia   teniendo salién armas,
alegre va Mio Cid   con todas sus compañas.

If you treat them well, you will be more than proud."
The Carrión brothers agreed to everything.
And then my Cid's four married children
Were given what he had ordered for them.
When their hands received those things,
The Carrión brothers had them loaded.
Valencia was much excited by their going:
Men put on their armor and galloped out
To escort the travelers on their way.
They were ready. But before they could leave,
The sisters, Doña Elvira and Doña Sol,
Fell to their knees, in front of their father:
"Father, we ask a favor, in the name of the Lord!
You created us, our mother brought us into the world:
We kneel to you both, our mother and father.
You're sending us, now, to Carrión,
And it is our duty to do as you say.
But we ask the two of you
To send us messages, in that faraway land."
My Cid agreed, and embraced them.

125

And then their mother said and did the same things:
"Go, daughters, and may God protect you as you leave!
You have your father's blessing, as well as mine.
Go to Carrión and enjoy your wedding gifts.
It seems to me you've married well."
They kissed their father's hands, and their mother's.
My Cid and all the others rode out with them,
All dressed to the hilt, all armored.
Thus the Carrións left Valencia, that shining city,
Saying farewell to the ladies, and to all the men,
Riding, escorted, across the farmers' fields,
My Cid and everyone else immensely pleased.
He who first lifted his sword at just the right time

Violo en los avueros   el que en buen ora cinxo espada
que estos casamientos   non serién sin alguna tacha;
nos' puede rrepentir,   que casadas las ha amas.

126

"¿Ó eres mio sobrino,   tú, Félez Muñoz?
Primo eres de mis fijas amas   d'alma e de coraçón.
Mándot' que vayas con ellas   fata dentro en Carrión,
verás las heredades   que a mis fijas dadas son,
con aquestas nuevas   vernás al Campeador."
Dixo Félez Muñoz: "Plazme d'alma e de coraçón."
Minaya Álbar Fáñez   ante Mio Cid se paró;
"Tornémosnos, Cid,   a Valencia la mayor,
que si a Dios ploguiere   e al padre Criador,
ir las hemos ver   a tierras de Carrion."
"A Dios vos acomendamos,   don Elvira e doña Sol,
atales cosas fed   que en plazer caya a nós."
Rrespondién los yernos: "¡Assí lo mande Dios!"
Grandes fueron los duelos   a la departición,
el padre con las fijas   lloran de coraçón,
assí fazían   los cavalleros del Campeador.
"¡Oyas, sobrino,   tú, Félez Muñoz!
Por Molina iredes,   í yazredes una noch,
saludad a mio amigo   el moro Avengalvón;
rreciba a mios yernos   como él pudier mejor.
Dil' que enbío mis fijas   a tierras de Carrión,
de lo que ovieren huebos   sírvalas a so sabor,
desí escúrralas fasta Medina   por la mi amor;
de quanto él fiziere   yol' dar[é] por ello buen galardón."
Cuemo la uña de la carne   ellos partidos son,
yas' tornó pora Valencia   el que en buen ora nasció.
Piénsanse de ir   los ifantes de Carrión,
por Sancta María d'Alvarrazín   fazían la posada.
Aguijan quanto pueden   ifantes de Carrión:
felos en Molina   con el moro Avengalvón.
El moro, quando lo sopo,   plógol' de coraçón,

Could see these marriages were far from perfect,
But he who had made them could not regret them.

126

"My nephew," he called, "Félix Muñoz, where are you?
My daughters' first cousin, who loves them with all his soul!
Let me send you with them, as far as Carrión;
Look at the lands they've both received
As wedding gifts. Come back and tell me what you've seen."
Félix Muñoz said, "With all my heart and soul."
Minaya Alvar Fáñez then intervened:
"My Cid, our escorting is done, we ought to turn back.
If it pleases God and our Lord,
Later we'll see them once more in Carrión."
And to the girls he said: "We commend you to God.
May good things come to you."
Their husbands answered: "May God command it!"
At this point true departure began, and brought sorrow with it:
Father and daughters wept from deep in their hearts,
As did the Warrior's men.
"Hear me, my nephew, Félix Muñoz!
Go to Molina, spend the night,
And greet my friend, Abengalbón, the Moor;
Ask him to give my sons-in-law a friendly welcome.
Tell him I've sent my daughters to Carrión.
I'd like him to do whatever needs to be done for them:
Whatever he does, I'll pay him back, and more."
Saying goodbye was like tearing flesh.
Then he who was born at the right time rode home.
The Carrións started off, planning to spend the night
At Santa María de Albarracín,
By riding as fast as they might.
Then they stopped at Molina, with the Moor, Abengalbón,
Who was pleased that they had come,
Receiving them with real affection.

saliólos rrecebir   con grandes avorozes,
¡Dios, qué bien los sirvió   a todo so sabor!
Otro día mañana   con ellos cavalgó,
con dozientos cavalleros   escurrirlos mandó;
ivan trocir los montes,   los que dizen de Luzón.
A las fijas del Cid   el moro sus donas dio,
buenos seños cavallos   a los ifantes de Carrión.
Trocieron Arbuxuelo   e llegaron a Salón,
ó dizen el Ansarera   ellos posados son.
Tod' esto les fızo el moro   por el amor del Cid Campead[or].
Ellos veyén la rriqueza   que el moro sacó,
entr'amos ermanos   consejaron tración:
"Ya pues que a dexar avemos   fijas del Campeador,
si pudiéssemos matar   el moro Avengalvón,
quanta rriquiza tiene   aver la iemos nós.
Tan en salvo lo abremos   como lo de Carrión,
nunqua avrié derecho de nós   el Cid Campeador."
Quando esta falsedad   dizién los de Carrión,
un moro latinado   bien ge lo entendió;
non tiene poridad,   díxolo [a] Avengalvón:
"Acayaz, cúriate d'éstos,   ca eres mio señor,
tu muert oí cossejar   a los ifantes de Carrión."

127

El moro Avengalvón   mucho era buen barragán,
co[n] dozientos que tiene   iva cavalgar,
armas iva teniendo,   parós' ante los ifantes,
de lo que el moro dixo   a los ifantes non plaze:
"¡Dezidme qué vos fız,   ifantes de Carrión!
Yo sirviéndovos sin art   e vós, pora mí, muert consejastes.
Si no lo dexás   por Mio Cid el de Bivar,
tal cosa vos faría   que por el mundo sonás
e luego levaría sus fijas   al Campeador leal;
vós nu[n]qua en Carrión   entrariedes jamás.

Lord, he did all he could to delight them!
When they left, early the next morning,
He and two hundred horsemen went with them, as an escort;
They rode together, across the heights of Luzón.
The Moor gave each of my Cid's daughters a horse,
And one to each of the Carrión brothers.
They reached the shores of the Arbujuelo, then the Jalón,
And stopped for the night at Ansarera.
The Moor did these things for love of our Warrior.
But the Carrións saw what wealth the Moor
Possessed, and planned to betray him:
"We know we'll soon be rid of these girls.
If we can kill Abengalbón, this Moor,
Everything he owns will be ours:
That's as sure as what we own in Carrión.
Warrior Cid can't do anything to us."
These treacherous words were overheard
By a Moor who understood Spanish,
Who went straight to Abengalbón:
"My lord, watch out for them:
These Carrión fellows are plotting your death."

127

Abengalbón was sturdy, young, and bold,
Riding with two hundred men of his own,
Well-armored. He came to the Carrións,
And what he said was hardly music to their ears:
"Tell me, please, what I have done to you noblemen?
I've gone far out of my way—and you're planning my death?
Love for my Cid is all that keeps me
From doing things to you that would ring in the whole world's
    ears!
And then I'd bring his daughters back to the Warrior.
You'd never see Carrión again!

128

"Aquím' parto de vós   como de malos e de traidores.
Iré con vuestra gracia,   don Elvira e doña Sol,
poco precio las nuevas   de los de Carrión.
Dios lo quiera e lo mande,   que de tod' el mundo es señor,
d'aqueste casamiento   que grade el Canpeador."
Esto les ha dicho   e el moro se tornó,
teniendo iva armas   al trocir de Salón,
cuemo de buen seso   a Molina se tornó.
Ya movieron del Ansarera   los ifantes de Carrión,
acójense a andar   de día e de noch,
a siniestro dexan Atienza,   una peña muy fuert,
la sierra de Miedes   passáronla esto[n]z,
por los Montes Claros   aguijan a espolón,
a siniestro dexan a Griza   que Álamos pobló,
allí son caños   dó a Elpha encerró,
a diestro dexan a Sant Estevan,   más cae aluén.
Entrados son los ifantes   al rrobredo de Corpes,
los montes son altos,   las rramas pujan con las núes;
¡e las bestias fieras   que andan aderredor!
Fallaron un vergel   con una linpia fuent,
mandan fincar la tienda   ifantes de Carrión,
con quantos que ellos traen   í yazen essa noch,
con sus mugieres en braços   demuéstranles amor,
¡mal ge lo cunplieron   quando salié el sol!
Mandaron cargar las azémilas   con grandes averes,
cogida han la tienda   dó albergaron de noch,
adelant eran idos   los de criazón,
assí lo mandaron   los ifantes de Carrión
que non í fincás ninguno,   mugier nin varón,
sinon amas sus mugieres   doña Elvira e doña Sol:
deportarse quieren con ellas   a todo su sabor.
Todos eran idos,   ellos *quatro* solos son,
tanto mal comidieron   los ifantes de Carrión:
"Bien lo creades,   don Elvira e doña Sol,

128

"I turn my back to you, here—you scum, you traitors.
With your permission, Doña Elvira and Doña Sol:
I think very little of these Carrión fellows!
May God, who rules the world, take care
That my Cid does not regret this marriage affair."
He'd spoken his mind; the Moor swung around
And, riding sensibly and carefully,
He and his men returned to Molina.
The Carrións left Ansarera,
Not stopping by day or night,
Passing to the left of the Atienza cliff,
Over the Miedes mountains,
Dashing over the hills of Claros,
Riding to the left of Griza, built by Alamos—
In the caves where he left Elpha in chains—
Went hurriedly by San Esteban, to the right,
And came to the Corpes woods,
Where oaks grow so tall their branches almost scrape the sky,
And fierce wild beasts are everywhere.
They found a clearing, through which a spring went running,
And ordered a tent set up.
They slept there, that night, with all their men,
Often embracing their wives, and showing their love—
But how terribly they repaid it, after the sun came up!
They ordered their precious belongings loaded;
The tent they had slept in was folded,
Along with their personal things.
Then the Carrións ordered that no one stay,
Not one man or woman,
Except their wives, Doña Elvira and Doña Sol:
They wished to enjoy them, completely alone.
Everyone left, as they'd been commanded.
The Carrións' plan was a foul one:
"Pay close attention, Doña Elvira and Doña Sol:

aquí seredes escarnidas   en estos fieros montes.
Oy nos partiremos   e dexadas seredes de nós,
non abredes part   en tierras de Carrión.
Irán aquestos mandados   al Cid Campeador,
nós vengaremos por aquésta   la [*desondra*] del león."
Allí les tuellen   los mantos e los pelliçones,
páranlas en cuerpos   e en camisas e en ciclatones.
Espuelas tienen calçadas   los malos traidores,
en mano prenden las cinchas   fuertes e duradores.
Quando esto vieron las dueñas,   fablava doña Sol:
"¡Por Dios vos rrogamos,   don Diego e don Ferrando!
Dos espadas tenedes   fuertes e tajadores,
al una dizen Colada   e al otra Tizón,
cortandos las cabeças,   mártires seremos nós,
moros e cristianos   departirán d'esta rrazón,
que por lo que nós merecemos   no lo prendemos nós.
Atan malos ensienplos   non fagades sobre nós;
si nós fuéremos majadas,   abiltaredes a vós,
rretraer vos lo an   en vistas o en cortes."
Lo que rruegan las dueñas   non les ha ningún pro,
essora les conpieçan a dar   los ifantes de Carrión,
con las cinchas corredizas   májanlas tan sin sabor,
con las espuelas agudas   dón ellas an mal sabor
rronpién las camisas e las carnes   a ellas amas a dos,
linpia salié la sangre   sobre los ciclatones;
ya lo sienten ellas   en los sos coraçones.
¡Quál ventura serié ésta,   si ploguiesse al Criador,
que assomasse essora   el Cid Campeador!
Tanto las majaron   que sin cosimente son,
sangrientas en las camisas   e todos los ciclatones.
Cansados son de ferir   ellos amos a dos,
ensayandos' amos   quál dará mejores colpes.
Ya non pueden fablar   don Elvira e doña Sol;
por muertas las dexaron   en el rrobredo de Corpes.

Today, in these fierce mountains, we'll whip the skin off your flesh.
Then we'll leave you, abandon you here.
You'll never own Carrión land.
Tell this to your Warrior father, the Cid:
Here is our revenge for all that lion business!"
Then they pulled off the girls' mantles and capes,
Stripped them to their shifts and their filmy silk cloaks.
They put on their spurs, these miserable traitors,
Then unbuckled the heavy saddle straps, and pulled them free,
And took the hardened leather in their hands.
Seeing all this, Doña Sol spoke:
"We beg you, husbands, in the name of God!
Take your two swords, sharp and strong—
One named Colada, and the other Tizón—
Cut off our heads, let us be martyred!
Moors and Christians will cry out against you,
We have not deserved what you're doing to us.
What a horrible shame to commit!
If we are beaten and dishonored
It will fall on you, by law or in the king's court."
The brothers did not hear a word they said,
But began to beat them, whipping at their heads
And bodies, digging sharp spurs into their flesh,
Ripping both their clothes and skin.
Blood stains grew on their long silk cloaks.
How deep in their hearts they suffered!
What wonderful fortune it would have been
Had God, at just that moment, sent Warrior Cid to the scene!
The girls were whipped so hard they had no feeling,
Bloody shifts sodden, blood dragging long silk cloaks to the
      ground.
Both brothers attacked and whipped away,
Yelling, competing who could whip better,
Until the girls were barely conscious, and the Carrións tired.
They left them for dead on the forest floor.

129

Leváronles los mantos   e las pieles armiñas,
mas déxanlas marridas   en briales e en camisas
e a las aves del monte   e a las bestias de la fiera guisa.
Por muertas la[s] dexaron,   sabed, que non por bivas.
¡Quál ventura serié   si assomás essora el Cid Campeador!

130

Los ifantes de Carrión en el rrobredo de Corpes | por muertas las
    dexaron
que el una al otra   nol' torna rrecabdo.
Por los montes dó ivan   ellos ívanse alabando:
"De nuestros casamientos   agora somos vengados;
non las deviemos tomar por varraganas | si non fuéssemos
    rrogados,
pues nuestras parejas   non eran pora en braços.
La desondra del león   assís' irá vengando."

131

Alabandos' ivan   los ifantes de Carrión,
mas yo vos diré   d'aquel Félez Muñoz:
sobrino era   del Cid Campeador;
mandáronle ir adelante,   mas de su grado non fue.
En la carrera dó iva   dolió l' el coraçón,
de todos los otros   aparte se salió,
en un monte espesso   Félez Muñoz se metió
fasta que viesse venir   sus primas amas a dos
o qué an fecho   los ifantes de Carrión.
Violos venir   e oyó una rrazón,
ellos nol' v[e]yén   ni dend sabién rraçión;
sabet bien que si ellos le viessen   non escapara de muert.

129

They rode away with costly cloaks and furs,
Leaving their wives lying, half-naked,
For mountain birds and forest beasts to eat as they pleased.
They were sure the girls were dead.

130

What luck it would have been, had Warrior Cid appeared!
But the noble Carrións rode through the woods,
Their wives apparently dead,
Unable to help each other or themselves.
They went galloping down the mountain:
"Now we've had our revenge for these weddings!
They weren't worth taking as mistresses,
Had we been properly approached;
They surely weren't good enough for marriage.
Now we've had our revenge for that lion business!"

131

And on they went, boasting as they rode.
Now I need to tell you what Félix Muñoz,
Warrior Cid's nephew, had been doing.
He too had been ordered to leave, but did not want to.
He went down the road, his heart heavy,
But stayed away from the troupe
Of Carrión servants. He went off the road,
Into a thick wood from which he hoped to see his cousins
    coming
And learn what the Carrións were up to.
He heard their horses and heard their talk;
They did not see him or suspect his presence,

Vanse los ifantes,   aguijan a espolón;
por el rrastro   tornós' Félez Muñoz,
falló sus primas   amortecidas amas a dos.
Llamando: "¡Primas, primas!,"   luego descavalgó,
arrendó el cavallo,   a ellas adeliñó:
"¡Ya primas, las mis primas,   don Elvira e doña Sol,
mal se ensayaron   los ifantes de Carrión!
¡A Dios plega e a Sancta María   que dent prendan ellos mal
    galardón!"
Valas tornando   a ellas amas a dos,
tanto son de traspuestas   que non pueden dezir nada.
Partiéronsele las telas   de dentro del coraçón,
llamando: "¡Primas, primas,   don Elvira e don Sol!
¡Despertedes, primas,   por amor del Criador!
¡Mie[n]tra es el día,   ante que entre la noch,
los ganados fieros   non nos coman en aqueste mont!"
Van rrecordando   don Elvira e doña Sol,
abrieron los ojos   e vieron a Félez Muñoz:
"¡Esforçadvos, primas,   por amor del Criador!
De que non me fallaren   los ifantes de Carrión,
a grant priessa   seré buscado yo;
si Dios non nos vale   aquí morremos nós."
Tan a grant duelo   fablava doña Sol:
"Sí vos lo meresca, mio primo,   nuestro padre el Canpeador,
¡dandos del agua,   sí vos vala el Criador!"
Con un sonbrero   que tiene Félez Muñoz,
nuevo era e fresco,   que de Valéncial' sacó,
cogió del agua en él   e a sus primas dio,
mucho son lazradas   e amas las fartó.
Tanto las rrogó   fata que las assentó,
valas conortando   e metiendo coraçón
fata que esfuerçan,   e amas las tomó
e privado   en el cavallo las cavalgó,
con el so manto   a amas las cubrió.
El cavallo priso por la rrienda   e luego dent las part[ió],
todos tres señeros   por los rrobredos de Corpes,
entre noch e día   salieron de los montes,
a las aguas de Duero   ellos arribados son,

But had they seen him, believe me, it would have meant his
    death.
The Carrións went by, galloping fast.
Then Félix Muñoz retraced their tracks,
And found his cousins, both half-dead.
Crying, "O cousins, my cousins," he leaped from his horse,
Tied its reins to a tree, and went to the girls:
"Ah, cousins, my cousins Doña Sol and Doña Elvira!
What horrible things these Carrións have done!
May it please the Lord and his mother that they pay for this!"
He carefully turned them over,
But their bodies had been too shocked, they could not speak.
He felt the strings of his heart breaking apart,
And cried, "Cousins! Cousins! Doña Elvira, Doña Sol!
Wake up, cousins, in the name of God!
It's still daylight, but the night is coming,
Wild mountain beasts will eat us all!"
They started coming back to themselves,
Opening their eyes, and recognizing Félix Muñoz.
"Quick, cousins, for the love of God!
When they find I've left them, they'll hurry back here,
And without God's help, this is where we'll die."
Slowly, clearly suffering, Doña Sol spoke:
"Cousin, as you value my father, the Warrior,
Give us water, in the name of God!"
Using a clean new hat—just bought
In Valencia—Félix Muñoz
Brought water for them both,
And in their great pain they drank it down.
He kept insisting that they sit up,
Urging, consoling. At last they were sitting,
And he urged them on, until at last
He got them to his horse, lifted them up,
Covering them both with his cloak,
Then quickly took the reins and led them away.
Completely alone, in the Corpes forest,
He got them out of the mountains by the end of the day.
When they got to the river Duero, he made his way

a la torre de don Urraca   elle las dexó.
A Sant Estevan   vino Félez Muñoz,
falló a Diego Téllez,   el que de Álbar Fáñez fue.
Quando él lo oyó,   pesól' de coraçón,
priso bestias   e vestidos de pro,
iva rrecebir   a don Elvira e a doña Sol;
en Sant Estevan   dentro las metió,
quanto él mejor puede   allí las ondró.
Los de Sant Estevan   siempre mesurados son,
quando sabién esto,   pesóles de coraçón,
a llas fijas del Cid   danles esfuerço;
allí sovieron ellas   fata que sanas son.
Alabandos' seían   los ifantes de Carrión.
De cuer pesó esto   al buen rrey don Alfonso.
Van aquestos mandados   a Valencia la mayor,
quando ge lo dizen   a Mio Cid el Campeador,
una grand ora   pensó e comidió;
alçó la su mano,   a la barba se tomó:
"Grado a Christus,   que del mundo es señor,
quando tal ondra me an dada   los ifantes de Carrión;
par aquesta barba   que nadi non messó,
non la lograrán   los ifantes de Carrión,
¡que a mis fijas   bien las casaré yo!"
Pesó a Mio Cid   e a toda su cort
e [a] Álbar Fáñez   d'alma e de coraçón.
Cavalgó Minaya   con Pero Vermúez
e Martín Antolínez,   el burgalés de pro,
con *dozientos* cavalleros   quales Mio Cid mandó;
díxoles fuertemientre   que andidiessen de día e de noch,
aduxiessen a sus fijas   a Valencia la mayor.
Non lo detardan   el mandado de su señor,
apriessa cavalgan,   andan los días e las noches,
vinieron a Gormaz,   un castiello tan fuert,
í albergaron   por verdad una noch.
A Sant Estevan   el mandado llegó
que vinié Minaya   por sus primas amas a dos.
Varones de Sant Estevan   a guisa de muy pros
rreciben a Minaya   e a todos sus varones,

To Doña Urraca's tower, and left them there.
He went on to San Esteban, and located
Diego Téllez, one of Alvar Fáñez's men,
Who was deeply upset by what he heard.
Quickly gathering horses and fine clothes,
He went to welcome the great Cid's daughters,
And took them to San Esteban,
Honoring them as warmly as he could.
San Esteban's people are even-tempered, thoughtful:
When they heard what had happened, it hurt them,
And they took care of my Cid's daughters,
Who stayed there until they were well again.
The Carrións went on boasting, glorifying themselves.
Good King Alfonso was deeply moved.
Word of what had happened reached Valencia,
And when my Cid, the Warrior, was told,
He spent a long, long time thinking it over;
He raised his hand and tugged at his beard:
"I'm thankful to Christ, Lord of this world,
For the honor I've had from the Carrión heirs!
By this beard, which no one has ever pulled,
These Carrións won't be exulting for long,
Because I let them marry my daughters!"
He was troubled at heart, as were Alvar Fáñez
And all the members of his court.
My Cid sent Minaya, with Pedro Bermúdez,
And that fine man from Burgos, Martín Antolínez,
And two hundred well-armed men,
Telling them to ride all day and all night
And bring his daughters back to Valencia.
They did not keep him waiting:
They galloped hard, all day and all night,
Until they came to San Esteban's fortress, Gormaz,
Where, truth to tell, they rested one night.
San Esteban had heard, by this time,
That Minaya was coming for his two cousins;
The people there were glad to welcome
Minaya and all his companions,

presentan a Minaya   essa noch grant enfurción,
non ge lo quiso tomar,   mas mucho ge lo gradió:
"Gracias, varones de Sant Estevan,   que sodes coñoscedores,
por aquesta ondra que vós diestes   a esto que nos cuntió;
mucho vos lo gradece,   allá dó está, Mio Cid el Canpeador,
assí lo fago yo   que aquí estó.
Afé Dios de los cielos   que vos dé dent buen galardón."
Todos ge lo gradecen   e sos pagados son,
adeliñan a posar   pora folgar essa noch.
Minaya va ver   sus primas dó son,
en él fincan los ojos   don Elvira e doña Sol:
"Atanto vos lo gradimos   como si viéssemos al Criador
e vós a él lo gradid   quando bivas somos nós.

132

"En los días de vagar   toda nuestra rrencura sabremos contar."
Lloravan de los ojos   las dueñas e Álbar Fáñez
e Pero Vermúez   otro tanto las ha:
"Don Elvira e doña Sol,   cuidado non ayades
quando vós sodes sanas e bivas   e sin otro mal.
Buen casamiento perdiestes,   mejor podredes ganar.
¡Aún veamos el día   que vos podamos vengar!"
Í yazen essa noche   e tan grand gozo que fazen.
Otro día mañana   piensan de cavalgar,
los de Sant Estevan   escurriéndolos van
fata Rrío d'Amor,   dándoles solaz;
d'allent se espidieron d'ellos,   piénsanse de tornar
e Minaya con las dueñas   iva cabadelant.
Trocieron Alcoceva,   a diestro dexan Gormaz,
ó dizen Bado de Rrey   allá ivan pas[s]ar,
a la casa de Berlanga   posada presa han.
Otro día mañana   métense a andar,
a qual dizen Medina   ivan albergar
e de Medina a Molina   en otro día van.
Al moro Avengalvón   de coraçón le plaz,

Offering them a fine feast, that night,
Which Minaya really did not want, and gracefully declined:
"My thanks, people of San Esteban, for your thoughtfulness,
You who know the misfortune that has fallen on us.
We are very grateful, both my Cid, the Warrior,
And I, who am going to be so briefly here.
God on high will surely reward you!"
His graciousness was pleasing to them all;
Everyone went to take their rest.
Minaya went to where his cousins were lodged.
When Doña Elvira and Doña Sol saw him
They said: "You're as welcome to our eyes as God himself!
You find us alive only because of him.
When things are calmer, we'll tell you what we have suffered."

132

Both ladies wept, and so did Alvar Fáñez,
And Pedro Bermúdez told them:
"Doña Elvira, Doña Sol: don't upset yourselves,
You're healthy, you're alive, there's no need to worry.
You've lost a good marriage, but you might get a better one.
Just you wait till we can revenge you!"
They rested there, that night, feeling very happy.
The next morning, when they were ready to ride,
San Esteban people escorted them as far
As Rio d'Amor, to help keep things cheerful,
Then said their farewells and went home.
Minaya and the ladies traveled on,
Crossing Alcoceba, with Gormaz to their right,
Going toward Vado de Rey, on the way
To Berlanga, the town where they would rest.
Early the next morning they traveled on,
Toward a town called Medinaceli, where they rested again,
Then spent the next day riding to Molina.
There, Albengalbón, the Moor, greeted them warmly,
Riding out to show his welcome;

saliólos a rrecebir   de buena voluntad,
por amor de Mio Cid   rrica cena les da.
Dent pora Valencia   adeliñechos van;
al que en buen ora nasco   llegava el mensaje,
privado cavalga,   a rrecebirlos sale,
armas iva teniendo   e grand gozo que faze,
Mio Cid a sus fijas   ívalas abraçar,
besándolas a amas,   tornós' de sonrrisar:
"¡Venides, mis fijas,   Dios vos curie de mal!
Yo tomé el casamiento,   mas non osé dezir ál.
Plega al Criador,   que en cielo está,
que vos vea mejor casadas   d'aquí en adelant.
¡De mios yernos de Carrión   Dios me faga vengar!"
Besaron las manos   las fijas al padre.
Teniendo ivan armas,   entráronse a la cibdad,
grand gozo fizo con ellas   doña Ximena su madre.
El que en buen ora nasco   non quiso tardar,
fablós' con los sos   en su poridad,
al rrey Alfonso de Castiella   pensó de enbiar:

133

"¿Ó eres, Muño Gustioz,   mio vassallo de pro?
¡En buen ora te crié   a ti en la mi cort!
Lieves el mandado   a Castiella al rrey Alfonso,
por mí bésale la mano   d'alma e de coraçón,
cuemo yo só su vassallo   e él es mio señor,
d'esta desondra que me an fecha   los ifantes de Carrión
quel' pese al buen rrey   d'alma e de coraçón.
Él casó mis fijas,   ca non ge las di yo;
quando las han dexadas   a grant desonor,
si desondra í cabe   alguna contra nós,
la poca e la grant   toda es de mio señor.
Mios averes se me an levado,   que sobejanos son,
esso me puede pesar   con la otra desonor.
Adúgamelos a vistas,   o a juntas o a cortes
como aya derecho   de ifantes de Carrión,

Out of love for my Cid, he gave them a great banquet.
The next day they rode straight to Valencia.
When he who was born at a lucky hour heard
They were close to the city, he galloped out
And welcomed them with a show of arms and great joy.
Smiling with pleasure, he kissed them both:
"You're here, my daughters? May God keep you from harm!
I did not dare refuse your marriage.
May God, high in his heaven, let me see you
Better married in days to come!
And may he grant me revenge on my Carrión sons-in-law!"
His daughters kissed their father's hands.
Everyone making a show of arms, they rode to the city;
How happy the girls were, seeing Doña Jimena, their mother!
And he who was born at just the right time held a secret
Conference, at once, with the best of his men,
Discussing how best to present their case to the king.

133

"So there you are, Muño Gustioz, one of my finest!
It was a fortunate hour, when I took you into my court!
Carry my message to Don Alfonso, King of Castile;
Kiss his hand for me, with all my heart and my soul,
For I am in his service, and he is my lord:
What the Carrións have done to me
Should sicken the king's heart and soul.
I did not give my daughters in marriage:
When they were dishonored and abandoned
What shame falls upon us is small,
Compared to that directed against my lord.
My sons-in-law have ridden off with vast sums of money,
Which seems to me yet another dishonor.
They must be called before an assembly, or court,
So justice can be done

ca tan grant es la rrencura   dentro en mi coraçón."
Muño Gustioz   privado cavalgó,
con él dos cavalleros   quel' sirvan a so sabor
e con él escuderos   que son de criazón.
Salién de Valencia   e andan quanto pueden,
nos' dan vagar   los días e las noches;
al rrey   en San Fagunt lo falló.
Rrey es de Castiella   e rrey es de León
e de las Asturias   bien a San Çalvador,
fasta dentro en Sancti Yaguo   de todo es señor,
e llos condes gallizanos   e él tienen por señor.
Assí como descavalga   aquel Muño Gustioz,
omillós' a los santos   e rrogó a[l] Criador;
adeliñó pora'l palacio   dó estava la cort,
con él dos cavalleros   quel' aguardan cum a señor.
Assí como entraron   por medio de la cort,
violos el rrey   e connosció a Muño Gustioz,
levantós' el rrey,   tan bien los rrecibió.
Delant el rrey fincó los inojos   aquel Muño Gustioz,
besávale los pies   aquel Muño Gustioz:
"¡Merced, rrey Alfonso,   de largos rreinos a vós dizen señor!
Los pies e las manos   vos besa el Campeador,
ele es vuestro vassallo   e vós sodes so señor.
Casastes sus fijas   con ifantes de Carrión,
alto fue el casamien[t]o   ca lo quisiestes vós.
Ya vós sabedes la ondra   que es cuntida a nós,
cuemo nos han abiltados   ifantes de Carrión:
mal majaron sus fijas   del Cid Campeador,
majadas e desnudas   a grande desonor,
desenparadas las dexaron   en el rrobredo de Corpes,
a las bestias fieras   e a las aves del mont.
Afelas sus fijas   en Valencia dó son.
Por esto vos besa las manos   como vassallo a señor
que ge los levedes a vistas,   o a juntas o a cortes;
tienes' por desondrado,   mas la vuestra es mayor,
e que vos pese, rrey,   como sodes sabidor;
que aya Mio Cid derecho   de ifantes de Carrión."
El rrey una grant ora   calló e comidió:

For what has pierced and pained my heart."
Muño Gustioz departed quickly,
Along with a pair of knights to assist him
And several servants of his own.
They left Valencia and rode
As fast as they could, by day and by night.
They found the king in Sahagún—
Don Alfonso, ruler of Castile and León,
Lord of Asturias, and the city of Oviedo,
And the land far as Santiago,
His lordship acknowledged by all the Galician counts.
When Muño Gustioz dismounted,
He prayed to God and his saints,
Then he and the men who rode with him
Went to the palace where the king held court.
From where he was sitting, King Alfonso
Saw them and recognized Muño Gustioz,
And at once arose and greeted them warmly.
Muño knelt in front of him
And kissed his feet, saying:
"A favor, King Alfonso, lord of many lands.
The Warrior kisses your feet and hands—
He who is in your service and acknowledges you his lord.
He gave his daughters to the Carrión heirs
Largely because you wanted the match.
You have heard what sort of honor they've done us,
Just how disgracefully
They've beaten the daughters of Warrior Cid,
Whipped them long and hard, and stripped them,
Then left them for dead in the Corpes forest,
Food for the wild beasts and birds of the mountains.
His daughters are now with the Warrior, in Valencia.
He kisses your hands—he in your service, you his lord—
And wishes the Carrións brought to an assembly or court.
You have been dishonored still more than my Cid,
And it is to you, wise king, on whom we call,
So my Cid can have justice against these Carrións!"
The king sat silent, thinking, for some time.

"Verdad te digo yo   que me pesa de coraçón
e verdad dizes en esto,   tú, Muño Gustioz,
ca yo casé sus fijas   con ifantes de Carrión;
fízlo por bien   que fuesse a su pro.
¡Si quier el casamiento   fecho non fuesse oy!
Entre yo e Mio Cid   pésanos de coraçón,
ayudar le [é] a derecho,   ¡sín' salve el Criador!
Lo que non cuidava fer   de toda esta sazón,
andarán mios porteros   por todo mio rreino,
pora dentro en Toledo   pregonarán mi cort,
que allá me vayan   cuendes e ifançones,
mandaré cómo í vayan   ifantes de Carrión
e cómo den derecho   a Mio Cid el Campeador,

134

"e que non aya rrencura   podiendo yo vedallo.
Dezidle al Campeador,   que en buen ora nasco,
que d'estas *siete* semanas   adobes' con sus vassallos,
véngam' a Toledo,   éstol' do de plazo.
Por amor de Mio Cid   esta cort yo fago.
Saludádmelos a todos,   entr'ellos aya espacio,
d'esto que les abino   aún bien serán ondrados."
Espidiós' Muño Gustioz,   a Mio Cid es tornado.
Assí como lo dixo,   suyo era el cuidado,
non lo detiene por nada   Alfonso el castellano,
enbía sus cartas   pora Léon e a Sancti Yaguo,
a los portogaleses   e a galizianos
e a los de Carrión   e a varones castellanos,
que cort fazié en Toledo   aquel rrey ondrado,
a cabo de *siete* semanas   que í fuessen juntados;
qui non viniesse a la cort   non se toviesse por su vassallo.
Por todas sus tierras   assí lo ivan pensando
que non falliessen   de lo que el rrey avié mandado.

"You are right, I am heavy at heart,
And I tell you, Muño Gustioz, you are doubly right:
I did indeed make this marriage.
I did it, hoping to help your Warrior.
How I wish it had never been done!
My Cid and I are both heavy at heart.
I will help him have justice, in the name of God!
It has been a long time since I did this,
But now I will send my heralds through all of Castile,
Calling my nobles to court, in Toledo—
And every count, every man who has a title.
And I'll summon the Carrións to come
And do justice to my Cid, the Warrior:
He will not have suffered for nothing, if I can help it.

134

"Tell the Warrior, that man born in a good hour,
To be ready, he and his men, to come to Toledo
In seven weeks: that will be how long it takes.
I call this court for love of my Cid.
Greet them all for me, tell them to be patient:
This disaster they endured may yet be turned to honor!"
Muño Gustioz said his farewells, and returned to my Cid.
The king made sure that what he had said was exactly what was
    done:
Alfonso, King of Castile, let nothing stand in his way.
He sent word to León and Santiago,
To the Portuguese and Galicians,
To the Carrións and his own Castilians,
Announcing their honored king was holding court in Toledo,
Where they should arrive in seven weeks, no later.
A nobleman who did not come no longer served Alfonso.
Every one of his subjects felt quite sure
The good king's notice should not be ignored.

135

Ya les va pesando   a los ifantes de Carrión
porque en Toledo   el rrey fazié cort;
miedo han que í verná   Mio Cid el Campeador.
Prenden so consejo   assí parientes como son,
rruegan al rrey   que los quite d'esta cort.
Dixo el rrey: "No lo feré,   ¡sín' salve Dios!
Ca í verná   Mio Cid el Campeador;
dar le [e]des derecho,   ca rrencura ha de vós.
Qui lo fer non quisiesse   o no ir a mi cort,
quite mio rreino,   ca d'él non he sabor."
Ya lo vieron que es a fer   los ifantes de Carrión,
prenden consejo   parientes como son;
el conde don García   en estas nuevas fue,
enemigo de Mio Cid   que mal siémprel' buscó,
aquéste consejó   los ifantes de Carrión.
Llegava el plazo,   querién ir a la cort,
en los primeros va   el buen rrey don Alfonso,
el conde don Anrrich   e el conde don Rremond,
aquéste fue padre   del buen enperador,
el conde don Fruella   e el conde don Beltrán.
Fueron í de su rreino   otros muchos sabidores,
de toda Castiella   todos los mejores.
El conde don García   con ifantes de Carrión
e As[s]ur González   e Gonçalo Assúrez,
e Diego e Ferrando   í son amos a dos,
e con ellos grand bando   que aduxieron a la cort:
e[n]baírle cuidan   a Mio Cid el Campeador.
De todas partes   allí juntados son.
Aún non era llegado   el que en buen ora nació,
porque se tarda   el rrey non ha sabor.
Al quinto día   venido es Mio Cid el Campeador,
[a] Álbar Fáñez   adelántel' enbió
que besasse las manos   al rrey so señor:
bien lo sopiesse   que í serié essa noch.
Quando lo oyó el rrey,   plógol' de coraçón,

135

How it troubled the Carrións,
The king calling this court in Toledo!
They were afraid my Cid, the Warrior, would come.
The whole family discussed the problem,
Then begged the king to exempt them.
He replied: "I will do no such thing!
My Cid, the Warrior, is coming,
And needs to have justice for what you've done.
Whoever does not attend
Had better leave this land, for he loses my favor."
The Carrións saw it was going to happen;
The entire family discussed the problem.
Count Don García Ordóñez took part—
My Cid's enemy, always trying to hurt him—
And gave the Carrións his advice.
The time came, they had to attend.
Among the first to arrive were King Alfonso,
Count Don Enrique, and Count Don Ramón—
Count Ramón was the good emperor's father—
Count Don Fruela, and Count Don Beltrán.
Many deeply learned men attended the court,
The best of all there were, from all Castile.
Count Don García was there, along with the Carrións,
And Ansur González, Suero González,
And Diego and Fernando, our pair of Carrión brothers,
And with them a horde, their men and others,
Assembled for assaulting my Cid, the Warrior.
Members of the court had come from all over,
But he who was born at a fortunate hour
Was late, and the king was annoyed.
On the fifth day my Cid, the Warrior, appeared;
He had sent Alvar Fáñez in advance,
To show respect for the king, his lord, and to kiss his hands
And say he was coming that night.
Hearing this, the king was delighted,

con grandes yentes   el rrey cavalgó
e iva rrecebir   al que en buen ora nació.
Bien aguisado viene   el Cid con todos los sos,
buenas conpañas   que assí an tal señor.
Quando lo ovo a ojo   el buen rrey don Alfonso,
firiós' a tierra   Mio Cid el Campeador,
biltarse quiere   e ondrar a so señor.
Quando lo oyó el rrey   por nada non tardó:
"¡Par Sant Esidro   verdad non será oy!
Cavalgad, Cid, si non,   non avría de[n]d sabor,
saludar nos hemos   d'alma e de coraçón.
De lo que a vós pesa   a mí duele el coraçón,
¡Dios lo mande que por vós   se ondre oy la cort!"
"Amen," dixo   Mio Cid el Campeador,
besóle la mano   e después le saludó:
"Grado a Dios   quando vos veo, señor.
Omíllom' a vós   e al conde do Rremond
e al conde don A[n]rrich   e a quantos que í son,
¡Dios salve a nuestros amigos   e a vós más, señor!
Mi mugier doña Ximena,   dueña es de pro,
bésavos las manos,   e mis fijas amas a dos,
d'esto que nos abino   que vos pese, señor."
Rrespondió el rrey: "Sí fago, ¡sín' salve Dios!"

136

Pora Toledo   el rrey tornada da,
essa noch Mio Cid   Tajo non quiso passar:
"¡Merced, ya rrey,   sí el Criador vos salve!
Pensad, señor,   de entrar a la cibdad
e yo con los míos   posaré a San Serván;
las mis compañas   esta noche llegarán.
Terné vigilia   en aqueste sancto logar,
cras mañana   entraré a la cibdad
e iré a la cort   enantes de yantar."
Dixo el rrey: "Plazme de veluntad."
El rrey don Alfonso   a Toledo es entrado,

And with many others rode out to welcome
The man born at an hour so right.
My Cid came well prepared, with all his knights,
Men who were worthy of him, their lord; they knew how to fight.
Seeing Don Alfonso, his king,
Warrior Cid dismounted,
Intending to honor his noble lord.
But immediately the king forbade it:
"In the name of Saint Isidore, don't do that, today!
Keep riding, my Cid, or I'll be angry.
We'll greet each other only in our hearts and souls.
Your suffering presses hard on my heart:
May this court be led by God, and do you honor!"
"Amen!" replied my Cid, the Warrior,
Kissing the king's hands, and then his mouth.
"My lord," he said, "I'm grateful to you for appearing here!
My humble greetings to you, and to Count Ramón,
And Don Enrique, and all those who are here.
God save our friends, and especially you, my lord!
Doña Jimena, my worthy wife,
Kisses your hands, and so do my daughters,
Since you have shared our misfortune, and felt its importance."
"I do," said the king. "By God, I do!"

136

The king then turned, intending to ride to Toledo.
But my Cid did not want to cross the Tagus that night.
"A favor, my king! May God give you salvation.
Proceed to Toledo, my lord,
And I and my men will rest at San Servando.
The rest of my men will meet us there,
And in that holy place we'll say our prayers together.
I plan to ride to Toledo, in the morning,
And go to the court before we eat."
"I gladly consent," said the king,
Who then proceeded to Toledo,

Mio Cid Rruy Díaz   en San Serván posado.
Mandó fazer candelas   e poner en el altar,
sabor á de velar   en essa santidad,
al Criador rrogando   e fablando en poridad.
Entre Minaya   e los buenos que í ha
acordados fueron   quando vino la man.
Matines e prima   dixieron faza'l alba.

137

Suelta fue la missa   antes que saliesse el sol
e su ofrenda han fecha   muy buena e conplida.
"Vós, Minaya Álbar Fáñez,   el mio braço mejor,
vós iredes comigo   e el obispo don Jerónimo
e Pero Vermúez   e aqueste Muño Gustioz
e Martín Antolínez,   el burgalés de pro,
e Álbar Álbarez   e Álbar Salvadórez
e Martín Muñoz,   que en buen punto nació,
e mio sobrino   Félez Muñoz;
comigo irá Mal Anda,   que es bien sabidor,
e Galind Garcíez,   el bueno d'Aragón;
con éstos cúnplanse ciento   de los buenos que í son.
Velmezes vestidos   por sufrir las guarnizones,
de suso las lorigas   tan blancas como el sol;
sobre las lorigas   armiños e pelliçones
e, que non parescan las armas,   bien presos los cordones,
so los mantos las espadas   dulces e tajadores;
d'aquesta guisa   quiero ir a la cort
por demandar mios derechos   e dezir mi rrazón.
Si desobra buscaren   ifantes de Carrión,
dó tales ciento tovier,   bien seré sin pavor."
Rrespondieron todos: "Nós esso queremos, señor."
Assí como lo á dicho,   todos adobados son.
Nos' detiene por nada   el que en buen ora nació:
calças de buen paño   en sus camas metió,
sobr'ellas unos çapatos   que a grant huebra son,
vistió camisa de rrançal   tan blanca como el sol,

While Ruy Díaz, my Cid, remained in San Servando.
He had candles placed on the altar, in that holy place,
Meaning to spend the night praying,
Quietly begging God for his favor.
Minaya and my Cid's other good men
Were more than ready, when daylight came.

137

Mass and morning prayers had been said
Before the sun appeared.
They left many generous offerings.
"You, Minaya Alvar Fáñez," said my Cid,
"You, my right arm, and Bishop Don Jerónimo, will come
    with me,
And Pedro Bermúdez, and our Muño Gustioz,
And Martín Antolínez, that fine fellow from Burgos.
And Alvar Alvarez, and Alvar Salvadórez,
And Martín Muñoz, born at the right time,
And my nephew, Félix Muñoz.
I'll also take Mal Anda, a learnèd man of law,
And Galín García, from Aragon: a good man to have.
Fill up my hundred with other good men, and that will be all.
Wear padded vests under your armor,
And then your mail shirts, gleaming like the sun,
And over them your fur-lined capes—
To let your armor shine, tie them tight at the waist,
But hide your sweet sharp swords beneath them.
This is how I'll go to court
And ask for justice, stating my case.
If the Carrións look for trouble, I can't be afraid,
Followed by a hundred men this good!"
They shouted: "We'll do whatever you ask!"
Saying this, they got themselves ready.
He who was born at a fortunate hour didn't sit around waiting:
He pulled on a pair of well-woven stockings

con oro e con plata   todas las presas son,
al puño bien están,   ca él se lo mandó;
sobr'ella un brial   primo de ciclatón,
obrado es con oro,   parecen por ó son;
sobr'esto una piel vermeja,   las bandas d'oro son,
siempre la viste   Mio Cid el Campeador;
una cofia sobre los pelos   d'un escarín de pro,
con oro es obrada,   fecha por rrazón,
que non le contal[l]assen los pelos   al buen Cid Canpeador;
la barba avié luenga   e prísola con el cordón,
por tal lo faze esto   que rrecabdar quiere todo lo suyo;
de suso cubrió un manto,   que es de grant valor.
En él abrién que ver   quantos que í son.
Con aquestos ciento   que adobar mandó
apriessa cavalga,   de San Serván salió;
assí iva Mio Cid   adobado a lla cort.
A la puerta de fuera   descavalga a sabor,
cuerdamientre entra   Mio Cid con todos los sos:
él va en medio   e los ciento aderredor.
Quando lo vieron entrar   al que en buen ora nació,
levantós' en pie   el buen rrey don Alfonso
e el conde don Anrrich   e el conde don Rremont
e desí adelant,   sabet, todos los otros;
a grant ondra lo rreciben   al que en buen ora nació.
Nos' quiso levantar   el Crespo de Grañón,
nin todos los del bando   de ifantes de Carrión.
El rrey dixo al Cid: "Venid acá ser, Campeador,
en aqueste escaño   quem' diestes vós en don;
maguer que [a] algunos pesa,   mejor sodes que nós."
Essora dixo muchas mercedes   el que Valencia gañó:
"Sed en vuestro escaño   como rrey e señor,
acá posaré   con todos aquestos míos."
Lo que dixo el Cid   al rrey plogo de coraçón.
En un escaño torniño   essora Mio Cid posó,
los ciento quel' aguardan   posan aderredor.
Catando están a Mio Cid   quantos ha en la cort,
a la barba que avié luenga   e presa con el cordón,
en sos aguisamientos   bien semeja varón,

And handsomely crafted shoes;
His linen shirt was white as the sun,
With cuff links of silver and gold,
Made to his instructions,
And over it a tunic of the finest silk,
Brocaded with gold, and glittering.
Over this he wore a coat, lined with purple fur—
And this was how my Cid, the Warrior, always dressed.
His head was crowned by a linen cap,
Gold-brocaded, meant to ensure
No one could pull his hair.
His great long beard was tied and shortened by a cord,
So whoever might want to pull his beard couldn't.
And over all the rest he wore a costly cloak
Which caught the eye of anyone who saw it.
With the hundred men he'd summoned
He galloped away from San Servando:
My Cid had readied himself for court.
At the outer gate, he dismounted,
With him in the middle, his men all around him,
He went in, carefully surrounded.
At the sight of this man born at a fortunate hour,
Good King Don Alfonso rose,
And so did Count Don Enrique, and Count Don Ramón.
And, let me tell you, almost everyone else.
He who was born at the right time was given high honors.
But Count Don García Ordóñez did not feel like standing,
Nor did the Carrións or any of their men.
"Come sit with me, Warrior," said the king,
"On this bench of mine, a gift from you.
No matter who thinks different, you're better than us all!"
He who had conquered Valencia answered, most politely:
"Stay where you are, seated as king and my lord;
I'll sit over there, with my men."
The king took deep pleasure in this reply.
So my Cid seated himself on a well-made bench,
And his hundred warriors sat around him.
Everyone there was staring at him,

nol' pueden catar de vergüença   ifantes de Carrión.
Essora se levó en pie   el buen rrey don Alfonso:
"¡Oíd, mesnadas,   sí vos vala el Criador!
Yo, de que fu rrey,   non fɪz más de dos cortes,
la una fue en Burgos   e la otra en Carrión;
esta tercera   a Toledo la vin fer oy
por el amor de Mio Cid,   el que en buen ora nació,
que rreciba derecho   de ifantes de Carrión.
Grande tuerto le han tenido,   sabémoslo todos nós;
alcaldes sean d'esto   el conde don Anrrich e el conde don
    Rremond
e estos otros condes   que del vando non sodes.
Todos meted í mientes,   ca sodes coñoscedores,
por escoger el derecho,   ca tuerto non mando yo.
D'ella e d'ella part   en paz seamos oy:
juro par Sant Esidro,   el que bolviere mi cort
quitar me á el rreino,   perderá mi amor.
Con el que toviere derecho   yo d'essa parte me só.
Agora demande   Mio Cid el Campeador;
sabremos qué rresponden   ifantes de Carrión."
Mio Cid la mano besó al rrey   e en pie se levantó:
"Mucho vos lo gradesco   como a rrey e a señor
por quanto esta cort   fɪziestes por mi amor.
Esto les demando   a ifantes de Carrión:
por mis fɪjas quem' dexaron   yo non he desonor,
ca vós las casastes, rrey,   sabredes qué fer oy;
mas quando sacaron mis fɪjas   de Valencia la mayor,
yo bien los quería   d'alma e de coraçón,
diles dos espadas   a Colada e a Tizón,
éstas yo las gané   a guisa de varón,
ques' ondrassen con ellas   e sirviessen a vós;
quando dexaron mis fɪjas   en el rrobredo de Corpes
comigo non quisieron aver nada   e perdieron mi amor;
denme mis espadas   quando mios yernos non son."
Atorgan los alcaldes: "Tod' esto es rrazón."
Dixo el conde don García: "A esto fablemos nós."
Essora salién aparte   iffantes de Carrión
con todos sus parientes   e el vando que í son,

And at his long beard, tied up by a cord:
He was every inch a man!
The Carrións were too ashamed to look.
Then good King Alfonso rose:
"Hear me, gentlemen, in the name of God!
Since I've been king, I've called only two courts,
One in Burgos, and one in Carrión.
This third one has been called, here in Toledo,
For love of my Cid, he who was born at a blessèd time,
To give him justice against the Carrión heirs.
We all know the immense wrongs they have done him.
The judges, here, will be Count Don Enrique and Count Don
    Ramón,
Along with counts who are not allied to the accused.
Pay close attention, and as the learnèd men you are
Determine what is proper, for I do not enforce malice.
Let everyone be peaceful, today,
For I swear by Saint Isidore that he who disrupts this court
Will be sent into exile, and will lose my favor.
I am on whichever side is proven right.
My Cid, the Warrior, will present his claim,
And then we'll hear what the Carrións say."
My Cid kissed the king's hands, and rose to his feet:
"I am deeply grateful to you, my king and lord,
For your concern in calling this court.
Here is what I ask of the Carrión heirs:
Deserting my daughters brings no dishonor to me,
Because it was you who gave them away, my king; you will do as
    you please.
But when you Carrións took my daughters away—
And I acted with love, from my heart and my soul—
I gave you two swords, Colada and Tizón,
Precious swords that I won
In battle, hoping they'd win more honor with you.
By abandoning my daughters, in the Corpes forest,
You broke all connection with me, and my love was lost:
Give back my swords, since you're no longer my sons-in-law!"
The judges agreed: "This is completely just."

apriessa lo ivan trayendo   e acuerdan la rrazón:
"Aún grand amor nos faze   el Cid Campeador
quando desondra de sus fijas   no nos demanda oy,
bien nos abendremos   con el rrey don Alfonso.
Démosle sus espadas   quando assí finca la boz,
e quando las toviere   partir se á la cort;
ya más non avrá derecho   de nós el Cid Canpeador."
Con aquesta fabla   tornaron a la cort:
"¡Merced, ya rrey don Alfonso,   sodes nuestro señor!
No lo podemos negar   ca dos espadas nos dio,
quando las demanda   e d'ellas ha sabor
dárgelas queremos   delant estando vós."
Sacaron las espadas   Colada e Tizón,
pusiéronlas en mano   del rrey so señor,
saca las espadas   e rrelumbra toda la cort,
las maçanas e los arriazes   todos d'oro son.
Maravíllanse d'ellas   todos los omnes buenos de la cort.
Rrecibió [el Cid] las espadas,   las manos le besó,
tornós' al escaño   dón se levantó,
en las manos las tiene   e amas las cató,
nos' le pueden camear   ca el Cid bien las connosce,
alegrós'le tod' el cuerpo,   sonrrisós' de coraçón,
alçava la mano,   a la barba se tomó:
"¡Par aquesta barba   que nadi non' messó,
assís' irán vengando   don Elvira e doña Sol!"
A so sobrino   por nónbrel' llamó,
tendió el braço,   la espada Tizón le dio:
"Prendetla, sobrino,   ca mejora en señor."
A Martín Antolínez,   el burgalés de pro,
tendió el braço,   el espada Coládal' dio:
"Martín Antolínez,   mio vassallo de pro,
prended a Colada,   ganéla de buen señor,
del conde do Rremont Verenguel   de Barcilona la mayor.
Por esso vos la do   que la bien curiedes vós;
sé que si vos acaeciere . . . .
con ella ganaredes   grand prez e grand valor."
Besóle la mano,   el espada tomó e rrecibió.
Luego se levantó   Mio Cid el Campeador:

Count García Ordóñez said: "We'll talk about this."
They went off all together, the Carrión heirs,
Their family and friends. Their talk went quickly;
They all decided, almost at once, to give in on this:
"He's doing us a favor, Warrior Cid,
Not asking a thing for his daughters' dishonor.
We can settle up nicely, just with the king.
Let's give him the swords, since that's all he wants,
And once he's gotten them, he'll leave the court.
Then no more righteous claims for justice, from Warrior Cid!"
This decided, they went back to court:
"By your grace, King Don Alfonso and our lord!
We cannot deny that he gave us two swords.
Since he wants them back, and he has that right,
We'll gladly hand them over, here in your presence."
They brought the two swords, Colada and Tizón,
And put them in the king's hands.
He drew them, and they lit up the room,
Their pommels and hand guards made of gold:
All the good men in the court stared in wonder.
My Cid took them, kissed the king's hands,
Then turned and went back to his place,
Where he made a careful examination:
He couldn't be fooled, he knew them well.
His whole body spoke his joy; his heart was smiling.
He raised his hand, and grasped his beard:
"By my beard, which no one has ever pulled,
This begins my daughters' revenge!"
He called to his nephew, Pedro Bermúdez,
Took him by the arm and gave him Tizón.
"Take it, nephew: it suits you better."
Then he called to Martín Antolínez, worthy man from Burgos,
Took his arm, and gave him Colada:
"Martín Antolínez, my first-class warrior,
Accept Colada—which I won from a very fine lord,
Count Ramón Berenguer, from great Barcelona—
I make this gift knowing you will treat it well.
Take it; it will earn you honor and praise."

"Grado al Criador   e a vós, rrey señor,
ya pagado só de mis espadas,   de Colada e de Tizón.
Otra rrencura he   de ifantes de Carrión:
quando sacaron de Valencia   mis fijas amas a dos
en oro e en plata   tres mill marcos les di [y]o,
yo faziendo esto,   ellos acabaron lo so;
denme mis averes   quando mios yernos non son."
¡Aquí veriedes quexarse   ifantes de Carrión!
Dize el conde don Rremond: "Dezid de sí o de no."
Essora rresponden   ifantes de Carrión:
"Por éssol' diemos sus espadas   al Cid Campeador
que ál no nos demandasse,   que aquí fincó la boz."
"Si ploguiere al rrey,   assí dezimos nós:
a lo que demanda el Cid   quel' rrecudades vós."
Dixo el buen rrey: "Assí lo otorgo yo."
Levantós' en pie   el Cid Campeador:
"D'estos averes   que vos di yo
si me los dades,   o dedes [d'ello rraçón]."
Essora salién aparte   ifantes de Carrión,
non acuerdan en consejo   ca los haveres grandes son,
espesos los han   ifantes de Carrión.
Tornan con el consejo   e fablavan a so señor:
"Mucho nos afinca   el que Valencia gañó
quando de nuestros averes   assil' prende sabor,
pagar le hemos de heredades   en tierras de Carrión."
Dixieron los alcaldes   quando manifestados son:
"Si esso ploguiere al Cid,   non ge lo vedamos nós,
mas en nuestro juvizio   assí lo mandamos nós
que aquí lo enterguedes   dentro en la cort."
A estas palabras   fabló el rrey don Alfonso:
"Nós bien la sabemos   aquesta rraçón
que derecho demanda   el Cid Campeador.
D'estos *tres* mill marcos   los *dozientos* tengo yo,
entr'amos me los dieron   los ifantes de Carrión;
tornárgelos quiero,   ca *tan des*fechos son,
enterguen a Mio Cid,   el que en buen ora nació;
quando ellos los an a pechar,   non ge los quiero yo."
Fabló Ferrán Go[n]çález: "Averes monedados non tenemos nós."

His hand was kissed, the sword was given and received,
Then he rose, my Warrior Cid:
"Thanks to God, and to you, my lord the king,
My swords, Colada and Tizón, are mine again!
I have other complaints against the Carrión heirs:
When they took my daughters from Valencia,
I gave them three thousand marks in silver and gold.
I did my duty, but they did what they meant to do.
Give me back my money, for you are no longer my sons-in-law."
You should have seen the Carrións moaning and groaning!
Count Don Ramón of Burgundy: "Answer him, yes or no."
Then the Carrións said:
"The only reason we gave him back the swords
Was to stop him from claiming more, so this would end."
"We declare," said Don Ramón, "if the king so pleases,
That you must pay him what he asks."
The good king said: "I hereby confirm this."
Warrior Cid immediately rose:
"Either give me what I ask of you,
Or give some reason for refusing."
Then the Carrións went out to discuss this;
They could not satisfy the claim, it was huge,
And most of the money had been spent.
They came back in, and said:
"He who conquered Valencia asks too much,
But if he wants more of what we have,
We'll pay him with land in Carrión."
When they admitted this much, the judges said:
"If Warrior Cid approves, we'll allow it,
But we think he should receive his money
Here and now, right in this court."
At these words, Don Alfonso, the king, declared:
"We fully approve this claim,
Asserted here by Warrior Cid.
I have in hand two hundred marks,
Given me by the Carrións.
I wish to return this, their purses being so drained;
Let them hand it to him who was born at a lucky hour;

Luego rrespondió   el conde don Rremond:
"El oro e la plata   espendiésteslo vós,
por juvizio lo damos   ant'el rrey don Alfonso:
páguenle en apreciadura   e préndalo el Campeador."
Ya vieron que es a fer   los ifantes de Carrión:
veriedes aduzir   tanto cavallo corredor,
tanta gruessa mula,   tanto palafré de sazón,
tanta buena espada   con toda guarnizón;
rrecibiólo Mio Cid   como apreciaron en la cort.
Sobre los dozientos marcos   que tenié el rrey Alfonso,
pagaron los ifantes   al que en buen ora nasco,
enpréstanles de lo ageno,   que non les cumple lo suyo,
mal escapan jogados,   sabed, d'esta rrazón.

138

Estas apreciaduras   Mio Cid presas las ha,
sos omnes las tienen   e d'ellas pensarán,
mas quando esto ovo acabado   pensaron luego d'ál:
"¡Merced, ya rrey señor,   por amor de caridad!
La rrencura mayor   non se me puede olbidar.
Oídme toda la cort   e pésevos de mio mal:
de los ifantes de Carrión,   quem' desondraron tan mal,
a menos de rriebtos   no los puedo dexar.

139

"Dezid, ¿qué vos merecí,   ifantes [de Carrión],
en juego o en vero | o en alguna rrazón?
Aquí lo mejoraré   a juvizio de la cort.
¿A quém' descubriestes   las telas del coraçón?
A la salida de Valencia   mis fijas vos di yo
con muy grand ondra   e averes a nombre;
quando las non queriedes,   ya canes traidores,

Seeing how much they must pay, I don't want to keep this."
Fernando González said: "There is no money in our purse."
Then Count Don Ramón replied:
"Since you have spent all the silver and all the gold,
With the king's approval we judges decide
Payment must be made in kind, if Warrior Cid accepts this."
And now the Carrións understood what had to be done.
You should have seen the racing horses brought in,
The fat mules, the first-rate palfreys,
Good swords with their accouterments.
My Cid accepted them, as the court had decreed.
In addition to two hundred marks the king had been holding,
The Carrións paid and paid Warrior Cid, born at a lucky hour,
Borrowing from whoever would lend, for they had to.
The court, please understand, had squeezed them dry as a bone.

138

My Cid took all of this property.
His men took it, and would guard it.
With this issue settled, he presented another:
"I ask your favor, my king and lord, in charity's name.
I cannot forget my most bitter complaint.
Let the court hear me, today, and feel my pain.
The Carrión heirs have so maliciously dishonored me,
I cannot accept anything less than a challenge to battle.

139

"Tell us what I deserved from you Carrións—
In jest? in truth? or some other way?
Let your actions be judged by this court.
Why did you pull at the deepest strings of my heart?
When you left Valencia, I gave you my daughters
With great honor and many gifts.
If you did not want my daughters—ah, you treacherous dogs!—

¿por qué las sacávades   de Valencia sus honores?
¿A qué las fıriestes   a cinchas e a espolones?
Solas las dexastes   en el rrobredo de Corpes
a las bestias fıeras   e a las aves del mont;
por quanto les fıziestes   menos valedes vós.
Si non rrecudedes,   véalo esta cort."

                              140

El conde don García   en pie se levantava:
"¡Merced, ya rrey,   el mejor de toda España!
Vezós' Mio Cid   a llas cortes pregonadas;
dexóla crecer   e luenga trae la barba,
los unos le han miedo   e los otros espanta.
Los de Carrión   son de natura tal
non ge las devién querer   sus fıjas por varraganas,
o ¿quién ge las diera   por parejas o por veladas?
Derecho fızieron   por que las han dexadas.
Quanto él dize   non ge lo preciamos nada."
Essora el Campeador   prisos' a la barba:
"¡Grado a Dios   que cielo e tierra manda!
Por esso es lue[n]ga   que a delicio fue criada;
¿qué avedes vós, conde,   por rretraer la mi barba?
Ca de quando nasco   a delicio fue criada,
ca non me priso a ella   fıjo de mugier nada,
nimbla messó   fıjo de moro nin de cristiana,
como yo a vós, conde,   en el castiello de Cabra;
quando pris a Cabra   e a vós por la barba,
non í ovo rrapaz   que non messó su pulgada.
La que yo messé   aún non es eguada."

                              141

Ferrán Go[n]çález   en pie se levantó,
a altas vozes   odredes qué fabló:
"Dexássedes vós, Cid,   de aquesta rrazón;

Why did you steal them from their life in Valencia?
Why did you beat them with buckles and spurs?
You abandoned them, alone in the Corpes forest,
Food for wild beasts and mountain birds.
What you did to them was shameful, infamous!
Let this court pass judgment, if you refuse our challenge."

140

Count Don García Ordóñez rose:
"May I speak, O greatest king in Spain?
Warrior Cid is an old hand at courts like this;
He carefully lets his beard grow long,
So some will fear him, and others will shake in terror.
The Carrións come from such noble stock
They couldn't conceivably want these girls as mistresses!
Who was it that gave them as wives and lawful spouses?
The Carrións were right to desert them.
Everything Cid says amounts to nothing whatever!"
Warrior Cid took hold of his beard:
"Thanks to God, who made heaven and earth!
This beard is long because he wants it long.
What has my beard done to you, Count, to be scolded like this?
I have loved and cherished it all my life,
No man born of woman has ever pulled it,
No son of Moor or Christian birth—
As happened to you, Count, in Cabra castle!
When I took that castle, I pulled your beard,
Every single Moorish boy took his turn—
And what I pulled out still hasn't grown back!"

141

Fernando González stood up,
Shouting what he thought honorable:
"Enough of this, Cid, enough, stop this!

de vuestros averes   de todos pagado sodes.
Non creciés varaja   entre nós e vós.
De natura somos   de condes de Carrión,
deviemos casar con fijas   de rreyes o de enperadores,
ca non pertenecién   fijas de ifançones.
Por que las dexamos   derecho fiziemos nós;
más nos preciamos,   sabet, que menos no."

142

Mio Cid Rruy Díaz   a Pero Vermúez cata:
"¡Fabla, Pero Mudo,   varón que tanto callas!
Yo las he fijas   e tú primas cormanas;
a mí lo dizen,   a ti dan las orejadas.
Si yo rrespondier,   tú non entrarás en armas."

143

Pero Vermúez   conpeçó de fablar,
detiénes'le la lengua,   non puede delibrar,
mas quando enpieça,   sabet, nol' da vagar:
"¡Dirévos, Cid,   costu[m]bres avedes tales,
siempre en las cortes   'Pero Mudo' me llamades!
Bien lo sabedes   que yo non puedo más;
por lo que yo ovier a fer   por mí non mancará.
Mientes, Ferrando,   de quanto dicho has,
por el Campeador   mucho valiestes más.
Las tus mañas   yo te las sabré contar:
¡miémbrat' quando lidiamos   cerca Valencia la grand!
Pedist las feridas primeras   al Canpeador leal,
vist un moro,   fústel' ensayar,
antes fuxiste   que a'l te allegasses.
Si yo non uviás,   el moro te jugara mal;
passé por ti,   con el moro me of de ajuntar,
de los primeros colpes   ofle de arrancar;
did' el cavallo,   tóveldo en poridad,

You've gotten back what you lost, you've been paid;
We have no wish to fight with you.
We were born to be counts of Carrión!
We ought to be married to the daughters of kings, or emperors;
Even second-class nobles are unworthy of us.
Deserting your daughters was our right;
It does not hurt but elevates our honor: do you hear me?"

142

My Cid, Ruy Díaz, turned to Pedro Bermúdez:
"Speak, Pedro the Mute, who keeps his words to himself!
These are my daughters and your first cousins;
They've been talking to me, but pulling your ears.
If I make the challenge, you won't get another chance."

143

Pedro Bermúdez tried to talk;
His tongue stopped him, would not let a word come out—
But once he began, believe me, no one could stop him!
"Cid, that's becoming a habit!
Especially at court, you call me Dumb Pedro!
You know, in fact, I can't talk better—
But nothing's ever missing from what I *do*.

"Fernando, everything you've said is a lie!
Being with Warrior Cid improved your reputation.
I know some Fernando tales worth telling:
Remember, we fought in front of Valencia?
You begged the Cid to let you strike first,
You saw a Moor, and began to ride at him—
Then you turned and ran before you reached him!
He was ready to beat you black and blue,
But I galloped past you and attacked him.
I killed him with a couple of strokes.

fasta este día   no lo descubrí a nadi.

Delant Mio Cid e delante todos   ovístete de alabar
que mataras el moro   e que fızieras barnax;
croviérontelo todos,   mas non saben la verdad.
¡E eres fermoso,   mas mal varragán!
Lengua sin manos,   ¿cuémo osas fablar?

144

"Di, Ferrando,   otorga esta rrazón:
¿non te viene en miente   en Valencia lo del león,
quando durmié Mio Cid   e el león se desató?
E tú, Ferrando,   ¿qué fızist con el pavor?
¡Metístet' tras el escaño   de Mio Cid el Campeador!
Metístet', Ferrando,   por ó menos vales oy.
Nós cercamos el escaño   por curiar nuestro señor,
fasta dó despertó Mio Cid,   el que Valencia gañó;
levantós' del escaño   e fues' pora'l león.
El león premió la cabeça,   a Mio Cid esperó,
dexós'le prender al cuello   e a la rred le metió.
Quando se tornó   el buen Campeador,
a sos vassallos   violos aderredor,
demandó por sus yernos,   ¡ninguno non falló!
Rriébtot' el cuerpo   por malo e por traidor,
éstot' lidiaré aquí   ant' el rrey don Alfonso
por fıjas del Cid,   don Elvira e doña Sol,
por quanto las dexastes   menos valedes vós;
ellas son mugieres   e vós sodes varones,
en todas guisas   más valen que vós.
Quando fuere la lid,   si ploguiere al Criador,
tú lo otorgarás   a guisa de traidor;
de quanto he dicho   verdadero seré yo."
D'aquestos amos   aquí quedó la rrazón.

Then I let you take his horse,
And never said a word, until today.
I heard you boasting to Cid, and everyone else,
About your great conquest.
Not knowing the truth, they all believed you.
You look good on a horse, but you're a coward!
You talk, you don't *do*! How dare you talk?

144

"Tell me, Fernando, admit it.
Didn't you run from the lion, in Valencia,
When my Cid was sleeping and the beast got out?
And you, Fernando, what did fear make you do?
You hid beneath the bench where Cid was sleeping!
You hid, and now I'm telling the truth!
The rest of us rallied around my Cid,
To protect our sleeping lord,
Until he woke, walked over to the lion,
Which stopped and waited, bending its head,
And Warrior Cid led him, by the mane, back to his cage.
And then my Cid saw you were missing
And asked his men where you were. No one knew!

"And now I challenge you, you scoundrel, you traitor.
And we will fight here, in front of King Alfonso,
In the names of Doña Elvira and Doña Sol!
What you did to them destroys your honor!
They're women, and you're supposed to be a man,
But they own far greater honor than you.
When we come to blows—God willing—
I'll make you confess you're a traitor,
And every word I've spoken is true."
And that was the end of this argument.

145

Diego Gonçález   odredes lo que dixo:
"De natura somos   de los condes más li[m]pios,
estos casamientos   non fuessen aparecidos,
por consagrar   con Mio Cid don Rrodrigo.
Porque dexamos sus fıjas   aún no nos rrepentimos,
mientra que bivan   pueden aver sospiros;
lo que les fıziemos   ser les ha rretraído,
esto lidiaré   a tod' el más ardido,
que porque las dexamos   ondrados somos nós."

146

Martín Antolínez   en pie se levantava:
"¡Calla, alevoso,   boca sin verdad!
Lo del león   non se te deve olbidar,
saliste por la puerta,   metístet' al corral,
fústed' meter   tras la viga lagar,
¡más non vestist   el manto nin el brial!
Yo llo lidiaré,   non passará por ál,
fıjas del Cid   porque las vós dexastes;
en todas guisas, sabed,   que más valen que vós.
Al partir de la lid   por tu boca lo dirás
que eres traidor   e mintist de quanto dicho has."
D'estos amos   la rrazón fıncó.

147

Assur Gonçález   entrava por el palacio,
manto armiño   e un brial rrastrando,
vermejo viene,   ca era almorzado,
en lo que fabló   avié poco rrecabdo:

145

Now hear what Diego González said:
"We are by birth the purest blood in Spain!
These marriages should never have taken place,
Mingling our blood with that of Warrior Cid!
We're not the least bit sorry we deserted your daughters,
But they'll regret it as long as they live:
It will always be thrown in their faces.
I will defend us against the bravest challenger:
What we did has earned us tremendous honor!"

146

Martín Antolínez jumped to his feet:
"Shut up, traitor, who cannot speak truth!
Don't forget what happened with the lion.
You ran out the door, and hid in the yard,
Behind the filthy wine press.
You couldn't wear those clothes again!
I have to fight you on this:
You deserted the Cid's two daughters,
But everyone gives higher honor to them.
I'll make you admit, when the fighting is done,
That you're a traitor, you lie like a drunken sot!"
And thus the two challenges were arranged.

147

Then Ansur González came in,
Dragging his ermine cloak and his coat behind him.
His face was beet red, from eating and drinking,
And his words were tumbled all out of order.

THE SONG OF THE CID

148

"Ya varones, ¿quién vio nunca tal mal?
¿Quién nos darié nuevas   de Mio Cid el de Bivar?
¡Fuesse a Rrío d'Ovirna   los molinos picar
e prender maquilas,   como lo suele far!
¿Quíl' darié   con los de Carrión a casar?"

149

Essora Muño Gustioz   en pie se levantó:
"¡Calla, alevoso,   malo e traidor!
Antes almuerzas   que vayas a oración,
a los que das paz   fártaslos aderredor.
Non dizes verdad   [a] amigo ni a señor,
falso a todos   e más al Criador;
en tu amistad   non quiero aver rración.
Fazer te lo [é] dezir   que tal eres qual digo yo."
Dixo el rrey Alfonso: "Calle ya esta rrazón.
Los que an rrebtado   lidiarán, ¡sín' salve Dios!"
Assí como acaban   esta rrazón,
afé dos cavalleros   entraron por la cort,
al uno dizen Ojarra   e al otro Yéñego Siménez,
el uno es [del] ifante de Navarra | e el otro [del] ifante de
    Aragón.
Besan las manos   al rrey don Alfonso,
piden sus fijas   a Mio Cid el Campeador
por ser rreínas   de Navarra e de Aragón
e que ge las diessen   a ondra e a bendición.
A esto callaron   e ascuchó toda la cort.
Levantós' en pie   Mio Cid el Campeador:
"¡Merced, rrey Alfonso,   vós sodes mio señor!
Esto gradesco yo   al Criador,
quando me las demandan   de Navarra e de Aragón.
Vós las casastes antes,   ca yo non,
afé mis fijas   en vuestras manos son;

148

"Hey, good men! Who ever saw such an awful thing?
Has anyone heard of this Cid from Vivar?
Send him to sharpen his millstones, next to a river,
Let him earn his fees, like he always did!
Who said he could marry a Carrión?"

149

Muño Gustioz stood up:
"Shut up, traitor, evil and dangerous!
You eat before you've said a single prayer,
Your greeting kiss stinks like your breath.
You don't speak truth to friends or lords;
You lie to everyone, and mostly to God.
I have no interest in friendship with you:
I'll make you admit you are what I say you are!"
King Alfonso declared: "This matter is closed.
We must proceed to combat, in the name of God!"

Just as they finished this long discussion,
Two messenger knights suddenly entered the court.
One was Ojarra, from the Prince of Navarre,
The other, Iñigo Jiménez, from the Prince of Aragon.
They kissed King Alfonso's hands,
Then turned to Warrior Cid and asked for his daughters
As queens of Aragon and Navarre,
Each one wed to a prince, in full ceremony and honor.
The court was silent, awaiting my Cid's response.
Warrior Cid arose:
"Bless you, King Alfonso, my lord!
I'm grateful to God on high
That Navarre and Aragon have asked for them!
It was you who gave them away, before,
So I hereby place them in your hands again:

sin vuestro mandado   nada non feré yo."
Levantós' el rrey,   fizo callar la cort:
"Rruégovos, Cid,   caboso Campeador,
que plega a vós   e atorgar lo he yo,
este casamiento   oy se otorgue en esta cort,
ca crece vos í ondra   e tierra e onor."
Levantós' Mio Cid,   al rrey las manos le besó:
"Quando a vós plaze,   otórgolo yo, señor."
Essora dixo el rrey: "¡Dios vos dé dén buen galardón!
A vós, Ojarra,   e a vós, Yéñego Ximénez,
este casamiento   otórgovosle yo
de fijas de Mio Cid,   don Elvira e doña Sol,
pora los ifantes   de Navarra e de Aragón,
que vos las den   a ondra e a bendición."
Levantós' en pie   Ojarra e Íñego Ximénez,
besaron las manos   del rrey don Alfonso
e después de Mio Cid   el Campeador,
metieron las fes   e los omenajes dados son
que cuemo es dicho   assí sea, o mejor.
A muchos plaze   de tod' esta cort,
mas non plaze   a los ifantes de Carrión.
Minaya Álba[r] Fáñez   en pie se levantó:
"¡Merced vos pido   como a rrey e a señor
e que non pese esto   al Cid Campeador:
bien vos di vagar   en toda esta cort,
dezir querría   yaquanto de lo mío."
Dixo el rrey: "Plazme de coraçón;
dezid, Minaya,   lo que oviéredes sabor."
"Yo vos rruego   que me oyades toda la cort,
ca grand rrencura he   de ifantes de Carrión.
Yo les di mis primas   por mandado del rrey Alfonso,
ellos las prisieron   a ondra e a bendición;
grandes averes les dio   Mio Cid el Campeador,
ellos las han dexadas   a pesar de nós.
Rriébtoles los cuerpos   por malos e por traidores.
De natura sodes   de los de Vanigómez
onde salién condes   de prez e de valor;
mas bien sabemos   las mañas que ellos han.

Whatever you wish will be done."
The king arose, asking for silence and order:
"Magnificent Warrior, I ask you to accept
These marriages, which I hereby authorize—
If it pleases you as it pleases me.
They will bring you blessings, honor, and lands."
My Cid rose and kissed his king's hands:
"Since it pleases you, my lord, I agree."
The king replied: "May God reward you!
Ojarra and Iñigo Jiménez, you have my authority
To proceed with the making of these marriages—
My Cid's daughters, Doña Elvira and Doña Sol,
With the heirs of Aragon and Navarre,
Conducted with full ceremony and honor."
Ojarra and Iñigo Jiménez rose
And kissed King Don Alfonso's hands,
Then did the same with my Warrior Cid;
They solemnly swore, and gave their oaths
That all would be as they had said, or better.
Most members of the court were delighted,
Though the Carrións were not.
Then Minaya Alvar Fáñez rose:
"I ask permission from my lord and king—
And hope I do not displease my Warrior Cid!
I have been silent in these proceedings,
But now I ask your permission to say something for myself."
The king said: "Yes, Minaya, with all my heart.
Say whatever you wish to."
"I would like the entire court to hear me, as I address
The profound quarrel I have with the Carrións.
I gave away those girls, my cousins, at the king's command;
The Carrións took them, in marriages solemnly made.
My Warrior Cid gave them immense gifts,
But they abandoned their wives most painfully.
I challenge them as malicious traitors!
You Carrións belong to the Beni-Gómez line,
From which have come counts courageous and wise.
But we know the evil ways of their descendants!

Esto gradesco yo   al Criador
quando piden mis primas   don Elvira e doña Sol
los ifantes de Navarra   e de Aragón.
Antes las aviedes parejas   pora en braços las tener,
agora besaredes sus manos   e llamar las hedes señoras,
aver las hedes a servir,   mal que vos pese a vós.
¡Grado a Dios del cielo   e [a] aquel rrey don Alfonso
assil' crece la ondra   a Mio Cid el Campeador!
En todas guisas   tales sodes quales digo yo:
si ay qui rresponda   o dize de no,
yo só Álbar Fáñez   pora tod' el mejor."
Gómez Peláyet   en pie se levantó:
"¿Qué val, Minaya,   toda essa rrazón?
Ca en esta cort   afarto[s] ha pora vós
e qui ál quisiesse   serié su ocasión.
Si Dios quisiere   que d'ésta bien salgamos nós,
después veredes   qué dixiestes o qué no."
Dixo el rrey: "Fine esta rrazón,
non diga ninguno   d'ella más una entención.
Cras sea la lid,   quando saliere el sol,
d'estos *tres* por tres   que rrebtaron en la cort."
Luego fablaron   ifantes de Carrión:
"Dandos, rrey, plazo,   ca cras ser non puede,
armas e cavallos tienen   los del Canpeador,
nós antes abremos a ir   a tierras de Carrión."
Fabló el rrey   contra'l Campeador:
"Sea esta lid   ó mandáredes vós."
En essora dixo Mio Cid: "No lo faré, señor;
más quiero a Valencia   que tierras de Carrión."
En essora dixo el rrey: "A osadas, Campeador.
Dadme vuestros cavalleros   con todas vuestras guarnizones,
vayan comigo,   yo seré el curiador,
yo vos lo sobrelievo   como a buen vassallo faze señor
que non prendan fuerça   de conde nin de ifançón.
Aquí les pongo plazo   de dentro en mi cort,
a cabo de tres semanas   en begas de Carrión
que fagan esta lid   delant estando yo:

I thank our God in heaven
That these girls, my cousins, will marry
The heirs of Navarre and Aragon!
They were yours, you Carrións, to have and to hold,
And now you'll call them 'my lady' and kiss their royal hands.
You'll have to serve them, in spite of yourselves!
I thank both God and our good king, Don Alfonso,
For the honor this gives my Cid, the Warrior!
You Carrións are exactly what I have called you—
If anyone says you're not,
I am Alvar Fáñez, and every bit as good as you!"
Gómez Peláez arose:
"What's the use, Minaya, of all this discussion?
Many in this court would like to fight you;
There's no denying that.
Wait and see how God decides,
And then we'll know who's wrong and right."
The king declared: "All talking is done.
No one declares a further position.
The fighting begins tomorrow at dawn,
Three pairs of those who argued in court."
Then the Carrión heirs spoke up:
"Give us time to get ready; tomorrow's too soon.
The Warrior has our horses and armor;
We have to ride to Carrión to equip ourselves."
The king turned to my Cid:
"Should they fight tomorrow? The choice is yours."
Warrior Cid replied: "I make no choice,
Except that I prefer Valencia to Carrión."
The king said: "Of course, Cid.
Let me have your challengers, fully equipped;
They'll come with me as their guardian.
You are in my service, and as your lord
I guarantee there'll be no problems
With any Carrión count or lord.
Here in my court I fix the time for battle:
Three challenges shall be fought in my presence

quien non viniere al plazo   pierda la rrazón,
desí sea vencido   e escape por traidor."
Prisieron el juizio   ifantes de Carrión.
Mio Cid al rrey   las manos le besó
e dixo: "Plazme, [señor].
Estos mis tres cavalleros   en vuestra mano son,
d'aquí vos los acomiendo   como a rrey e a señor;
ellos son adobados   pora cumplir todo lo so,
¡ondrados me los enbiad a Valencia,   por amor del Criador!"
Essora rrespuso el rrey: "¡Assí lo mande Dios!"
Allí se tollió el capiello   el Cid Campeador,
la cofia de rrançal,   que blanca era como el sol,
e soltava la barba   e sacóla del cordón.
Nos' fartan de catarle   quantos ha en la cort;
adeliñó a él el conde don Anrich   e el conde don Rremond.
Abraçólos tan bien   e rruégalos de coraçón
que prendan de sus averes   quanto ovieren sabor.
A éssos e a los otros   que de buena parte son,
a todos los rrogava   assí como han sabor,
tales í á que prenden,   tales í á que non.
Los *dozientos* marcos   al rrey los soltó,
de lo ál tanto priso   quant ovo sabor.
"¡Merced vos pido, rrey,   por amor del Criador!
Quando todas estas nuevas   assí puestas son,
beso vuestras manos   con vuestra gracia, señor,
e irme quiero pora Valencia,   con afán la gané yo."

[*At this point, an entire parchment page,
roughly fifty lines, is missing.*]

150

El rrey alçó la mano,   la cara se sanctigó:
"¡Yo lo juro par Sant Esidro   el de León
que en todas nuestras tierras   non ha tan buen varón!"
Mio Cid en el cavallo   adelant se llegó,

On the open meadows of Carrión.
Whoever fails to appear has lost his cause,
And will be known as a traitor."
The Carrións accepted these orders.
My Cid kissed the king's hand,
And said: "I agree, my lord.
I put these three knights in your hands.
They serve you, now, you are their lord.
Send them back with honor, in the name of God!"
The king replied: "May the Lord so arrange it!"
Warrior Cid pulled back his cap,
White linen as white as the sun,
Untied and shook out his beard.
People at the court couldn't stop gaping.
Count Don Ramón approached him, and Count Enrique:
He hugged them both and warmly offered
Anything he had that they might want.
He gave the king back his two hundred marks;
Don Alfonso took what he liked.
And to all the others who'd taken Cid's side
The Warrior offered what they desired.
"And now, my king, for the love of God,
Since all these affairs are settled and gone,
Let me kiss your hands, and with your permission
I'd love to go home to Valencia, which I fought for and won."

[*At this point, an entire parchment page,
roughly fifty lines, is missing.*]

150

The king raised his hand, and made the sign of the cross:
"Cid, I swear in the name of Saint Isidore of León
No knight as good as you exists in all this land!"
My Cid rode closer and kissed the hand

fue besar la mano   a Alfonso so señor:
"Mandástesme mover   a Bavieca el corredor,
en moros ni en cristianos   otro tal non ha oy,
y[o] vos le do en don,   mandédesle tomar, señor."
Essora dixo el rrey: "D'esto non he sabor;
si a vós le tolliés   el cavallo no havrié tan bue[n] señor.
Mas atal cavallo cum ést   pora tal como vós
pora arrancar moros del canpo   e ser segudador,
quien vos lo toller quisiere   nol' vala el Criador,
ca por vós e por el cavallo   ondrados somo[s] nós."
Essora se espidieron   e luegos' partió la cort.
El Campeador a los que han lidiar   tan bien los castigó:
"Ya Martín Antolínez   e vós, Pero Vermúez | e Muño Gustioz,
firmes sed en campo   a guisa de varones;
buenos mandados me vayan   a Valencia de vós."
Dixo Martín Antolínez: "¿Por qué lo dezides, señor?
Preso avemos el debdo   e a passar es por nós,
podedes oír de muertos,   ca de vencidos no."
Alegre fue d'aquesto   el que en buen ora nació,
espidiós' de todos   los que sos amigos son;
Mio Cid pora Valencia   e el rrey pora Carrión.
Las tres semanas de plazo   todas complidas son.
Felos al plazo   los del Campeador,
cunplir quieren el debdo   que les mandó so señor,
ellos son en p[o]der   del rrey don Alfonso el de León;
dos días atendieron   a ifantes de Carrión.
Mucho vienen bien adobados   de cavallos e de guarnizones
e todos sus parientes   con ellos son,
que si los pudiessen apartar   a los del Campeador
que los matassen en campo   por desondra de so señor.
El cometer fue malo,   que lo ál nos' enpeçó,
ca grand miedo ovieron   a Alfonso el de León.
De noche belaron las armas   e rrogaron al Criador.
Trocida es la noche,   ya quiebran los albores,
muchos se juntaron   de buenos rricos omnes
por ver esta lid,   ca avién ende sabor;
demás sobre todos   í es el rrey don Alfonso
por querer el derecho   e non consentir el tuerto.

Of his lord and king, Don Alfonso:
"You asked me to show you Babieca in action.
No Moor, no Christian, owns so fine a horse.
And I hereby give him to you, my lord. Accept him."
"No," said the king, "I cannot accept this.
Were you to give him to me, he'd lose a better rider.
A horse like this deserves a rider like you,
A man who beats Moors in battle, then chases them down.
Accepting this horse from you, I'd offend our Lord:
You and the horse together bring us honor!"
They said their farewells and left the court.
Then Warrior Cid cheered on those who were fighting:
"Eh, Martín Antolínez, and you, Pedro Bermúdez
And Muño Gustioz, ride hard like the fighters you are.
Let's have good news of you in Valencia!"
Martín Antolínez said: "Why say this, my lord?
We have a job to do and it's up to us to do it.
Maybe you'll hear we're dead—but defeated? No!"
Then my Cid and his friends rode to Valencia;
The king and his friends rode to Carrión.

The three-week intermission was over;
The Warrior's men were there, and ready to fight,
As Warrior Cid had ordered,
Protected by Don Alfonso of León.
They waited two days for the Carrións to come,
And they came, with fine horses and equipment,
Supported by their entire family—
Who longed to catch the Warrior's men alone
And kill them, to dishonor my Cid.
They had this planned, but didn't attempt it,
For fear of Alfonso de León.
The Cid's men sat and prayed that night.
Darkness ebbed, dawn was about to break,
When a crowd of well-bred knights assembled,
Anxious to watch these fights.
But most important of all was King Alfonso,
Affirming justice and blocking what was wrong.

Yas' metién en armas   los del buen Campeador,
todos tres se acuerdan,   ca son de un señor.
En otro logar se arman   los ifantes de Carrión,
sediélos castigando   el conde Garcí Ordóñez:
andidieron en pleito,   dixiéronlo al rrey Alfonso,
que non fuessen en la batalla   las espadas tajadores | Colada e
    Tizón,
que non lidiassen con ellas   los del Canpeador,
mucho eran rrepentidos los ifantes   por quanto dadas son,
dixiérongelo al rrey,   mas non ge lo conloyó:
"Non sacastes ninguna   quando oviemos la cort;
si buenas las tenedes,   pro abrán a vós,
otros[s]í farán   a los del Canpeador.
Levad e salid al campo,   ifantes de Carrión,
huebos vos es que lidiedes   a guisa de varones,
que nada non mancará   por los del Campeador.
Si del campo bien salides,   grand ondra avredes vós,
e si fuére[de]s vencidos,   non rrebtedes a nós,
ca todos lo saben   que lo buscastes vós."
Ya se van rrepintiendo   ifantes de Carrión,
de lo que avién fecho   mucho rrepisos son;
no lo querrién aver fecho   por quanto ha en Carrión.
Todos tres son armados   los del Campeador,
ívalos ver   el rrey don Alfonso;
dixieron   los del Campeador:
"Besámosvos las manos   como a rrey e a señor
que fiel seades oy   d'ellos e de nós;
a derecho nos valed,   a ningún tuerto no.
Aquí tienen su vando   los ifantes de Carrión,
non sabemos   qués' comidrán ellos o qué non;
en vuestra mano   nos metió nuestro señor:
¡tenendos a derecho,   por amor del Criador!"
Essora dixo el rrey: "¡D'alma e de coraçón!"
Adúzenles los cavallos   buenos e corredores,
santiguaron las siellas   e cavalgan a vigor,
los escudos a los cuellos   que bien blocados son,
e[n] mano prenden las astas   de los fierros tajadores,
estas tres lanças   traen seños pendones,

The Warrior's men put on their armor,
Three who were as one, serving one lord.
In a different spot, the Carrións put on their armor,
Count García Ordóñez advising and instructing;
Then they approached the king, protesting
That Colada and Tizón, those gleaming swords, should be
    barred
From this battle. They now regretted handing them over.
They told the king this, but their plea was rejected:
"You made no objection when this was discussed in court.
If you have good swords, let them serve you well;
This also applies to the Warrior's men.
Carrións: rise and take the field!
Words won't help you: all you need
Is to fight like men. No man on the Warrior's side will yield
To words. You'll gain great honor if you win,
But don't blame us if you lose:
You asked for this, and here it is."
The Carrión heirs were sick at heart,
Deeply regretting all the part they'd played.
All of Carrión would gladly be paid
If they could escape. The Warrior's men were waiting.
King Alfonso paid them
An inspection visit, and they said to him:
"Please let us kiss your hands, our king and lord,
For you will ensure that justice is done today.
That's all we ask for. Give us no favor.
Supporters are all around the Carrións:
Who knows what they might plan, what might be done?
We place ourselves in your hands, O lord!
Give us justice, for the love of God!"
The king replied: "With all my heart!"
Their horses were brought, swift and strong;
First they blessed the saddles, then mounted,
Shields hung down from the neck.
They took up sharp-pointed lances,
Three banners fluttering on each.
Many fine fighters around them,

e derredor d'ellos   muchos buenos varones.
Ya salieron al campo   dó eran los mojones.
Todos tres son acordados   los del Campeador
que cada uno d'ellos   bien fos ferir el so.
Fevos de la otra part   los ifantes de Carrión,
muy bien aconpañados,   ca muchos parientes son.
El rrey dioles fieles   por dezir el derecho e ál non,
que non varajen con ellos   de sí o de non.
Dó sedién en el campo   fabló el rrey don Alfonso:
"Oíd qué vos digo,   ifantes de Carrión:
esta lid en Toledo la fiziérades,   mas non quisiestes vós.
Estos tres cavalleros   de Mio Cid el Campeador
yo los adux a salvo   a tierras de Carrión;
aved vuestro derecho,   tuerto non querades vós,
ca qui tuerto quisiere fazer,   mal ge lo vedaré yo,
en todo mio rreino   non avrá buena sabor."
Ya les va pesando   a los ifantes de Carrión.
Los fieles e el rrey   enseñaron los mojones,
librávanse del campo   todos aderredor;
bien ge lo demostraron   a todos *seis* cómo son,
que por í serié vencido   qui saliesse del mojón.
Todas las yentes   esconbraron aderredor,
más de *seis* astas de lanças   que non llegassen al mojón.
Sorteávanles el campo,   ya les partién el sol,
salién los fieles de medio,   ellos cara por cara son,
desí vinién los de Mio Cid   a los ifantes de Carrión
e llos ifantes de Carrión   a los del Campeador,
cada uno d'ellos   mientes tiene al so.
Abraçan los escudos   delant los coraçones,
abaxan las lanças   abueltas con los pendones,
enclinavan las caras   sobre los arzones,
batién los cavallos   con los espolones,
tembrar querié la tierra   do[n]d eran movedores.
Cada uno d'ellos   mientes tiene al so,
todos tres por tres   ya juntados son;
cuédanse que essora cadrán muertos   los que están aderredor.
Pero Vermúez,   el que antes rrebtó,

My Cid's men rode to the well-marked field of battle:
They had agreed how each
Would strike the man he'd challenged.
Across from them were the Carrións,
Many men around them, mostly family.
The king appointed judges, to say what was fair or not;
Once they decided, no one could dispute them.
Six fighters were on the field, and the king declared:
"Listen to me, you Carrións!
You could have fought in Toledo; you refused.
These three of Warrior Cid's good men
Are under my personal care.
Behave yourselves, do nothing unfair,
For I will be harsh on anyone playing tricks:
He'll never be seen in Castile again."
The Carrións were clearly unhappy at these words.
The king and his judges rode around the field,
Displaying the boundaries; then the field was cleared.
All six fighters were told, and very plainly,
That to cross the boundaries meant defeat.
No one watching could approach a boundary
Closer than the length of six lances.
They drew lots for positions; no one got the sun in his eyes.
The judges stood beside the field, at its center; it was time
    to fight.
As my Cid's good men attacked
The Carrións, too, advanced,
Each aiming straight at his man.
They pulled their shields over their chests,
Lowered lances hung with banners,
Bent their heads toward the saddlebows,
And spurred their horses forward.
The earth seemed to tremble with the sound of the charge.
Each aiming straight at his man,
Three on three they fought:
The watchers thought they'd all fall dead at once!
Pedro Bermúdez, who'd made the first challenge,

con Ferrá[n] Gonçález   de cara se juntó,
firiénse en los escudos   sin todo pavor.
Ferrán Go[n]çález a Pero Vermúez   el escúdol' passó,
prísol' en vazío,   en carne nol' tomó,
bien en dos logares   el astil le quebró.
Firme estido Pero Vermúez,   por esso nos' encamó,
un colpe rrecibiera   mas otro firió:
quebrantó la b[l]oca del escudo,   apart ge la echó,
passógelo todo,   que nada nol' valió,
metiól' la lança por los pechos,   que nada nol' valió.
Tres dobles de loriga tenié Fernando,   aquéstol' prestó,
las dos le desmanchan   e la tercera fincó:
el belmez con la camisa   e con la guarnizón
de dentro en la carne   una mano ge la metió,
por la boca afuera   la sángrel' salió,
quebráronle las cinchas,   ninguna nol' ovo pro,
por la copla del cavallo   en tierra lo echó.
Assí lo tenién las yentes   que mal ferido es de muert.
Él dexó la lança   e al espada mano metió,
quando lo vio Ferrán Go[n]çález   conuvo a Tizón,
antes que el colpe esperasse   dixo: "Vençudo só."
Atorgárongelo los fieles,   Pero Vermúez le dexó.

1 5 1

Martín Antolínez e Diego Gonçález   firiéronse de las lanças,
tales fueron los colpes   que les quebraron amas.
Martín Antolínez   mano metió al espada,
rrelumbra tod' el campo,   tanto es linpia e clara;
diol' un colpe,   de traviéssol' tomava,
el casco de somo   apart ge lo echava,
las moncluras del yelmo   todas ge las cortava,
allá levó el almófar,   fata la cofia llegava,
la cofia e el almófar   todo ge lo levava,
rráxol' los pelos de la cabeça,   bien a la carne llegava,
lo uno cayó en el campo   e lo ál suso fincava.

Was face to face with Fernando González,
Each bravely striking the other's shield.
Fernando's blow went through Pedro's,
But ended in empty air, not touching flesh,
And his lance was snapped in two.
Pedro Bermúdez sat straight in his saddle, unshaken;
He'd taken one blow, yet gave back another,
Smashing through the shield, which broke apart, useless,
As the lance drove through, almost
Reaching the heart, but the third of Fernando's mail shirts
—His last line of defense—
Saved him, as the first and second were pierced.
But the blow drove fragments of metal
A full hand deep in the flesh,
So that blood gushed from his mouth,
And the horse's belts and straps were broken, nothing held,
And Fernando fell backward, straight to the ground.
Everyone thought he was fatally wounded.
Pedro dropped his lance and drew his sword,
But Fernando recognized Tizón
And called, before the blow fell, "I am beaten!"
The judges agreed, and Pedro left him where he was.

151

Martín Antolínez and Diego González each struck so hard
That both their lances shattered.
Martín Antolínez drew his sword,
Shining so clear and bright it lit the whole field.
He struck a sidewise blow
That smashed the top of Diego's helmet,
Slicing through the metal and all the straps,
Reaching the woolen lining, cutting it away,
Scraping off much hair and not a little flesh.
When precious Colada struck this blow,
Diego saw he could not escape

Quando este colpe á ferido   Colada la preciada,
vio Diego Gonçález   que no escaparié con el alma,
bolvió la rrienda al cavallo   por tornasse de cara.
Essora Martín Antolínez   rrecibiól' con el espada,
un cólpel' dio de llano,   con lo agudo nol' tomava.
Diago [Go]nçález espada tiene en mano,   mas no la | ensayava,
essora el ifante   tan grandes vozes dava:
"¡Valme, Dios, glorioso señor,   e cúriam' d'este espada!"
El cavallo asorrienda   e mesurándol' del espada
sacól' del mojón;   Martín Antolínez en el campo fincava.
Essora dixo el rrey: "Venid vós a mi compaña,
por quanto avedes fecho   vencida avedes esta batalla."
Otórgangelo los fieles   que dize verdadera palabra.

152

Los dos han arrancado,   dirévos de Muño Gustioz,
con Assur Gonçález   cómo se adobó.
Firiénse en los escudos   unos tan grandes colpes;
Assur Gonçález,   furçudo e de valor,
firió en el escudo   a don Muño Gustioz,
tras el escudo   falsóge la guarnizón,
en vazío fue la lança   ca en carne nol' tomó.
Este colpe fecho,   otro dio Muño Gustioz,
tras el escudo   falsóge la guarnizón:
por medio de la bloca   el escúdol' quebrantó,
nol' pudo guarir,   falsóge la guarnizón;
apart le priso,   que non cab' el coraçón,
metiól' por la carne adentro   la lança con el pendón,
de la otra part   una braça ge la echó;
con él dio una tuerta,   de la siella lo encamó,
al tirar de la lança   en tierra lo echó,
vermejo salió el astil   e la lança e el pendón.
Todos se cuedan   que ferido es de muert.
La lança rrecombró   e sobr'él se paró,
dixo Gonçalo Assúrez: "¡Nol' firgades, por Dios!"

With his life, and pulled his horse to the side,
Turning his head away, and Martín Antolínez reined in
His sword blow, hitting with the flat of the blade.
Diego's sword was in his hand, but he did not use it,
Shouting as loud as he was able:
"God in heaven help me! Save me from this sword!"
He swung his horse around, his eyes on the blade,
And rushed off the field, leaving Martín Antolínez alone.
To whom the king said: "Come here to me.
You've done enough; it's over, you've won."
The judges affirmed this decision.

152

Two had been beaten; I'll tell you how Muño Gustioz
Did with Ansur González,
Beating each other's shields with powerful blows.

Ansur González was brave and strong:
His lance pierced Muño's shield and armor,
But ended in air, touched no flesh.
Muño hit back, straight through
Both shield and armor, a sideward blow
That could not be stopped, hitting flesh
But not the heart, lance point and hanging banners
Coming out in back, with bits
Of mail shirt and lining, the full length
Of an arm. Muño pulled hard on the reins,
Stayed firm in the saddle, and twisted
The lance, yanking it back. Ansur was pitched
To the ground, his saddle was drenched in blood.
Everyone watching was convinced
Ansur González would soon be dead.
Muño stood over him, lance in hand,

Vençudo es el campo   quando esto se acabó,
dixieron los fieles: "Esto oímos nós."
Mandó librar el canpo   el buen rrey don Alfonso,
las armas que í rrastaron   él se las tomó.
Por ondrados se parten   los del buen Campeador,
vencieron esta lid,   grado al Criador.
Grandes son los pesares   por tierras de Carrión.
El rrey a los de Mio Cid   de noche los enbió
que no les diessen salto   nin oviessen pavor.
A guisa de menbrados   andan días e noches,
felos en Valencia   con Mio Cid el Campeador;
por malos los dexaron   a los ifantes de Carrión,
conplido han el debdo   que les mandó so señor,
alegre fue d'aquesto   Mio Cid el Campeador.
Grant es la biltança   de ifantes de Carrión:
qui buena dueña escarnece   e la dexa después
atal le contesca   o siquier peor.
Dexémosnos de pleitos   de ifantes de Carrión,
de lo que an preso   mucho an mal sabor;
fablémosnos d'aqueste   que en buen ora nació.
Grandes son los gozos   en Valencia la mayor
porque tan ondrados fueron   los del Canpeador.
Prisos' a la barba   Rruy Díaz so señor:
"¡Grado al rrey del cielo,   mis fijas vengadas son!
Agora las ayan quitas   heredades de Carrión.
Sin vergüença las casaré   o a qui pese o a qui non."
Andidieron en pleitos   los de Navarra e de Aragón,
ovieron su ajunta   con Alfonso el de León,
fizieron sus casamientos   con don Elvira e con doña Sol.
Los primeros fueron grandes,   mas aquéstos son mijores,
a mayor ondra las casa   que lo que primero fue.
¡Ved quál ondra crece   al que en buen ora nació
quando señoras son sus fijas   de Navarra e de Aragón!
Oy los rreyes d'España   sos parientes son,
a todos alcança ondra   por el que en buen ora nació.
Passado es d'este sieglo   el día de cinquaesma;
. . . .   ¡de Christus aya perdón!
¡Assí fagamos nós todos   justos e pecadores!

And Suero González cried out: "Don't hit him
Again! You've won, it's over and done!"
The judges said: "The victory's confirmed."
Good King Alfonso ordered the field to be emptied;
He kept for himself whatever lay on the ground.

The Warrior's men rode home with honor:
Thanks to the Lord, they had won their battles!
The Carrión people were deeply sorrowful.
King Alfonso had the victors leave at night,
So they could ride, not fearing men in hiding.
Sensible men, they traveled both night and day,
And reached Valencia safely.
They had shamed the Carrión heirs,
Paid their debt to Warrior Cid, as they'd sworn
To do. He was absolutely delighted.
The Carrións were left in disgrace:
Whoever beats a good woman, and then abandons her,
Should be in great trouble—or worse!
But that's enough of the Carrións' woes:
Let's talk of a man born at a good hour.
Valencia, too, was delighted at the honors
Won by Warrior Cid's men.
Ruy Díaz pulled at his beard:
"My daughters have been revenged: I thank the King of heaven!
They're free of all Carrión links!
Nothing is wrong, now, with giving them in marriage."
The kings of Navarre and Aragon had face-to-face
Talks with Alfonso of León, arranging
It all. The girls' first marriages had been grand,
But there was far more honor in these.
Just see what had come to my Cid, born at a good hour,
As his daughters ascended thrones in Aragon and Navarre!
Two Spanish kings were his close relations,
And he had brought honor to them.
My Cid left this world at Pentecost time:
May Christ have mercy on his soul,
As he will have for us all, both right and wrong!

Éstas son las nuevas   de Mio Cid el Canpeador,
en este logar   se acaba esta rrazón.

[*The copyist of the manuscript adds:*]

Quien escrivió este libro, ¡dél Dios paraíso, amen!
Per Abbat le escrivió en el mes de mayo
en era de mill r.C.C   xL.v. años.

This the tale of my Cid, the Warrior,
And here my story is done.

[*The copyist of the manuscript adds:*]

May God grant paradise to the man who transcribed this book. Amen!
Written out by Per Abbat in the month of May
In the year of our Lord 1207.

Notes

Number in parentheses indicates stanza number.

Alvar Fáñez (2): The Cid's closest confidant and his conduit to Alfonso in the poem. Historical records document his successful military career in service to the king but in fact he seems never to have been part of the Cid's entourage in exile. Also referred to as Minaya, meaning "my brother" (a fusion between the Castilian possessive *mi* and the Basque *anai*, "brother").

various names of the Cid (3): Ruy is the diminutive form of Rodrigo, and most often used when the patronymic Díaz follows immediately; *Campeador*, which could be translated as "Battler" or "Conqueror," as well as "Warrior," derives from the Latin *Campi Doctoris*, literally, "Master of the Battlefield." Not only is Cid itself the direct Castilian adaptation of Arabic *sayyid*, but the somewhat unusual practice of calling him *mio Cid* derives from an understanding, and translation, of this honorific form of address in Arabic, *sayyidi*, "my lord."

Saint Mary's cathedral (4): The old cathedral of Burgos, built by Alfonso but torn down in the thirteenth century to make way for the Gothic cathedral that dominates the city today, and where the Cid and his wife, Jimena, are now buried.

Martín Antolínez (5): Almost certainly a completely fictional character, in the poem he is characterized as an exemplary citizen of Burgos, and serves as the head of the Cid's household.

"[he who was] born at a lucky hour" (5): This formulaic epithet for the Cid, and variants on it, is repeated throughout, reminding us of the oral nature of the poem and other epics.

Raguel and Vidas (7–11): This famous episode shows the Cid hatching a plan that will allow him to deceive a pair of Jewish moneylenders. They will reappear briefly in the second canto, begging Alvar Fáñez to convey to the Cid that they'll be ruined if he doesn't repay their loan, but the matter is left unresolved in the poem.

"to either Moors or Christians" (9): The expression as it is used here means "everybody/anybody" as in "Swear you won't reveal this to anyone." This first of many instances in the text of the word "Moor" underlines its commonplace meaning as "Muslim," that is, as one of the three possible religious categories of citizens of medieval Spain.

San Pedro de Cardeña (11): One of the most important Benedictine monasteries of Castile, founded in the ninth century, and the most important center of the cult of the Cid, who was reburied here in 1102. When the Cid had died in Valencia in 1099 his wife, Jimena, had remained in control of the city, but three years later it was taken by the Almoravids. At that point Jimena took the Cid's body to be buried in Cardeña, and asked to be buried there herself, although both were disinterred in the twentieth century and transferred to the cathedral of Burgos. The relationship between the monastery and its monks and the various historical and poetic traditions about the Cid has been the object of much scholarly curiosity and speculation, and some believe the poem's author must have emerged from that environment.

"you, who wear so flowing a beard!" (16): The Cid's beard symbolizes honor and virility and there are constant references to it within the poem. In this some scholars see the influence of other epic figures, and especially so from the depiction of Charlemagne's legendary beard; there is, however, also the traditional practice of leaving one's beard untrimmed as a marker of grief from ancient times. The Cid's heart is said to be as soft as his beard, and at another point he proclaims, "No scissors will touch it, not a single hair will be cut," out of love of his king. Further on, and at various critical junctures in the poem, it is prominently noted that no one has ever pulled the Cid's beard, and this is clearly a great source of pride. When the Cid's nemesis Don García Ordóñez later seeks to insult him, stating that his rival's (unruly) beard is intended to inspire fear and terror, the Cid reminds the count that when the Warrior seized Cabra castle from him, not only did he pull the count's beard but "Every single Moorish boy took his turn." The count's emasculation remains evident in that his beard "still hasn't grown back."

"Spain" (23): *España* is used here to mean what we would call Islamic Spain, or al-Andalus, as it was called in Arabic.

Pedro Bermúdez (30): Plays the role of the Cid's nephew and standard-bearer, although no documentary evidence of such a historical character exists.

King of Valencia (32): Identified a few lines later as Tamín, this is a fictitious ruler, as are many of the poem's Muslim leaders (although some may be very loosely based on historical figures, or allude to them via vaguely reminiscent names), including Fáriz and Galvé, Tamín's visitors in this episode.

Saint James (36): Santiago, patron saint of Spain, whose remains are traced in legend to an eighth-century discovery by a monk (who found the apostle's body washed up on the Galician shores, covered in scallop shells) and whose burial site in what would become the cathedral city of Compostela constitutes the center of one of Europe's most popular and enduring pilgrimage routes, also known in English as the Way of Saint James. In medieval representations Santiago is known sometimes as the Pilgrim but also—as here—as Santiago Matamoros, Saint James the Moorslayer.

Félix Muñoz (37): Another fictional character identified in the poem as the Cid's cousin and thus, of particular importance in later developments in the poem, as devoted first cousin to the Warrior's daughters.

Count of Barcelona (55): Berenguer Ramón II, known as the Fratricide, for the murder, in 1082, of his brother, who was himself a count of Barcelona, and whose name is the rather confusing mirror-image (Ramón Berenguer) and thus almost certainly mistakenly named later in the poem (137). The historical Cid did in fact defeat Berenguer Ramón twice—in 1082, while the Cid was working for the Taifa of Saragossa, and in 1090, during his campaign to take control of Valencia. María, one of the Cid's daughters (in life they were named María and Cristina), in fact married the nephew and son of the count brothers of Barcelona, Ramón Berenguer III.

Colada (59): This name is said to derive from *acero colado* (cast steel). The sword itself is lost (although "replicas" are available everywhere in Spain today). The Cid eventually bequeaths both Colada and Tizón (the sword he wins from the Moor Búcar, see note below) to his unworthy sons-in-law, who must eventually surrender these symbols of honor back to him. In the end, the two swords are awarded to far better men, Martín Antolínez and Pedro Bermúdez, who have proven their loyalty and devotion to the Cid—and who ultimately use these same weapons to challenge, humiliate, and defeat Diego and Fernando in battle.

King of Morocco (72): One of the clearest references to a historical ruler, Yusuf Ibn Tashufin, first Almoravid caliph of Morocco (1059–1106). It is, however, not at all clear just who the other king is with whom he is at war, but there may be a historical confusion in the reference to the king of the Atlas mountains: the poem uses the later, Almohad term *Montes Claros* to refer to the Atlas mountain region, suggesting this is an anachronistic reference to the later rivalry and war between Almoravids of the Cid's lifetime and their successors, the Almohads, who arose as a power in the Atlas region in the 1120s and eventually defeated the Almoravids in 1145.

lord of Seville (75): Although he is not named specifically here, this is likely an allusion to the king of Seville during this period, the memorable poet-king al-Mutamid, whose court the historical Cid almost certainly visited, to collect *parias* on behalf of Alfonso. Al-Mutamid's accomplished poetry as well as his role as the patron of many other poets of this era earn him an important role in the literary history of the period. He was also a pivotal political figure, instrumental in the invitation to the Almoravids to cross the Strait of Gibraltar and aid the Andalusian Muslims against Alfonso, after the Castilian took Toledo, only to be eventually imprisoned by his erstwhile allies.

Bishop Don Jerónimo (78): Jerome of Perigord was brought to Spain by Bernard of Sedirac, the first archbishop of Toledo after its Castilian conquest in 1085, to take part in the Cluniac reform. In 1098, four years after Rodrigo's capture of Valencia, Jerome was made bishop of Valencia by Bernard—at the behest of the Cid himself, according to some.

"He asked for Alfonso, and where he might find him" (80): This reminds us explicitly that the medieval capitals were often completely moveable, and that kings were rarely to be found in one permanent residence. In this instance Alfonso is found in Carrión, but later on, the king is in residence in Sahagún (133) and when he ultimately convenes his court to judge the Carrión brothers, it is in Toledo.

Saint Isidore (82): Immensely learned church father known for his voluminous *Etymologiae*, an encyclopedic compilation of knowledge including medicine, law, geography, theology, and much else. Canonized in 1598, he has in recent years been further elevated, by the Vatican, into the patron saint of the Internet. He served as bishop of Seville from 599 to 636 and is most frequently referred to as Isidore of Seville, although the poem also refers to him as Isidore of León (100), alluding to the important church (the Real Colegiata) dedicated to Saint Isidore in León, where many of the early kings and queens of Castile and León are buried.

Count García Ordóñez (82): This historical count of Nájera was in fact an important figure at Alfonso's court, who may have been influential in the Cid's exile in 1081. In the poem he is unambiguously the leader of anti-Cid sentiment at the court.

nobles of Carrión (82): Diego and Fernando González, grandsons of counts of Carrión and part of a politically powerful family of the period in both Castile and León, although their characters and roles in the poem appear to be highly fictionalized: they are named as *infantes* (younger sons of kings, destined to never ascend to power) yet they held no such title, nor is there any historical record of their ever having married the Cid's daughters or having had any other connection with Rodrigo Díaz. Occasionally referred to by their surname (González) in the poem, Diego and Fernando are also often called the Carrións in this translation.

Abengalbón (83): There are records of a Muslim ruler on which the character of Abengalbón of Molina, the literary Cid's faithful and highly trusted ally (the Cid more than once relies on him for safe transport of his wife and daughters), may be based, although once again the dramatic events of the poem, and the pivotal role in the domestic drama of the Cid's family, are certainly fictionalized.

"Babieca was famous all over Spain" (86): Indeed, the Cid's horse has even been immortalized in a legend recounted by Gustavo Adolfo Bécquer (1836–1870), in which Babieca falls to its knees before the mosque of Bab al-Mardum in Toledo, thus revealing that there was a church where the mosque was later built; legend also had it that the horse was eventually buried at San Pedro de Cardeña along with the rest of the family, although there is no indication the horse's remains were later transferred to the cathedral of Burgos along with Rodrigo and Jimena.

King Búcar (113): Unclear if any specific historical character is an intended allusion, although it is clear that Búcar is the Hispanized form of the rather common Arabic name Abu Bakr, and among the possible historical figures whose name does echo here is Abu Bakr ibn Abd al-Aziz, the ruler of Valencia who appears as Tamín earlier in the poem.

Tizón (118): The other famous sword, together with Colada, which comes into the Cid's possession through battle. Unlike the assumed-lost Colada, however, a sword that some claimed to be Tizón was long displayed at the Military Museum in Madrid and was sold to the cathedral of Burgos in 2007, only to have its authenticity officially questioned by the state.

"a Moor who understood Spanish" (126): Multilingualism was widespread in medieval Spain, and just as the very name of the Cid reveals commonplace familiarity with Arabic among some Christians (and this includes some communities, such as the Mozarabs, whose native language was in fact Arabic), the *moro latinado* here alludes to the access that many Muslims had to "Latin"—that is, to the variety of spoken languages that derive from Latin, of which Castilian was but one.

"where [Alamos] left Elpha in chains" (128): The provenance and meaning of these toponyms have never been discovered.

"What shame falls upon us is small, / Compared to that directed against my lord" (133): The dishonor done by the Carrión brothers is far greater to the king, for it was Alfonso who sanctioned their marriage, and the Cid's own reservations were such that although he obeyed his monarch in agreeing to the arrangement, he had Alvar Fáñez stand in for him in the public ceremony.

Don Enrique (135): Grandson of Robert I, duke of Burgundy and nephew of Queen Constanza, Alfonso VI's wife, and by 1095, he had married Alfonso's illegitimate daughter Teresa and was governor of Portugal. This is the beginning of a parade of nobles all intimately connected to each other through marriages as well as interfamily rivalries, and also includes Don Ramón, count of Amous, Enrique's cousin and sometimes bitter rival. Ramón had married Alfonso's legitimate daughter, Urraca, and was made governor of Galicia; their son would inherit the throne as Alfonso VII.

San Servando (136): The fortified castle outside Toledo's city walls, transformed into a fortified monastery by Alfonso, after his conquest of the city in 1085, and in the possession of Cluny at the time of the Cid. The imposing building is located directly across the Tagus from the entrance to Toledo, across the Alcántara bridge (and note that the name of the bridge derives directly from *al-qantara*, the word for "bridge" in Arabic).

"Two messenger knights suddenly entered the court. / One was Ojarra, from the Prince of Navarre, / The other, Iñigo Jiménez, from the Prince of Aragon" (149): These are much more prestigious and honorable marriages for the Cid's daughters, who would now be queens (and, as is soon pointed out, the Carrión brothers would then have to serve their former wives). Although the daughters' first, failed marriages to the infantes are fully fictionalized, these second, successful marriages certainly echo the historical daughters' marriages into the highest royal ranks of Navarre and Barcelona. At stake, in the poem's hagiography of the Warrior, was not only the prestige of his daughters' alliances—which of course speaks to his own restored prestige inside the Castilian court—but the role he thus played in bringing together a number of rivalrous families and warring Christian principalities and kingdoms.